"Melissa," He Whispered,

"may I have tonight? Tonight, and tomorrow night, and all the nights after?"

She didn't answer; she couldn't. She wished fervently that she could stop being afraid of the future, stop thinking about the real barrier that lay between them. Maybe she'd been foolish to avoid discussing it during their magic interval, and he seemed to have forgotten. They had shared something, something uncomplicated and right, if only for a little while. Melissa felt that she deserved that, at least. She simply wouldn't think about tomorrow, or the real world that was lying in wait for them.

PAT WALLACE

lives in New York's Greenwich Village with her husband, who is the inspiration for all her heroes. She is also devoted to their several cats and to her writing, which has been her very successful career for many years.

Dear Reader,

Thank you so much for the many letters I have received from you praising our Silhouette Special Edition series. Your comments and views have proved to be very informative and have been a great help to us in establishing Special Edition as a firm favourite amongst romance readers.

Special Editions have all the elements you enjoy in Silhouette Romances and more. These stories concentrate on romance in a longer, more realistic and sophisticated way, and they feature greater sensual detail.

I hope you enjoy this book and all the wonderful romances from Silhouette.

Please continue sending your suggestions and comments by writing to me at this address:

Jane Nicholls
Silhouette Books
PO Box 177
Dunton Green
Sevenoaks
Kent
TN13 2YE

PAT WALLACE
Shining Hour

Silhouette

Special Edition

Published by Silhouette Books

Grateful acknowledgement to Roger Pavris for
permission to reprint 'Parable of the Fixed Stars', 'Buffalo
Waits in Cove of Dragons' and 'The Squanderer' from
Parable of the Fixed Stars by Ree Dragonette, published
in 1968 by Allograph Press.

Map by Ray Lundgren

First printing 1984

British Library C.I.P.

Wallace, Pat
    Shining hour.—(Silhouette special edition)
    I. Title
    813'.54[F]   PS3573.A4269/

    ISBN 0 340 35743 6

Printed and bound in Great Britain for
Hodder and Stoughton Paperbacks, a
division of Hodder and Stoughton Ltd.,
Mill Road, Dunton Green, Sevenoaks,
Kent (Editorial Office: 47 Bedford
Square, London, WC1 3DP) by
Richard Clay (The Chaucer Press) Ltd.,
Bungay, Suffolk

For Andrea Cirillo
In loving memory of Ree Dragonette
For her children, Juanita, John
and Ralph Corsiglia

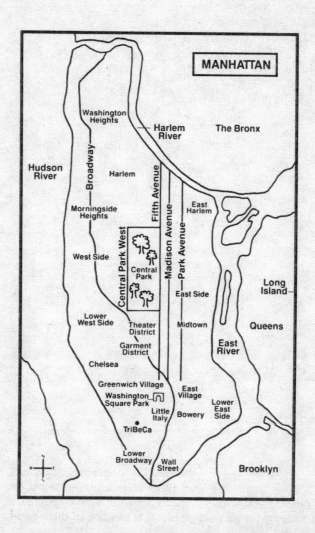

MANHATTAN

The Bronx

Harlem River

Washington Heights

Hudson River

Broadway

Harlem

Fifth Avenue

East Harlem

Morningside Heights

Central Park West

Central Park

Madison Avenue

Park Avenue

Long Island

West Side

East Side

Queens

Lower West Side

Theater District

Midtown

East River

Garment District

Chelsea

Greenwich Village

East Village

Lower East Side

Washington Square Park

Little Italy

Bowery

TriBeCa

Lower Broadway

Wall Street

Brooklyn

Chapter One

"This is quite a place." The voice was deep and resonant.

Melissa Grey paused in the act of raising her window gate and turned around. The voice belonged to a tall red-haired man parked on a motorcycle in front of the shop. He looked up at the building's facade, then back at her. She took a quick, shallow breath.

He was wonderful-looking. His shock of bright hair gleamed in the early September sun, a white smile slashed his tanned face; the contrasts were dazzling. He had eyes the color of a fox's. Melissa had never seen him before and yet he strongly reminded her of someone.

"Thank you." Tentatively she returned his smile and went back to her task, after a glance down the short, tree-lined block on East Eighteenth Street. She inhaled the air with pleasure; it was one of those lucid, just-right mornings, her birthday morning. "The day we have Indian summer in New York," as Ansel put it in his dry Maine way.

Country Things wasn't open yet, but then Ansel Harper was always late. Melissa waved to Martha Stanton, who was unlocking Patchwork, a shop selling quilted items, and to Michel St. Clair. His store, Frère Michel, offered beautiful old furniture.

"Can I help?"

Melissa heard the biker's question with amusement. The grille was counterweighted aluminum; the gate slid up like a feather at the touch of her delicate fingers. Those fingers had mastered antique clock-works for a decade, since she was fifteen years old. Everything mechanical worked for Melissa Grey, even if, as some said, she should be dancing a minuet and not picking at clocks' innards. Melissa knew she looked like an eighteenth-century figurine, yet inside she was anything but.

"No, thanks," she called back over her shoulder, hoping the man wouldn't turn out to be a pest. Generally, though, pests didn't look that good. With her back still turned to the man she smiled broadly. Then out of the corner of her eye she saw him get off his motorcycle and saunter toward the shop.

"I see I'm early."

He was standing close to her, reading her sign—two joined grandfather clocks in cardboard whose hands pointed to the 10 A.M. opening, the 6 P.M. closing.

"A phenomenon, I might add." His grin, a strange-ly rueful one, broke out and she realized who he reminded her of—Gavin. Gavin, who'd played such havoc with her life two years ago. He hadn't had the vital thatch of fiery hair, but they shared the same playful, arrogant look; that remote gentleness; that odd smile with something almost sad in it. A Pisces smile.

Her heart thudded but she said calmly, "It is a little early. That's okay, come in." It seemed ungracious to quibble over minutes with such an eager customer. Time Was dealt in some very expensive merchandise.

A shaft of sun sliced the pristine window glass with gold, then danced on the items in the store, playing over their scalloped gilt, rich wood and polished marble. When they went in, her trained ear registered the flawless ticking of various old clocks on shelves and tables and the deeper, more virile tocks of grandfathers, one on either side of the door. Melissa shut it and automatically went to her French desk to turn on the radio. The bright, graceful strains of Vivaldi's "Four Seasons" rippled softly out.

"Nice," the red-haired man said. "All this and Vivaldi, too."

He'd made himself very much at home, wandering around to look at the displays. He had a lithe, loose stride and there wasn't a superfluous ounce of flesh on his body, from the massive shoulders in the sweaty T-shirt to the lean middle and long legs frankly outlined by tight, faded jeans. His boots were scuffed and disreputable, and still he had the manner of a man used to giving orders and having them obeyed.

Melissa had oddly conflicting feelings; it warmed her that he liked her own favorite composer and yet something about him obscurely riled her. But she asked politely, "What can I show you?"

He turned, holding a small gilt clock in his hands, and gave her a long once-over. He took her in, starting at her dark gold hair coiled neatly at the back of her head, and her small-featured face, then traveling down the lines of her body hinted at by the gauzy lavender top and gray cotton slacks, all the way to her sandaled feet.

It was an insolent survey, yet in spite of herself she felt a quick dart of excitement.

"Where's the old gnome with the squint . . . from the brothers Grimm? In back?" he demanded suddenly.

"Chained in the cellar. The gnome you see is the gnome you get."

He laughed and his expression admired her quickness. "Some gnome." Then he threw her off balance by reverting to business. "This is attractive"—he looked down at the gilt clock—"but that's sensational." He nodded toward the rare bronze domed clock set like a royal crown on a footed rectangle.

"You have good taste," she admitted. "My grandfather made that." It was an exact copy of a lantern clock with a bob pendulum in a London museum. "Unfortunately, it's not—"

"—for sale," he concluded, reading from the neat card on the lantern clock's base. He looked up at her again and his fox-colored eyes gleamed. "This place has been here a long time, hasn't it?"

"Since 1892."

He checked out the windows and the moldings. "I take it you own the building. You *did* say 'thank you' before."

She nodded, wondering why he'd asked. Then an alarming answer occurred to her. Maybe he was a real estate developer, sounding her out; that had happened before. She'd once been harassed by a developer eager for her to sell out. Even if this man looked more like a terrorist at the end of a hard bombing, you never could tell.

Eager to change the subject, she asked, "What kind of clock are you looking for?"

"A birthday present for a lady. The party's tonight . . . so I'd better get cracking." He caught her expression.

It was such a coincidence she couldn't help smiling.

"Did I say something funny?" He studied her.

"Oh, no," she assured him quickly. "It's just that . . ." Why was she making such a federal case out of it? ". . . It's my birthday, too."

"Well, well. Happy birthday." His eyes gleamed more brightly. "I should have known."

This was getting too personal. Passing over his last puzzling comment, she rushed to speak. "Thanks. Maybe you'd like to look at some watches, too, as well as clocks? There are a lot of pretty things for a woman. Of course, that boudoir clock you're looking at is a beauty."

"Boudoir clock? Mmmm." He ran his big fingers over it.

Really, Melissa thought irritably. How persistent can you get? But she was more irritated at herself than at him. Usually when men were insinuating, and they often were, she could ignore them. She was annoyed with herself for feeling so flustered.

"It is pretty," he agreed. "But I'd like to get something more unusual."

She had to be some lady, Melissa thought. The clock that wasn't "unusual" enough was priced at three hundred dollars.

"She's a clock freak," he explained. "Another coincidence." He gave Melissa a quick, teasing glance; then he said, "Now . . . *this* is more like it." He was pointing to a unique nineteenth-century French clock. Its delicate round timepiece was set in the curving back of a swan.

"That's a very rare one," Melissa said. She had priced it at eighteen hundred dollars.

He picked it up and walked back with it to her desk. He set it down carefully. "Sold."

"You . . . er . . . saw the price."

He shook his head.

She gave it to him.

He slipped a credit card out of his wallet. "I'll take it," he said casually. That jolted her, but she was delighted. Generally people gave more thought to a purchase like that. "You accept this one, don't you?" The name on the card was Bart Freeman.

"Oh, yes." She dialed the credit card company, got the okay. "Everything's fine," she told him mildly, feeling elated. This was certainly a good way to start her birthday. "I'm sure the lady will love it. Let me gift wrap it for you."

She chose her favorite paper, a tiny pattern of lilies of the valley, a Virgo flower, on a smoky-blue background. Then she handed Bart Freeman a lily-shaped card, conscientious not to peek at what he wrote, which she had an absurd desire to do. Melissa was chagrined at that desire; she didn't even know this man.

Suddenly she noticed that he seemed to be waiting for something. She looked down and discovered that she had forgotten to give him his credit card and receipt; they were clutched in her hand. She handed them to him hastily, busying herself with ribbon. What had gotten into her? She tried to convince herself that she'd simply lost her cool because she had made such a huge sale so quickly with no effort at all.

She filled a box with lavender tissue and started to lift the clock.

"Here, let me do that. It's heavy," he said. As he took the clock from her their fingers brushed; the result was startling. There was a crackle of static electricity. That had happened once when she'd inserted her key in the door lock on a freezing day. Nothing like that had ever happened with a man . . . not even Gavin.

Bart Freeman gave a wordless exclamation. She could feel him staring at her. Perversely it almost annoyed her when he didn't make the expected comment about a "turn-on." On the contrary: When she glanced up at him briefly he had a very serious expression.

"Thanks," she murmured, and turned back to the wrapping. Her fingers were a little unsteady as she tied the package with narrow, shining-white ribbon fluffed into a rosette.

She attached a spray of silk valley lilies to the bow's center. Bart Freeman surveyed her handiwork. "That's beautiful," he said softly. "I can't haul that on the Harley. I'll pick it up later." His gaze returned to her. "Beautiful," he repeated softly. "Good Lord, you have purple eyes."

Her blue-gray eyes changed to reflect the colors she wore; the lavender tunic had given them that color today. Uneasily she felt his nearness magnetize her. He was incredibly appealing; a feverish warmth enveloped her. She could almost hear the vibrations sing between them. A fresh, exciting smell, like cedar shavings, emanated from his ruddy skin.

"Thanks a lot, Ms. Grey. What's the M for?" he demanded abruptly. Of course, he'd seen the "M. Grey" on the sign.

"Melissa," she murmured, making a great show of tidying up the already neat wrapping paper. He stood there until she finished her charade and there was nothing else to do but look at him again.

"Melissa. Melissa Grey. That's lovely."

His piercing stare bored into her. Then he said, slowly, "Oooh-kay . . ." while he kept on looking at her. In a brisker tone he added, "I'll be back for the package in a while."

"Fine," she said faintly. He went out and got on his bike, kicked it to life and roared away.

She stood there an instant, thinking with an irrational sense of loss, That's that. And immediately she asked herself, That's *what?* Charming as he was, too much about him bothered her; he seemed arrogant, irresponsible and very full of himself. Here today, gone tonight. She'd already been burned too deeply by a man like that. If there was anything she didn't need at all it was another third-degree burn.

Nevertheless when she slid open the door to the rear of the shop and stepped through, she glanced at herself in the mirror there. Her eyes *did* look purple. Their thick lashes were naturally darker than her hair; now her eyes looked wide and bright, absolutely glowing. If just talking to him for a half hour could put that look there, she couldn't help wondering what . . . other things would be like with him. She recalled that startling electricity in their fleeting touch.

Melissa made a face at herself. Maybe it was the eighteen-hundred-dollar sale that sparked that wattage. She had too much to do to stand there analyzing, anyway.

Four beautiful clocks that she'd gotten through canny auction bidding would be delivered that afternoon. The right place had to be found for each one. Then there was the heirloom watch to finish for the old lady who would be picking it up today . . . the Minnie Mouse watch to spruce up before 1:30 . . . Before she knew it, it was time for a quick lunch.

The next time she looked at the clocks, it was almost three. The pleased owner of the heirloom watch was just leaving when Melissa saw Bart Freeman at the door.

He held it open for the old lady, smiling at Melissa.

"Hello again." He was in the shop in one long stride, his rueful smile widening into a grin. "How about some lunch?"

"*Lunch!*" She had to laugh. "I had it three hours ago. It's almost three o'clock."

Bart Freeman looked at the grandfather clock. "So it is. What do you know?"

She noticed that his wrists were bare. "Don't you wear a watch?" She'd never known a man who didn't.

"Hate the things," he admitted, "if you'll pardon my rudeness. They remind me too much of—" He stopped short and her curiosity was aroused. She wondered what he did for a living, if anything.

"I've always thought it was more important to know what time is than what time it is," he drawled.

Oh, no. One of those mystic types, a so-called free spirit. Just like Gavin. Translation—messy, irresponsible and never on time, the kind who kept *other* people tied up and off balance.

"Time is a river, Melissa Grey. Let's float off on it for a while. It *is* your birthday. You should have champagne in a sidewalk café and watch the workaday world go by."

He made it sound marvelous. She wondered what it would be like just to lock up, wander out, drift along without any sense of responsibility at all. Maybe she was a little uptight, too regimented. . . .

But she couldn't. She really couldn't. A very good customer was coming in at 3:30, a woman she also liked, incidentally, and would hate to disappoint. Besides, there was that other nice client who was bringing in a Seth Thomas for an overhaul. He'd be fit to be tied if he had to carry it back home again.

"I'm sorry. I really can't. I have things I have to do, people depending on me. Don't you?"

His smile died. "Oh, yes, indeedy. Or at least they think so. But I'm playing hooky today and I wish you'd play it with me."

Something in his tone made her suspect he was married. She hadn't considered that before and it was a depressing idea.

"I'm sorry, Mr. Freeman. I can't."

"Won't, that is," he corrected in a doleful way. "All right, Melissa. I'll pick up my marbles and go." He hoisted the package. "But tomorrow's another day. I'll be back, some shining hour." He gave her a mock salute and left.

"Some shining hour," she murmured. Bart Freeman certainly didn't have a low opinion of himself, that was quite apparent. When the phone rang, she was relieved by the distraction.

"Hello, lovely lady." She recognized Ansel's Maine drawl right away. "All set for tonight?"

"Of course." Somehow with Ansel it was always "of course"; she took him very much for granted. There was an old-clothes comfort about him. Forty-ish, bearded Ansel had moved to New York from Maine a few years ago and ran his antique store with casualness, preferring chess at Jeff's Tavern to any amount of sales. She'd never looked on him as anything but a friend—and a surprisingly sharp adviser at auctions—but he kept on pursuing her in his polite, dogged way.

"Great. What time shall I pick you up . . . sevenish or so?"

"Seven's fine." They said good-bye.

There was something soothing about him. On the other hand Bart Freeman was about as soothing as hard rock. Just the kind of man she didn't need. But if that was the case, it was strange that he kept popping into her mind, over and over. She couldn't quite forget that strong sensation she'd felt when their fingers had accidentally met, that exciting crackle that had hinted at a future storm.

Just the kind of feeling, Melissa thought when she was locking up, that sang from her mother's poems.

Ria Draco the poet was born Honoria Drake, inheriting her passionate temperament, her great dark eyes and rigid code of honor from her Creole mother. Her curious intelligence and tow-colored hair had come from a New England father. Melissa's father, Harold Grey, had been the love of Ria's life, and Melissa looked exactly like him except for her sensuous mouth, which resembled Ria's. He had been a slender, reticent man as unlike Ria as the moon to the sun, a third-generation practitioner of watchmaking. He'd taught Melissa everything he knew and when he had died in her fifteenth year he'd bequeathed her his love of clocks and a future loyal clientele.

Melissa's great-grandfather, Josiah Grey, built the house containing Time Was in 1892, operating Grey Clocks on the street floor for many years. Melissa's grandfather Richard and her father Harold followed suit. When Melissa took over at nineteen, Grey Clocks became Time Was. She not only repaired and maintained antique timepieces but became a wizard at trading in them as well.

Then Gavin had come along—charming, lighthearted—to upset all her routines, laugh at her seriousness, never understanding what her work meant to her. Not telling her he was married until it was too late. But so charming.

Like the man called Bart Freeman, the very reincarnation in many ways of Gavin. She did not want a man like that to wreck her rebuilt life.

Going upstairs to her serene and beautiful apartment, Melissa made up her mind to forget him.

"Oo la la, and again oo la la," Ansel quipped, helping Melissa out of her black crepe cardigan jacket. He goggled at her off-one-shoulder jumpsuit, sooty-black with big powder-blue-and-magenta flowers. Her hair was hanging in loose, shining waves. "Terr-ific."

In the foyer of the spacious Gramercy Park apartment, Melissa's mother held out her arms. "Happy birthday, darling. You look so glamorous." Small Ria hugged Melissa to her. Her dark eyes glowed, her silver-gilt hair striking in contrast to her sherry-colored dress.

Melissa's stepfather, Mark Laine, towered behind Ria. He greeted Melissa in his growly baritone, leaning to kiss her cheek. Melissa liked this good-natured giant. Mark was a Columbia physicist with a staggering I. Q. who jogged in Gramercy Park and preferred the company of his pipe-smoking scientist cronies when Ria held her poetry classes.

Melissa shared his feelings; like Mark, she adored Ria and her poetry, but they both found the poets a bit much at times.

The bards were much in evidence tonight. There was a lot of hand-kissing and racy banter from the immense "street poet," Royal Jones; tender murmurs from Jake Palette, whose real name was Harvey Gold, and from blond Karel Larsson. Karel had always run after Melissa, even when she was seeing Gavin.

Antonio Pavone, whose last name was Italian for, appropriately, "peacock," burst into lyrical praise while his patient wife looked on.

"Peg!" Melissa was delighted to see her friend. It was a perfect excuse to escape the detestable Antonio.

Mark called Peg Walsh Linden the "only rational one in the bunch."

Peg embraced Melissa. "You look so good I'm sorry Carl's here. You'll steal him away!" She smiled up at her tall husband, a chemist who was a special pal of Mark's. They loved talking science and sports on these occasions.

"That'll be the day," Melissa mocked her. Peg and Carl were legendary for their closeness. Looking at them together now, Melissa felt a slight pang of envy.

"You've got that right," Mark commented. "Even our Marirose can't impress Carl." Mark cocked an ironic eye at Marirose Acerbo, who was seated across the room, showing a startling amount of skin. Marirose wrote violently erotic poetry and objectionable features on love techniques for some of the more sensational magazines. She was whispering in Royal Jones's ear. Melissa chuckled. Even Royal was blushing.

"But you're *glowing*," Peg murmured, when the men were in a solemn discussion of the World Series. "What's *happened?* You always look wonderful," she added loyally, "but there's something . . . special about you tonight. Could there be a new man in the wings? I don't think Faithful Harper's responsible."

Melissa laughed softly. Ansel was safely out of earshot, talking to Antonio and Sybilla Pavone. Maybe she *did* look different tonight. After all, what had happened today didn't happen that often—in fact, never. Bart Freeman had made her feel very alive, very vulnerable. It was an irony that she wasn't going to be allowed to forget him, much as she wanted to. But somehow she couldn't tell even Peg about today. That would really be jumping the gun. He might never come back.

So she said lightly, "Just birthday bubbles, I guess.

And an enormous sale at the shop the first thing this morning."

Peg's speculative look, however, had a distinctly *Oh, yeah?* flavor.

To distract her, Melissa remarked, "After all this time, it still amazes me." She looked around the motley gathering.

"What?"

"My mother and the poets. You're the only one with a life-style like hers; the others are pretty"—she turned to watch Marirose flirt with Antonio, who was not exactly discouraging her—"wild in some ways. Ria accepts things in them she'd never accept in herself."

"Look who's talking," Peg kidded, her eyes twinkling.

Melissa thought, I put my foot in it then. She's thinking about Gavin . . . and me. I put up with an awful lot from him. There was no getting away from love-talk tonight.

She was glad when Peg went on, "The bottom line is, they're dedicated to their craft. No matter what Ria thinks of their personal lives, you know she can't resist anyone who works hard, who tries."

"Mama mia! You're gorgeous." Sal Pensivo, the "bricklayer poet," was suddenly upon them, hugging Melissa. "If I weren't such an old crock . . ." The white dazzling smile in his weathered face was infectious. Melissa found herself enjoying all of them again, her uneasiness forgotten.

All of the poets had brought small gifts for her birthday. Melissa took a mischievous pleasure in the ones that twitted her astrological sign, Virgo, popularly thought of as compulsive, prissy and spinsterish, but deep down harboring strong feelings.

Ria scoffed at the vulgar, simplified horoscopes, but took it all good-naturedly. However, when the big, crowded reception was over, and the more intimate six—Ria, Mark, Peg, Carl, Melissa and Ansel—were sitting down to dinner, she said to Melissa, "You're the *real* Virgo, darling . . . just *seething* under that calm exterior."

That was true enough today, Melissa concluded.

"Just like Carl," Peg agreed fervently, giving her husband a tender look.

Relaxed and lazy after the fine wine and superb dinner, Melissa was content to listen to the others and withdraw into her private reflections. She'd always thought astrology was highly overrated, but after a good deal of observation she had to admit the same numbers kept turning up. She and Carl Linden shared neatness, precision and punctuality. Yet he was obviously capable of wild, stormy feelings for Peg.

And so was Melissa Grey. That morning a perfect stranger had aroused a volcanic excitement deep inside her.

Suddenly Melissa was shaken out of her pleasant somnolence by something Ansel was saying.

". . . just yesterday. Offered me a bundle . . . Melissa? I don't know. I haven't asked her yet . . . yes, the whole three blocks, evidently."

"Have they approached you yet, Melissa?" Mark asked.

"Who? I'm sorry, I missed all that." Noticing Ria's speculative glance Melissa added, "A little too much *vino.*"

"The Freeman Company's after your block," Mark explained. "Ansel says they've approached him about selling. I was wondering if they'd been to see you yet."

The *Freeman* Company. She knew about its subsidiaries, Freeman Precision Instruments, Freeman Time and others. Freeman Time. He'd said he hated watches, because they reminded him of . . . something he didn't mention. Could that be the same Freeman? It made sense. A self-styled gypsy like that would certainly hate precision.

"Have they?" Mark prompted, puzzled.

"I'm . . . not sure," she murmured without thinking.

"Not *sure?*" Ria chuckled. "You do need some coffee, darling. This sounds like *un*real estate."

Melissa tried to join the others' laughter. Finally she managed to answer with a measure of calm. "I meant I had a customer by that name today. He seemed interested in the building. He bought an eighteen-hundred-dollar clock."

Ansel whistled. "I wish I had some phoney customers like that."

"Why, those maneuvering sons of . . . guns," Mark muttered. "Probably snooping around." He took a pull on his pipe. "That's a hell of a way to do business."

"Well, they'll have no problem with 'incidental expenses,'" Carl offered. "They've got to be loaded. Freeman Precision furnishes us with about everything we've got. Probably you, too, Mark."

"Sure. They're incredibly diversified. And I must admit, my Freeman watch"—he pulled back his cuff, revealing the quartz watch on his heavy wrist—"is about tops." Glancing at Melissa and Ria, he said, "I still prefer your merchandise, Melissa."

She knew what Mark was doing—trying to change the subject. An anxiety-provoking topic like this didn't belong at a birthday party. Melissa could tell from her mother's uneasy expression that she was worried, too—afraid that the beloved building where she and Harold Grey had had such happiness might be destroyed.

Melissa felt a deep, irrational ache of betrayal. So that was what he'd come there for: to get the lay of the land, evaluate her business. To find out how little Freeman could get away with when they made their offer. And, who knew, maybe to romance her into an agreement? This hurt more than anything.

But the last thing she wanted was to let Ria know how upset she really was, least of all that she had any personal interest in these wretched Freemans.

She said brightly, "No more business. When do I get my presents?"

Peg clapped her hands. "Right. Where are you hiding them, Ria?"

For a while the gloomy discussion was forgotten. Gaily Melissa opened her gifts, exclaiming: an extravagant gift certificate and beautiful clock encyclopedia from Mark and Ria, a luxurious handbag of moss-green leather from Peg and Carl, a lovely amethyst pendant on a silver chain from Ansel.

There was no further mention of the Freeman threat when they parted. Ansel walked home with her to "help her with her loot."

She halfheartedly offered him a nightcap.

He put down the gifts on her pumpkin-colored couch and, studying her, shook his head. "Your heart's not in it, my dear. Another time. You're way off in outer space tonight, Melissa. I can't help thinking you're always that way, with me. It's not much good with us, is it?"

Melissa stood there staring at him, in the midst of the serene, harvest-hued living room. He looked and sounded so woebegone that she was touched. But it was true enough; things weren't that good between them, and it was time to admit it.

"Ansel, you've been a good friend to me, and that's meant a lot. . . ."

"But friendship isn't enough, Melissa. And you know it." That was true enough. There was no answer to that.

When he'd gone, she was surprised at how relieved she was. He couldn't have gone on waiting, she couldn't have gone on evading. But still, he'd always been there to depend on. She felt a sudden sharp loneliness; even the house seemed empty and hollow. The soft, familiar beauty of the living room with its shades of pumpkin, gold and mossy-green had a magazine look, not the feeling of a home.

"Baloney." She'd said it out loud. The house did not look like a magazine at all; it was only her mood that had made her think so. She loved this house, treasured it more than almost anything; the house where her people had lived for nearly a hundred years, where she'd lived all her life. Even now her parents' happiness seemed to fill every inch of space.

And she was proud of what she'd done to it. Over the years the house had undergone many improvements. When Ria had married again a few years ago, Melissa had resisted the idea of renting out all the living quarters. She couldn't have borne to move, and she hadn't wanted to intrude on Mark and her mother, even if they'd had plenty of room. She had decided to rent out only the top floor to a woman who was a talented painter.

Melissa got up and went downstairs, enjoying the sight of the beautiful dining room next to the kitchen. Where her grandfather's workshop had been, Ria had set up a rustic table and chairs; Melissa had had the walls painted golden-yellow to brighten this part of the house that didn't get much sun. A Seth Thomas clock adorned one wall and on another was a multicolored city scene painted by her fourth-floor tenant. The kitchen was a pretty bower of apple-red and spring-green.

She went back upstairs to the living room, gathered up her gifts and climbed a second flight of stairs to her bedroom floor. This had contained the dining room in the old days when servants were resigned to walking up two flights from the kitchen. Now it was a sunny boudoir decorated in pale turquoise and rosy tones.

This house was the Greys' castle and the Freeman Company would raze it to the ground. Not without a fight. They were not going to destroy this historic place if she could help it. Tomorrow she'd talk to Martha and Michel, check with the neighborhood association, the church . . . everyone in the area who wanted to preserve its gracious flavor.

Putting her gifts away, Melissa hardly took a second look at them. There was too much on her mind. A lot had happened today—that disturbing encounter this morning, the dismissal of Ansel, and now the shadow of loss that lay over the whole block where Time Was stood.

Suddenly Melissa smiled over the gift from poor Abigail. Abigail Cove was a sixty-year-old poet who still wore miniskirts and did her long dyed hair in a forties style. It was a hand-crocheted stole in shrieking magenta. Abigail wrote embarrassing poems about past affairs, maintaining that love was a woman's only possible goal.

Well, it wasn't Melissa's; she was going to put that at the bottom of the list for the duration of the property war with Freeman. Saving Time Was had to be the first order of business.

As far as Bart Freeman went—if he did come back, she could cope with him now. As a matter of fact, if he was one of the Freemans after her property, she'd be almost eager to see how far he would go to get what he wanted.

She'd just have to forget that phenomenal thing, that odd, electric reaction when his fingers had brushed hers.

Chapter Two

On a short, out-of-the-way block in downtown Manhattan, near New York Harbor, the original Freeman Building rose twenty-five modest stories over Cedar Street in sight of the World Trade Center and the glass-and-marble titans of its surrounding complex.

At eleven the next morning Bartholomew Alexander Temple Freeman parked his brown Jaguar in front of the Freeman Building across the street from the tiny Greek church and strode through the Freeman entrance. He was dressed in a neat, dark business suit worn as casually as his jeans; his wild thatch of hair was tamed but his eyes were shadowed from lack of sleep.

He waved to the man at the cigar stand. "Hiya, Fred." He asked the guard on duty, "How's your wife, Joe?"

Joe beamed. "A lot better, thanks. Good to see you back again, Mr. Freeman."

Bart got out of the elevator on the top floor and strolled through the outer office, speaking to the women there, and on into his secretary's office.

"Good afternoon," he said genially. "Any coffee?"

"Lots. Black as night, strong as the devil, hot as hell." His secretary answered his infectious grin.

"Deliver it, deliver it." Bart opened the door marked B. FREEMAN, PRESIDENT and sauntered through. That form of his name had been a sore point with his uncle Edward Freeman, chairman of the board, who said it had no clout. Bart had retorted that all his names would look like a law firm. When he had suggested "Bat," which represented his first three initials, his uncle had given up. His uncle also obviously disapproved of his constant comings and goings, yet he did nothing actively to discourage them.

Bart saw his crusty uncle now at the panoramic window, glowering at the unobstructed view of the harbor. To the left the verdigrised Statue of Liberty raised her torch above the gray-green, sun-bright water.

Edward turned. "I've been waiting almost an hour," he growled.

"I didn't know we had an appointment," Bart responded calmly. "And good morning to *you*." He edged past the steel-and-marble coffee table and leather couches of the conference area and sat down at his desk. Then he called through the open door, "Roberta . . . are you growing the beans? *Coffee,* if you have any mercy."

Roberta came hurrying in with a mug of coffee. Bart took it and sipped with a sigh of pleasure.

"Mr. Freeman?"

"No, thanks, Roberta. I had my breakfast at seven-thirty," Edward Freeman said politely, with heavy emphasis. "Would you close the door on your way out?"

"Certainly, sir. I was about to." A smile twitched at the corners of her generous mouth.

When the door was softly shut, Edward demanded, "What happened on your trip to the coast?"

Bart took another swig of coffee. "All sewed up. They're typing the report right now, I imagine." He swiveled his puffed leather chair for a harbor view.

"When did you have time to dictate it?" Edward sounded irritable. "You weren't in yesterday, and then there was your mother's party last night."

Bart swiveled again to face his uncle. "About two this morning, give or take." He glanced at the mail on his desk as a hint for Edward to come to the point.

Edward shook his stately head. "I wish I had your energy."

For emphasis Bart picked up the letter on top of the mail pile. "You're not here to discuss my nocturnal habits, Ned. What's up?"

"I want to know why you're making waves about the expansion plan," Edward said with uncharacteristic bluntness.

"Why go over this again? I have too many doubts—doubts about the cost, which I find prohibitive, and which we can better; there's too much waste over a four-block area. We can do it with three. I've told you that twice—should I put it on tape so I can just keep playing it?"

Edward looked nettled at his tone and Bart was a bit ashamed. He shouldn't talk like that to an older man.

He said more quietly, "And now I have additional doubts about the area."

"Why?" Edward demanded. "There are no landmarks in that whole four-block area, if that's what you're getting at."

"That's just what I'm getting at. True, there are no landmarks there now. But there are several buildings that could be declared landmarks before our planning gets off the ground."

"Where?" Edward persisted. "I've been over that area myself, all the way from Twenty-first to Eighteenth Street."

Eighteenth Street. Bart had a vivid image of the graceful old building that housed that shop. He'd never dreamed he'd find anything quite like that . . . or like her. He dismissed the distracting thought and said, "I made a very careful tour of that area yesterday. That space is surrounded by landmarks. You're in an historic area populated by some of the biggest guns in this city, people with the power and means to block us."

"Nonsense. You're inviting trouble. Why, already, some owners—" He stopped, biting his lip.

An uneasy suspicion dawned on Bart. "Some owners what?"

"Well," Edward began slowly, "I've been doing a little preliminary detective work. Someone's got to do it; you're too essential with out-of-town contacts to be burdened with all this."

That was always his uncle's refrain, Bart thought. Why? "You sent reps without my knowledge or consent?"

"Well, yes. Look, maybe we'd better table this until you come back from Chicago."

"I don't think I'm going this time," Bart said casually, surprising even himself. He'd made the decision on the spur of the moment.

"What?" He was amused at his uncle's look of

astonishment. But he saw something else—dismay. Now, that was interesting.

"I think I'll send Ransom, start grooming him for this kind of thing."

"Can Ransom handle it? You said yourself no one can handle these matters like you."

"Maybe I'm getting a little tired of running around." Bart studied his uncle. This time he was sure of it; his uncle looked positively disturbed. Bart added deliberately, "I thought this would please you and Mother."

Edward said hastily, "Your mother will be over-joyed. And so will I, of course." He did not sound too convincing. Bart wondered just what was behind it.

"Meanwhile," Edward went on pacifically, "I wish you'd let me carry the burden of this expansion thing. You've got a lot on your plate. And I think, after you consider it again, you'll find the whole plan is the best deal we could possibly make. I'll double-check this landmarks aspect."

Bart privately doubted it but kept silent.

He thought of how much he'd let slide at the home office while he was running all over the country, taking out the boat and water-skiing on summer afternoons, enjoying long winter weekends in the mountains. Not let slide, exactly; let slide from his immediate control, blithely assuming he could run the company with one hand.

Well, that was history now.

To set Edward off balance, he asked in a tangential way, "What were your reps' results?"

He'd achieved his purpose. Ned Freeman looked like a hard ball had just been slapped in his mitt. But he rallied. "Now you're listening to reason. The results were encouraging. For instance, there's a fellow on Eighteenth Street . . ." He gave the street number.

Melissa's block. This could get complicated, Bart thought.

". . . a fellow by the name of Harper. He runs a store called Country Stuff, or some such nonsense. It seems he likes taverns better than business, would sell like a shot. The same went for several other owners."

"Which ones exactly?" Bart asked casually. Edward listed them. Her name was not among them. Bart exhaled a breath of relief. "Now, what about those property costs?"

It seemed to him Edward was ruffled; maybe it was just his imagination. "We've gone over and over those," he said crabbily. "We're not buying farmland, you realize. Any child knows you have to buy Manhattan space by the square inch, practically."

Any child did know that. It was a pretty weak reply. "But other companies have done a lot better . . . Cranford, for one. I think we're dealing with the wrong people. I want to go over this thing with a microscope before I buy the idea."

"Well, I can see we're just getting redundant here." Edward rose huffily, glancing at his Freeman Precision watch. "I've got to get to a meeting. I'm late already. We'll take this up again later."

"Oh, that we will." Bart gave him a level look. His uncle stalked out.

Bart leaned back in his chair and stretched out his long legs, putting his feet on the desk. Something didn't quite compute. All of a sudden his Uncle Ned was awfully anxious to keep him out of the expansion.

There had been hints of that before, but he'd never tipped his hand so wide as this. Something was in the wind and Bart was damned-well going to find out what it was. But first things first right now.

He raced through the accumulated mail and dispatched it. Then he asked Roberta to go out and bring back certain data.

He glanced at his clock, smiling, dialed some numbers, gave orders.

Now, he judged with satisfaction, the only errand left was to get over to Broadway and buy a hat.

He wasn't going to be late for that lunch today.

Melissa finished reassembling the old Express English lever watch she had just cleaned, gave it a thorough polish and went in the back to wash her hands. She hung her smock on a hook and came back to the front, feeling strangely restless and dissatisfied.

It was another bright, wonderful day, crisper than the day before, but the ads for estate sales had yielded nothing of interest and she was facing a comparatively dull afternoon. She decided to go to lunch a little early.

As she was getting ready to leave she saw a brown Jaguar pull up outside Time Was. A tall man got out, his face obscured by an enormous ice bucket filled with dozens of yellow roses. A foil-wrapped bottle protruded from the roses. Something in his gestures struck her as familiar, but a hat hid his hair as completely as the bucket masked his face. Mystified, she realized he was heading straight for her door, the bucket still held high in front of him.

When she opened the door he lowered the container. Bart Freeman's face came into view. He was smiling at her, and there was a glint in his fox-colored eyes that slanted downward at the corners.

She was speechless; his tall leanness and comical burden filled the door. She could not help staring at his mouth, could not prevent the sudden breathless feeling that overtook her.

"A few belated birthday presents," he said lightly. "Where shall I put them?"

Melissa stepped back to admit him, a treacherous warmth invading her body. Laughter boiled in her and escaped. "On the desk."

"Yes, ma'am." He obeyed, withdrawing a bottle of French champagne from the midst of the roses. Fascinated in spite of herself, she watched him burrow among the flowers again and bring out two thin-stemmed glasses in Pliofilm envelopes. "Voilà!" Deftly he slipped the glasses from their coverings and set them on her desk.

"I couldn't persuade you yesterday," he said, "but now I've caught you, haven't I? This *is* your lunchtime, you told me."

"Am I having it with you?" she demanded. Excitement quickened in her body, all the countermoves she'd planned so coolly evaporating for the moment. It was maddening.

"That was the idea. I hope you will. How about a toast before lunch?" He uncorked the bottle with a flourish and poured wine into the glasses. He held out a glass to her.

She took it; the brush of their meeting fingers was swift and light as the wing of a moth and yet Melissa felt that amazing warmth, that jolt of sensation that she'd experienced the day before. His eyes gleamed more brightly. He touched his glass to hers, making them chime. "To your hour," he said in a husky voice.

Melissa raised her glass and tasted the glorious wine. Over the rim of his glass Bart Freeman took in her free-flowing hair, the soft green paisley dress that clung to her upper body. "Your hair is beautiful like that," he murmured when he put his glass down. "Your eyes are green today."

She didn't feel cool and rational now at all, as she had last night. Nevertheless she kept her reply light. "Thank you. You're a little crazy, Mr. Freeman." She grinned and his look dropped to her mouth.

"More than a little. Just one thing, though—I answer to Bart." She ignored that and he asked, "Ready for lunch?"

"As a matter of fact, I was just going out for that." The wine had soothed Melissa's nerves a little. After all, why not have lunch with him? This was the perfect chance to find out if he were one of *those* Freemans.

Out in the gentle sun, walking beside him, she stopped trying to fool herself. She could have asked him outright, without accepting his invitation to lunch. But it was delightful, being close to him like this, feeling his gaze on her, sensing that he shortened his long stride a bit to match her steps.

"Is the Green House all right?" His arm grazed hers when he turned to ask the question and she was startled all over again by the strong effect of that minute contact.

"It's fine," she murmured, hoping he hadn't guessed how much he moved her. Melissa Grey was always so together—but now she didn't feel together at all.

The Green House was an offbeat, multileveled restaurant just a block away; she'd been there only for dinner. It was not the kind of place a busy person dropped into for lunch, with its leisurely, unobtrusive service, its air of lazy rendezvous. They were escorted down wooden stairs to a secluded reserved table in a jungle of hanging plants, vines and flowers screening them from other diners.

"An expedition into darkest Gramercy," Bart quipped, seating himself across from Melissa. More than ever she felt that treacherous warmth, that insidious excitement. This was the first time she had really had the chance to look at him unobserved.

While he gave their drink order and studied the menu, she obliquely inventoried his crisp, vital hair with its irrepressible cowlick slanting over one rusty, straight brow; the virile, level brows contrasted sharply with the eyes that drooped slightly at the corners. If it had not been for the handsome, classic nose and well-shaped mouth, he would have looked like an intelligent clown. There were tiny laugh lines around his eyes and mouth.

She'd never seen a man who was so appealing without actual handsomeness. He looked up and gave her another of those odd, touching smiles that combined wistfulness and mischief in such a unique way.

Watch it, she told herself. This man is really getting to you.

"You had reservations," she remarked.

At once he caught her meaning—it was a polite way to ask if he were always so sure of himself.

"Only with hope," he admitted, leaning a little toward her. "You're the one with reservations, Ms. Grey. Isn't that so?"

Her face felt warm. This was not going the way it should. Not at all. "Yes."

"Something happened to you, didn't it?" he asked gently. "You've got 'burnt child' written all over you. I can almost see the bandages." He reached out and his fingers closed lightly over hers. "So was I," he added softly, "maybe in a different way from you. But I found out I had to keep living, stay open. We can't stay locked up, Melissa."

She withdrew her hand and took a sip of her drink. When he spoke in that tone she felt her resistance slip away. "That's what my mother says."

"What is she like?"

Relaxed by the drink and the champagne, Melissa told him.

"A poet for a mother," he commented in the same quiet tone. "A lady from antique time."

Melissa felt the throbbing of her pulse, magnetized by the gentleness of his voice, the surprising beauty of his words. Right now he didn't look at all like an arrogant playboy, another smooth male dedicated to "the score." It totally confused her.

She couldn't help wondering what his astrological sign was; he was so totally opposite to herself, with her caution and reserve, so free and open. Throughout Melissa's childhood Ria had steeped her in astrology, and while Melissa was still a bit skeptical about the whole thing, there was an almost eerie credibility to it, many times. His whimsy was Piscean.

Bart Freeman was still studying her intently. He moved back to allow the waiter to set their lunches before them; but as soon as the man was gone, he leaned forward again intently. "What is your father like?"

Even in the midst of her warm, vulnerable feelings, Melissa was dismayed by the direction the talk was taking. Everything was about her, nothing about him. Nevertheless she found herself compliant again, telling him all about her father and the generations of Greys.

As he ate, Bart Freeman seemed to be taking in every word. All the time he had a disturbing way of staring at her eyes and mouth and face and hair. Melissa poked at her lunch, hardly knowing what she was eating, feeling less and less in control.

She fell silent. A faint breeze moved the green, heavy vines, and the sun, through the glass greenhouse roof, was vivid on the masses of autumn flowers—gold and yellow, orange and burgundy, crimson and purple. Melissa took a quick, shaky breath, looking away from his own vividness.

"Please," he said so suddenly that even the low tone shook her. "Look . . . I'm sorry I came on so strong yesterday." He reached for her hand again and this time she did not withdraw it. "But I've never known anyone like you, Melissa. I was never hit so hard, so soon." He grinned his inimitable, sad grin. "But that's the way it is, isn't it? It's either instant or not at all, as far as I'm concerned."

Melissa studied him, almost wanting to believe him. But all at once she thought she saw a kind of triumph shining in his eyes, an easy satisfaction. She'd met him only yesterday, and now, after an hour with him, she was obviously succumbing. She slipped her hand from his grasp.

It wouldn't do. It wouldn't do at all. She still didn't even know who he was, whether all this was only a part of some plan of his.

"I'm sorry, I must go," she said. He looked startled, almost pained, and for an instant she wavered. It had been a very cold reply, she admitted to herself.

With greater softness, she repeated, "I really must go now."

He shook his head. "I've done it again. I'm sorry, Melissa. Please don't go yet." His eyes began to twinkle. "It's Wednesday—maybe we could see a matinee . . . go out to the track and watch the ponies. Couldn't we?"

When she didn't answer, he assured her, "I'll watch my words. Please."

It sounded very tempting. But she couldn't. She just couldn't let this go on. She didn't know a thing about him, wasn't really sure what he was after. And he could be married. The kind of gift he'd bought yesterday was for someone important—like a wife. It was an unpleasant idea.

All her doubts came rushing back. Yes, he might be married. And that notion broke the spell, tarnished the shining feelings she'd begun to feel, made a mockery of the lovely things he'd been saying. Why on earth hadn't that occurred to her before? That was probably one of the reasons he was so reticent about himself.

"I really can't," she said firmly.

"'Can't' again for 'won't,'" he retorted, but it was a rueful retort, not a rude one. That quality of gentleness was so disturbing; she was still drawn to him more than she wanted to be, could afford to be. "All right, Melissa, I give up . . . for now."

Out on the sidewalk the sun made a fiery mane of his vital, brilliant hair and her look was drawn irresistibly to it. Everything about him was so vital, supremely masculine. She gave him a glance, noticing on his face a disappointment that he couldn't hide. But she noticed something else, an expression of strong determination. Bart Freeman was not a man who gave up easily, she judged.

Yet she ventured, "You needn't walk me back."

He stopped and turned, staring down at her.

"I want to . . . thank you," she went on weakly, "for the 'birthday bubbles.' And lunch."

He shook his bright head and smiled. "I left my hat at your place. Very Freudian, you see . . . so I'd have an excuse to go back."

They walked on. "You don't look like the hat type to me," she commented.

"I'm not." The twinkling look he gave her set her pulses racing again. Her nostrils quivered at the pleasant, masculine aroma of him, that smell of cedar shavings.

He followed her into the shop. As soon as she closed the door he grabbed her in his arms and his mouth lowered to hers. Just before her closing lids blotted everything out, she was aware of the solemn excitement, the naked desire in his fox-colored eyes. At that moment she was lost to reason and to will; her arms stole around his sinewy neck and she was returning the kiss, returning it deeply and wildly, lost to the passionate tenderness of the mouth that had looked only humorous before.

A narrow flood of fire, like leaping mercury, raced throughout her every vein and she was moving into him, feeling the tremor in his big, hard body as she softened unthinking against him, caressing his neck with her fingers, learning the shape of his lean, fine head, the softness of his hair, the contours of his shoulders. Her hands were almost strange to her now, betraying her, hungry to know the outlines of his massive biceps, the sloping boxer's shoulders, the lobe of his shapely ear.

No, she thought hazily; merely taking him in with her eyes was no longer enough to satisfy; she wanted to touch him, and she had wanted to right from the very beginning.

He raised his lips from her mouth for a second, still holding her tightly, his eyes blazing down at her. "Melissa, Melissa," he said very softly; then his mouth was on hers again and she could feel herself letting go in a fiery weakness.

And then in another instant she had snapped to her senses: This is insane, insane, she was thinking; and she drew back shaken and a little shamed. "No," she protested in a quivering whisper, "no."

He would not let her go; his hands were hard and relentless on her waist, holding her near his body. She could feel that deep tremor in him still.

"Please," she said more firmly. "Let me go."

His big hands slackened their hold a trifle but he did not obey; the strong fingers still imprisoned her as he pleaded, "Don't send me away, Melissa. Don't send me away."

The touch of those hands was almost her undoing, but she shook her head, repeating, "No."

"Let's have this day together. You can't make me go . . . not after you kissed me like that."

"I'm sorry if I misled you, then," she said coldly. She supposed he expected her to pop into bed with him as a matter of course.

He reddened with annoyance and she could see a tendon flex in his jaw. "I didn't mean anything like that. I asked to spend the day with you, not the night. Although"— his smile started—"that's a fine idea."

She moved away from him and sat down at her desk, glad for the psychological barrier between them. The whole thing had gotten completely out of hand and everything she said seemed to make it worse. "Please go."

"Look, lady," he said, bending to place his big palms flat on the fragile desk and looking earnestly into her eyes, "maybe you've got the wrong idea about me. I think we should talk."

"I don't think so." It was impossible to talk rationally when he was that close to her.

He let out an exasperated breath and said, "Okay." He retrieved the hat and added, "For now." Then he walked to the door and turned. "I'll be in touch."

When he had gone out she went to the door and watched him drive away. At the corner she saw the hat skim out of the car window, like a discus, and land in a public trash basket. In spite of her distraught, confused emotions, laughter rose in her and broke free. He'd said he never knew anyone like her; well, she'd certainly never known anyone like *him*. Compared to Bart Freeman, Gavin had been as dull as bread.

She went back to the pleasant disarray of the wine and roses, not knowing for the moment where to begin. The whole episode had left her completely off balance.

There was no one clear-cut way to react to a man like that; it was hard to be angry at him, even harder to cope with the variety of emotions he aroused. Just when she was beginning to distrust him, his sincerity would reproach her. Then he undid her faint trust with his mysterious reticence, cooled her with his bland assumption that she would fall into his arms.

Well, she *had* fallen into his arms. Melissa had never been so confused about anyone or anything in her whole life. One thing was sure, she thought wryly. The roses needed water. She was distributing them into vases in the back when the buzzer sounded at the door. She came out carrying a filled vase.

She didn't know what she would do if he were back so soon. But to her surprise it was Ria. That was unusual; her mother wasn't one of those dropping-in mothers. She always phoned before she made one of her rare visits to the shop.

"Hello," Melissa said warmly, embracing Ria when she came in. Ria looked trim as usual, amazingly young in her corduroy trousers and soft blouson sweater, but there was a rather distracted expression on her face.

Catching sight of the champagne and roses, Ria commented, "Well, *well*. What's all this? Still celebrating? What's gotten into Ansel?"

"It wasn't Ansel," Melissa admitted. "Sit . . . while I straighten this out." She set the vase of roses down.

Ria obeyed, sitting at the desk. She lit a cigarette and observed as Melissa picked up the ice bucket containing the bottle and glasses. "Need any help?" she asked.

"No thanks. I'll be right back." Melissa stowed the bucket away in the back and returned.

"I'd be surprised," Ria commented, "if that stolid Capricorn did this." She waved at the roses. "This is very interesting." Her big black eyes gleamed. "A Piscean attention if I ever saw one. Delicious—your 'fatal opposite.'"

"I really wouldn't know." Melissa saw that her polite and sensitive mother had picked up on her unwillingness to discuss it. She was feeling more inept and foolish by the minute; she'd missed the chance at lunch with Bart Freeman to find out if he were one of the Freemans after their house. She couldn't possibly let Ria know that.

Tactfully Ria changed the subject. "I hope you're not too busy to talk. Something else has come up about that rotten building project."

"No, as a matter of fact, I have plenty of time this afternoon." Melissa sat down in the other chair, assailed with fresh apprehension.

"I've been talking to several people in the neighborhood association and they're calling an emergency meeting tomorrow night. Right now this Freeman plan is mostly just rumor and speculation, but we want to be prepared. You'll come, won't you?"

"Of course."

"Martha Stanton called me, too," Ria said, stubbing out her cigarette. "Someone approached her just this morning."

Melissa longed to ask Ria what the person had looked like, but there was no way to do that without inviting a lot of questions. She had a sneaking suspicion it could have been Bart Freeman himself. The whole wretched thing was utterly maddening. But Ria was staring at her, evidently a bit puzzled at her lack of response.

"And what happened?" Melissa asked hastily.

Ria chuckled. "You know Martha. She practically swept him out with a broom." Melissa grinned. Small blond Martha, who was five feet nothing and weighed about ninety-nine pounds wringing wet, had a sharp tongue and belligerent manner that could subdue the strongest man. "Patchwork means as much to her as Time Was does to us, you know. She said she tried to get you before, but you were probably out to lunch, and you weren't at the usual places."

Amused, Melissa heard her mother's Scorpionic curiosity surface with the last leading comment. Ria was too subtle to come right out and ask. Melissa wanted to tell her; she always liked talking things over with Ria. But now there were two reasons why she couldn't. Not only was there a Freeman involved, but her mother might also assume that Melissa was being "courted," to use Ria's term, and she didn't want to start a discussion in that direction. Melissa was always very aware that a good marriage for her was constantly on Ria's mind.

"Actually I was doing some shopping," she said mendaciously.

"Oh. Well, anyway, Martha seems to think there's mixed reactions on the block to this thing. A couple of people aren't averse to selling—our Ansel, for one." Ria's tone was dry. "He's always cared more about checkmates than checks, we all know. Checks he has to *work* for, that is."

"You've got that right. I tell you what, I'll give Martha a call, or drop in on her later. What time is the meeting tomorrow night?"

"Eight. At the church." Ria got up. "So we'll see you there, then?"

"Absolutely. But please don't go rushing off, Mother."

Ria smiled. "I must. Even if you're a lady of leisure today, I'm not. I promised Mark I'd do some research on the landmarks thing, and I have to read a new manuscript. A hundred other things."

Melissa could believe it. Her mother was always a dynamo of activity.

"All right. See you tomorrow."

When Ria had left, Melissa phoned Martha Stanton and Michel. They were both feeling nervous about the Freeman expansion plan, dreading the thought of eviction.

By the time Melissa locked up for the evening, the brief, hot, unexpected feelings kindled by Bart Freeman had cooled. She had an even stronger feeling that he was part of the whole conspiracy. And if that were so, what a low trick it had been—the champagne and flowers, the elaborate lunch, the poetic declarations. She wondered what ploys he was using with the other property owners.

And yet she couldn't help a faint ache of betrayal; he'd sounded so sincere and tender. Worse than that—his kiss, his touch had wakened desires in her that had been dormant for so long. That was something she couldn't get over in an afternoon.

After she'd checked the mail and changed into a T-shirt and jeans, Melissa descended to the kitchen to start dinner. She really didn't feel like eating much and was debating about whether to have dinner out when she heard the light running steps of a cat on the cellar stairs.

A lean black-and-white cat came bounding into the

kitchen and greeted her with a loud mew, staring up at her from his peridot-green eyes. His face was raffish and askew with a black splash on one side, white on the other, as if he'd fallen sideways into a bowl of ink.

"Philo!" Melissa stooped down to caress him. He was such an endearing animal; he always made her feel like smiling. He rubbed his head against her face.

Just then Melissa heard the call from above, on the outside stairs. "Philo! Where is that cacodemon?"

Melissa chuckled. It was her tenant and friend, Maria Deres, the painter who lived on the top floor. Maria had four charming cats that enjoyed running down the outside stairway to the garden. They rarely came into Melissa's quarters, but once in a while one of them made an unexpected entrance from somewhere.

Melissa went to the open window and called up. "Philo's with me, here in the kitchen."

"That cat, that cat," she heard Maria grumble in her deep voice. "I'm glad you're home," the voice called down. "I've got something for you." There was a pause and then the sound of her friend's steady footsteps descending.

Melissa went to open the garden door, admitting the smiling Maria. Philo shot out between their legs.

"I was going to feed him, but now . . ." Melissa laughed and grabbed Maria, hugging her.

"Feed him! I just stuffed him. Oh, you're cooking. I won't keep you. I just wanted to bring you this." Maria was holding a gaily wrapped package in her hand. "Happy birthday, a day late. I've been so wrapped up . . . *trying* to paint that night scene. I

swear moonlight is the worst thing in the world to get on canvas."

Melissa took the package. "Don't you dare run off," she ordered. "Let me give you some coffee.' Have dinner with me, please." It was not only politeness; all of a sudden Melissa was feeling very lonely. "There's plenty. It's stew."

"Oh, no," Maria protested. "Maybe just coffee." She came in and closed the door, sinking into one of the chairs at the rustic table. "I thought you'd be out with your beau tonight, celebrating your birthday at least for a week . . . like a Polish wedding." Maria smiled infectiously, the smile wrinkling her amiable, lined face. Maria Dereszewska was seventy-two years old and looked fifty. She signed her paintings "Maria Deres," remarking with dry humor that even she couldn't spell her full name and it looked better anyway on exhibition programs. Melissa loved her dearly; Maria was meticulous about respecting her privacy, and yet whenever she was needed, she was always on the spot. Over Melissa's protests, Maria had given her several beautiful paintings; one of them was the vivid city scene on the golden-yellow of the dining room wall.

Maria squinted up at the painting and remarked, "You know, that *is* a damned good picture." She added, with a twinkle in her heavy-lidded hazel eyes, "If I do say so myself."

"You're telling *me*," Melissa retorted and went to the kitchen to bring back a tray with a pot of coffee, cups and saucers. "The sugar's on the table," she prompted the absentminded Maria, who always seemed to be in a dreamworld of her own, a little like Ria. Melissa regarded her with affection; she was dressed in her habitual corduroy trousers and oversized plaid shirt. Her short gray-brown hair was ruffled, as if she'd been running her fingers through it as she struggled to get the moonlight right in her painting. There were traces of blue and white oil paint in the hair.

After Melissa poured out the coffee she opened her present.

"Oh, Maria, this is *gorgeous!*" Melissa unfolded the silk blouse.

"Isn't that the greatest shade of blue? It reminded me of asters . . . very appropriate for September. I guess I was thinking of that D. H. Lawrence poem about asters, whatever it was."

"Oh, yes. I know it. It's one of my favorites." A little dart of poignant feeling pierced her. Ria called D. H. Lawrence "the most passionate Virgo of them all," and Melissa remembered how deeply his love stories always affected her. He wrote of feelings as volcanic, as overwhelming, as the ones Bart Freeman had summoned up in her that very afternoon.

"Did I say something wrong?" Maria inquired gently. "You look like a rabbit ran over your grave, my dear. What's the matter?"

"Nothing. Nothing, really." Melissa folded the shining blouse and put it back in the box, then got up and put the box on the sideboard under the clock.

"Phooey," Maria scoffed. " 'Nothing, really' always means 'something.' "

Melissa could never fool the clear-sighted Maria; many times she'd found it easier to talk to her than to Ria, even.

"Well, I guess it's this real estate hassle," she admitted, which was at least partly true. For some reason she didn't feel like going into the other thing with Maria. Not yet. "You must have heard about it."

Maria let out a sigh. "And heard and heard. They

were talking about it in the grocery store . . . and the cleaners, and everywhere else I went today."

Looking at her friend Melissa was sorry she'd brought it up again. Maria looked desolate, frightened. "I don't know what I'd do if they tore down this house," Maria said in a burst of frankness. "Where is an old woman with four cats going to go in a hurry?"

Melissa felt awful. It would be bad enough for her and the others; for Maria, it would be disastrous. She'd told Melissa many times that her living there had been the happiest, most peaceful time of her life. The widowed Maria had led a fascinating and hectic life with her tempestuous husband, who had also been a painter. One of her constant sayings was "Peace, it's wonderful." New indignation fired Melissa; those blasted companies didn't give a damn about anything but money and progress. The fact that they were uprooting lives, destroying beauty, marring a venerable area, was nothing to them.

"Don't you worry," she said to Maria. "This neighborhood's not going to sit still for this. You can bet on it. There are still ways to stop it, and we'll use them all."

She was happy to see Maria brighten. "Now," she said briskly, "are you staying for dinner? If I know you, you'll gnaw on a piece of cheese if you're left to your own devices."

Maria rewarded her with a smile. Her indifference to food was too well known. "I do have a mouse meal up there," she confessed. "If you're sure it's not too much trouble."

"How could you be trouble?" Melissa patted Maria's face and went to the kitchen.

As if in tacit agreement, they didn't discuss the expansion plan again during dinner. Melissa told her all about the party, which Maria had had to miss because of a business commitment. She was in the midst of getting a show together and joked with Melissa about the exhibit program.

"They want me to write up something about how I paint. Can you imagine anything more ridiculous? I felt like saying, 'If I were a writer I wouldn't be painting.' What can I say, for heaven's sake? What I do is mix up paints and put them on canvas."

Melissa laughed, feeling better than she had all afternoon. She decided to ask her mother to help Maria with the difficult project.

They chatted awhile after dinner as Maria helped her tidy up.

"Come on up the inside stairs," Melissa urged her. "I don't want you bumbling out there in the dark."

Maria followed her up the inside stairs. On the bedroom floor they said good night. "How I love this house," the old woman murmured, glancing into the rosy bower of the bedroom.

"And we're going to keep it. Count on it," Melissa assured her.

Later, preparing for bed, Melissa wasn't as sure as she had tried to sound. Freeman Company was a big outfit, a powerful one. But then, she consoled herself, so were the interests of the people who lived in this area.

She left a dim light on and got into her brass bed, realizing for the first time how drained she was. Through her half-lowered lids she surveyed the beautiful room, and reflected how much time and thought, how much effort and care had gone into the decorating of this and all the other rooms in the treasured house.

The walls, like the coverings of the bed, were a

warm, rich pink, at once gentle and vivid, like a pale peony. On the wall facing the bed was her favorite painting of Maria's. Her friend styled it a "mystic Reginald Marsh, pretty obsolete."

In Melissa's judgment, it was anything but obsolete. The picture had, for her, a timeless fascination, a strange but remarkable subject.

It pictured the occupants of a subway car, weary, preoccupied and self-contained, hiding behind their newspapers and private anxieties, completely ignoring the striking figure of a clown who was riding among them. He lazed on a bench, his long legs stretched out in the aisle. The scene, instead of being realistically colored in the alternately dun and garish tones one always saw on a subway train, was all in dreamy pastels—rose and aquamarine, pale blues and lavender and green. In fact, Melissa had been so drawn to the coloring she'd decorated the whole bedroom around it, to Maria's delight.

Now she was struck by the face of the clown, as she had never been before. His face was wistful and mischievous and strong all at once, a triumph of portraiture. Melissa knew in an instant who he reminded her of, with his air of utter foreignness to the ordinary people on the train, his wise, twinkling eyes under their level brows regarding the others with compassionate amusement—his expression was like Bart Freeman's.

A man who was different from everyone, who went his own way, disguising a lonely sadness under careless humor.

"Ridiculous," she muttered and turned out the light, blotting the clown with darkness.

She must be out of her mind. She'd be better off leaving the fantasies to Maria and her mother. It was

silly to read so much into Bart Freeman's personality
. . . a man who was out to get her, in more ways than
one; out to get her family and neighbors and friends.

And yet, when he had kissed her—damn him,
anyway. She was going to put this afternoon right out
of her mind. She'd believed there was no one way to
take him, because he was so complicated. There was
just one way to consider him, after all. He was a
dangerous nuisance and her guard was going up again,
this time to stay.

Chapter Three

$\mathscr{I}$t wasn't quite nine the next morning when the Time Was phone rang. Melissa, working with the stem of a silver chatelaine, picked up the workshop extension with her other hand.

"You *are* there." She knew the deep, resonant drawl at once. "I couldn't get you last night. Some robot kept telling me you have an unlisted number."

Deliberately Melissa asked, "Who is this?"

There was a beat of silence, an indrawn breath. "Bart, Melissa. May I see you today . . . please?"

"I'm sorry," she said promptly. "That's impossible."

"Nothing's impossible. Except, possibly, me." Undiscouraged by her silence, he added, "I'd like to show you how well behaved I can be. Will you give me the chance?"

She was letting herself react to that caressing tone

and she mustn't. "I have a very full schedule today," she answered coolly.

"And tonight—are you working overtime? How about dinner?"

"I'm going to be busy all evening."

There was a deep sigh on the line. "I surrender. But only for the time being. Have a lovely day."

She hung up and went back to her task. He was exasperating, totally exasperating. She'd come downstairs that morning in a calm frame of mind and now all that was changed. Trying to adjust the stem on the old Waterbury "Lady L," she found that her fingers were unsteady, her concentration scattered.

Melissa put the delicate pieces away, turned out the light and busied herself with other things. She was relieved that there were no more calls from him the rest of the morning and throughout the afternoon. It was absurd to react like that, just to a man's voice, but somehow when she heard it she felt as if he were touching her.

It helped when things got going; all of a sudden about eleven, she was deluged with activity, and she spent part of the afternoon investigating some good buys in antique stores along lower Broadway. Closing time came upon her almost unawares, and then there was a rush to bathe and change, get to Ria's for dinner before the meeting.

Sitting with Mark and her mother in the church parish hall, surrounded by Martha, Maria and other familiar faces, she felt serene again, in control. The threat facing them was more important than anything else, and now, she thought gratefully, I can put my mind to it.

The president of the neighborhood association was talking to the group when Melissa's attention was distracted by a latecomer, a tall presence just on the edge of her vision. Involuntarily she turned and saw Bart Freeman.

She felt her face warming, sensed Ria's glance and turned a little away from her mother to hide her expression. As she did so, she met his eyes.

He nodded with a half smile on his sensuous lips, his dark eyes bright, and sat down in another row against the wall. His easy manner and negligent sprawl sparked Melissa's ire: That did it. He had to be here spying for that damned land-grabbing company. When this meeting was over she'd really let him have it.

Melissa had to force herself to listen to the rest of the meeting, follow the forming of committees. She herself volunteered for the one that would pursue the landmarks question, as did Ria and Mark.

At one point she heard Mark murmur to her mother, "Well, well, what's *he* doing here?" Melissa's heart thudded—did they know Bart Freeman? But when she followed the direction of her stepfather's eyes, she saw Ansel Harper.

Even more annoyed, she mentally echoed Mark's question. If Ansel was willing to sell out, it was strange that he was sitting in on this meeting.

After it adjourned, Melissa stood around talking with a number of people. She caught sight of Mark and her mother leaving; Ria gave her a casual wave.

Blast it. Seeing Ansel, they'd assumed he would walk her home, of course, so they hadn't asked if she wanted them to. The evening that had begun so serenely had become a mess, a tangle. Maria was going off with a friend; Melissa had heard her saying something about a drink at Jeff's Tavern, and Melissa didn't feel like intruding.

The main thing now was just to get out of there; she needed to be alone and sort things out. The only bright spot was that Bart Freeman seemed to have disappeared. Even he, she thought sourly, wouldn't have the nerve to keep after her now. His coming to the meeting had confirmed all her earlier suspicions.

She ran into Ansel by the door. "Melissa, how are you?" He was distant but amiable.

With a cool, civil answer, she went out. She'd felt like asking him what he was doing there at all, but the idea was distasteful. After all, she *had* rejected him and it was awkward. But she was still irritated with Ansel—he hadn't helped this situation to begin with, going against the rest of them.

He walked out chatting with Martha Stanton. Bart Freeman still hadn't surfaced and Melissa hardly knew whether she was sorry or glad; it would have been very satisfying to confront him, but it also could have been disturbing. She couldn't quite dismiss her confused and ambiguous emotions of the last two days and nights. Not to speak of that morning. He had a positive genius for rocking boats.

She saw Martha glance back, obviously puzzled that Melissa wasn't with Ansel. It was equally apparent that Martha felt uneasy with Ansel Harper herself; the news of Ansel's friendly reception of the buyer's representatives had raced like wildfire along the small world of Gramercy Park.

It was strange to be walking alone. Melissa moved on through the shadows of the venerable trees outside the church, casting their dark watery shapes on the pavement with the brilliant aid of a round harvest moon.

When she turned the corner, she heard her name quietly spoken. Bart Freeman was waiting for her.

"Please, ma'am," he said. Grinning, he tugged at the cowlick over his brow, mocking an ancient peasant. "May I speak to you, ma'am?"

She struggled between outrage and amusement. Something about it inevitably reminded her of the gamekeeper in *Lady Chatterley's Lover* and she was further dismayed by the acceleration of her traitorous pulse. Then anger won.

Walking toward him, she said coldly, "Let's get it out in the open. Just who *are* you, and what do you really want from me?"

He was utterly taken aback. But he rallied very quickly and answered, staring down at her. "You know who I am. All I want is to be with you, for us to get to know each other."

"You are really the most deceitful man I've ever met." She turned on her heel and walked away in the direction of Park Avenue South, too upset and angered to pursue the game. She'd never get a straight answer out of him. Ahead she saw Ansel and Martha in earnest conversation at the curb.

She heard Bart Freeman's footsteps behind her and hurried on. Then she noticed Martha walking away north, and Ansel, alone now, waiting to cross the street.

"Melissa! Let me talk to you!" Bart called to her.

"Just leave me alone," she retorted over her shoulder.

Ansel turned around, took in the situation and started walking toward her.

"Are you all right, Melissa?" His tone was belligerent, protective, and he glared at Bart.

Contrarily she resented Ansel's watchdog air; he sounded like the anxious father of an infant. "Perfectly," she said calmly. Ansel hesitated, shooting a bewildered glance at her and then at the man just behind her.

Finally Ansel shook his head, muttering, "Okay," and headed huffily south.

Bart Freeman fell into step with Melissa. "Who's the bodyguard?" he asked lightly. When she didn't answer, he said, "I'm glad you *had* one. It's not a great idea to run around alone at night."

Stung by the way he put it, she was impelled into a reply. "What do you mean, '*had* one'?" she demanded.

"Well, you won't be needing him anymore, ma'am," he retorted, slipping back into the imitation of the trusty servant. "I'm here to do the job."

This was past endurance. She just didn't know how to handle a man like this. He didn't know what a negative meant; he was like a rock. Worse than that; like constantly changing, moving water. No matter what you tossed into it, the water swallowed it up, reverting to its original form. But maybe there was one way to handle him, she decided.

They had reached the avenue and she desperately scanned the down-flowing traffic, eager for a chance to cross, perhaps elude him. However, she thought she knew how to get rid of him, once and for all.

"You're with Freeman Company, aren't you?" She turned and shot the question at him and something flickered in his eyes by the headlights' glare.

He held her look and let out a long breath. "Yes."

"I knew it," she muttered. "I knew it." Irritated, she saw there still wasn't an opening to cross. Then, when it seemed that an oncoming car was pretty far away, she started to dart across the avenue.

"Hold it!" The car was approaching faster than she'd reckoned. He grabbed her elbow and pulled her back to the curb. She was amazed at the panic in his tone and, glancing up at him, saw that he'd turned almost pale with his concern.

"Lady, lady." He shook his bright head. "I don't want to lose you now." His smile was shaky. "Now," he said. He took her firmly by the arm and they crossed the street. "Do you always do that?"

On the other side she started walking very fast. "I don't think I'm getting through to you. Just go away. Didn't it occur to you that I'd find out who you were, somewhere along the line?"

"Of course," he admitted, his long stride easily keeping pace. "But I wanted to put it off as long as possible."

"So you could romance me on the side?" She was furious now, no longer caring how crudely she expressed herself, although this was certainly not her style.

He obviously didn't think so, either, because she could feel his shocked surprise.

Before he could say anything else, she went on, "Is that the way you treat all the women owners? I'd like to know what ploys you used with the rest." Immediately she was chagrined that she'd put it on such a personal basis. "And then you came to our meeting to spy."

"Damn it! Look here, you stubborn little . . ." He grabbed her arm again and wheeled her around to face him.

But she wasn't through. "Why did you have to go through all that song and dance—the romantic gestures, the pretty speeches? Why didn't you just come right out and ask me to sell my property? What kind of person uses all that pretense?"

He had an expression of utter frustration, but there was naked hurt in his eyes. "That was no pretense, Melissa."

Impatiently she shook off his fingers and stalked off. Undiscouraged, he kept on at her side until Time Was came into view. "Would you let me come in a moment . . . give me a minute to explain?"

"You can't," she responded stiffly. "It's all too obvious."

In spite of her coldness he reached up and lightly touched her cheek. "Please," he said. His fingers had brushed her skin with such great gentleness, his voice was so beseeching that she was almost ashamed of her rage. That in itself was maddening.

"It's not obvious at all, Melissa. It's all very complicated. Can't we talk about it? Surely you can spare a man a cup of coffee."

Blast him, he put things in such a whimsical and absurd way that it made her feel like a perfect harridan to deny him. And he looked so eager and appealing—towering above her with that serious face —that she relented.

"All right," she said ungraciously. She unlocked the door and he followed right behind her. "All this and a garden, too," he murmured, closing the door. Melissa tossed her bag on one of the chairs and started into the kitchen, hearing him say, "This is lovely, Melissa Grey. Just like you."

Such unruffled good nature, such stubborn admiration, were hard to withstand. Somehow it always gave him a subtle advantage in their continuing duel. He was like a swordsman who only laughed when he was touched. She heated the coffee, listening to him prowl the dining area, apparently looking things over.

In direct line with her thought, he called out, "This is a wonderful painting."

"Yes . . . I love it." Melissa put the coffee things on a tray and carried them into the other room. His back was to her; he was examining the Seth Thomas clock. She had to admire the tall, hard shape of him—the back of his sinewy neck; the strong, sloping shoulders; the narrow hips in the tight tan trousers. He had a fantastic body, she admitted. "My mother would trade her whole bridge club for this one." He turned, grinning.

He saw the tray and came to relieve her of it. That reminded her of the way he'd helped her with the clock on that first morning, what had happened when their hands touched. "Thanks," she said calmly, this time taking care not to let their fingers meet. She needed all her marbles for this conference.

"Your mother likes clocks?" she asked neutrally as she sat down and poured the coffee.

He took the chair opposite. She was newly aware of his overwhelming masculinity, the way he seemed to fill the room with his presence. Other men had sat there, but the spacious area had never seemed to shrink, like this, when they had.

"She's the enthusiast I bought the clock for," he explained.

Elation buoyed her—his mother, not a wife or lover. But she tried to rein in her bubbling emotion; she hadn't invited him here to fall under that spell again.

"Why did you come to the meeting tonight?" she asked abruptly.

"To see you." He wasn't jarred a bit by the sudden question, the switch of subject. "It was the only way I could think of." The simple openness of that threw her a little off balance.

But she persisted. "It's very convenient that your company keeps such close tabs on us."

He waved his big hand as if to dismiss such a thought, but his earnest look still locked with hers. "Of course we do. That's the way everybody operates, surely you know that. But you haven't let me explain things to you." His hand crept toward hers on the table. She drew her own back.

Deliberately she took a sip of coffee before answering. She met his gaze, determined to win the staring game, to keep her cool. "I really don't see how you can," she said at last. "What's to explain—your company is after my house, and you weren't honest enough to identify yourself."

His russet lashes flicked and she could tell that the last words had hit home. "You're right. I'll identify myself now—with the whole package. Bartholomew Alexander Temple Freeman, president of Freeman Company, at your service." He gave her a crooked smile.

"President," she repeated, aghast.

"You make it sound like 'felon,'" he remarked ruefully, his look dancing from her eyes to her softly shining hair, then descending to linger on her short, straight nose and disapproving mouth. "You really are the most beautiful woman I've ever seen in my life," he said softly.

Fighting the melting warmth in her body, Melissa asked, as if he hadn't spoken, "Why all the deception?"

"Because I didn't want to mess things up right from the start. . . . I was trying to buy a little time. Time for us to . . . get to know each other. Sure, I knew this house was up for grabs. But you see, when it started—let me tell you how it was.

"I was riding around, looking the area over, checking things out. Farther uptown I couldn't see any problems at all; some pretty crummy places no one could miss. Then, when I got farther down, I began to realize what we were getting into. I saw this building, and your shop. You hadn't even opened yet. And when I looked in the window I saw that clock—it was a natural for my mother's birthday gift. That's what I had in mind. Then I saw you, and everything got complicated."

His voice was so gentle, he was so plausible and sincere, that she began to waver. But she couldn't. She just couldn't.

"That doesn't solve the problem," she answered coolly. "We're on opposite sides of the fence, and we'll stay that way as long as your company's trying to drive us out." He opened his mouth as if to speak, then closed it.

"I still can't trust you, Bart Freeman. You seemed to take me for some kind of fool," she went on bitterly.

"I'd never take you for any kind of fool," he said harshly. With a scrape of his chair, he was standing. Then before she knew it he had circled the table and was beside her, grabbing her hands, drawing her upward by her arms. His hold was gentle yet so firm that she couldn't extricate herself.

He was holding her close then, staring down into her eyes, and she felt herself begin to slide from the summit of her control, like a child at the top of a sliding board. His warm breath was on her mouth, the clean, male musk scent of him dragging at her senses.

"Melissa, oh, Melissa, be human, lady. All that's got nothing to do with this." And he bent his head until his quivering mouth touched her lips. She tried not to answer that mouth with hers, but it was no use. She was sliding downward now from that cool height, sliding with a wild and carefree exhilaration as her body moved closer to his.

Dizzily, hungrily, with closed eyes she felt her whole self go soft against him while her hands stroked his hair. She knew dimly that his fingers were at first cupping her face in their marvelous, tender power, then learning the outlines of her neck and shoulders, wandering to the slender curve of her waist, trailing up again to feel, in the forgetfulness of his starved embracing, the silkiness of her breasts budding to traitorous life through her thin shirt.

Melissa felt the sweet pressure of his wide chest and the amazing strength of those binding arms. This, then, she thought crazily, was what she had been so afraid of: She didn't want to let him go.

Why should I let him go? The hazy, dreamlike question sounded somewhere in her clouded consciousness. I've been so lonely, and alone. It's been so long.

Melissa opened her eyes as he raised his mouth for a breathless instant from her mouth; she saw in his own eyes two distant points of brightness, like a joyful, raging fire, that blazing light she had not seen for such a long and lonely time. Hungrily his look devoured her, as if he were trying to memorize the tumbled silk of her dark gold hair, her flushed face, her parted lips.

"I knew it, I knew it would be like this," he said hoarsely, his deep voice triumphant. And once again his hands explored her, tracing the form of her back, feeling the outward swell of her hips; he lowered his face to hers and took her mouth in a demanding kiss that dizzied her. She was shaken, helpless in his grasp, knowing a wonder almost painful in his seeking lips, his steely body. Her flesh went softer, more giving. All her sense of time and place and reason had departed; she was almost faint with desire.

She moved in his arms and withdrew a little from his grasp. She began to unbutton his shirt so she could feel his bare chest with her trembling hands. When she stroked him, he began to shake and it seemed they were both beyond all hesitation and control. Everything became a blur.

She was about to give herself to him, this maddening and bewitching stranger. This stranger.

The words sounded coldly and hollowly now in her

brain, exploding into dismay. She took her hands away from him.

"Melissa . . . what is it? What is it?" he asked her desperately.

He was a stranger, she repeated in silence. A man she still could not understand or bring herself to trust. In an awful instant she felt her wild desiring drain away, leaving her shamed and uncertain and chilled.

"What is it?" he demanded. "What's the matter?" He held her by the shoulders in bruising fingers. "What's turned you so cold to me? You were so . . . oh, Melissa, you . . ." He stopped in pained confusion, studying her, his eyes still reflecting the hunger of his desire.

"I can't . . ." she began miserably. "This can't . . . happen, Bart." She felt miserable and drained, but most of all she felt suffused with guilt and chagrin. There was a name for women who did things like that. And she had never, in all her life, been that kind of a woman.

And now she could see her own doubt mirrored in his expression. That was just what he would think she was. She knew then that she could not let this happen, could not let herself slip away into that wild forgetfulness. They were like strangers and there was too much unresolved between them; she was too uncertain of everything about him.

"Please, Bart, I must make you understand . . ." she began again.

"I understand all right, lady. You accused me of playing games. Compared to you, I'm an amateur. Have no fear, Melissa; I never forced myself on any woman, and I'm not about to start now. Good night."

Before she could say anything more, he'd stormed out the garden door, closing it firmly, and she could hear his quick, heavy step ascending the stairs.

She really didn't know whether to curse or cry. Now things were in a worse mess than ever. Why had she ever let him touch her like that, kiss her, in the first place? She should never, never have let it go that far.

But then her indignation overcame her hurt. How dare he talk like that to her? He had implied she'd purposely misled him.

She remembered his angry words, "Compared to you, I'm an amateur." Fuming, Melissa decided that that was the very last straw. If she ever spoke to him again she hoped someone would kick her. Hard.

Positively stimulated by her ire, Melissa tidied up and with an aggressive bang and rattle washed the coffee things, the pot and silver.

It would be a month of Sundays before she ever listened to anymore of his suggestions, as she had tonight.

Melissa was more dismayed than angry the next day when the memory of their encounter kept intruding. To make it worse, the remembrance of his mouth, the image of his body made her burn with savage frustration. She had wanted him every bit as much as he had wanted her—and to think he could call it a "game" on her part. She wondered what she'd say to him when he called, as he surely would.

But he didn't, that day or the next, and Melissa was wounded by his silence, even in the face of all that had happened.

She told herself that it was just as well; she'd gotten so busy that there wasn't time for much of anything but the shop and the neighborhood project. Already she'd met with the association committee, which was starting a letter and petition campaign, so all of them were swamped with clerical tasks and phoning. On top of that, Ria had a poetry reading scheduled for the following week, and Melissa offered to lend her a hand with programs and other matters.

And as if that weren't enough, she was obliged to go to another auction, one she really couldn't afford to miss. By the end of the week she'd just about had it, and was ready to relax. The greatest consolation was that she hadn't had a moment to brood over the abortive episode with Bart Freeman.

She took care of a minimum of business over the weekend, spent a serene Sunday with some friends and by Monday felt utterly renewed. Late on Monday afternoon she got a call from Peg Walsh Linden.

"I'm taking a day off tomorrow—they owe me," Peg said enthusiastically. "How about you? Let's go shopping, at least have lunch. It's been so *long*."

Melissa turned down the shopping expedition, but gladly accepted the lunch invitation.

"I'll be in midtown," Peg said. "You know that great old chophouse on Thirty-fourth and Eighth?"

Melissa said she knew it and loved it. They made an appointment to meet. She was putting away some new purchases when a bonded messenger appeared. Mystified, Melissa received a package. When the man had gone she unwrapped it. Within a larger box was a tiny satin hinged one. She opened the little box. In its gray velvet interior was a pair of exquisite sapphire earrings, her birthstone. A minute card was folded and stuck into the lid of the box.

Taking the card out she unfolded it and read, in a lilliputian handprint, "This is exactly how small I feel. Forgive me. These are the color of your eyes . . . and the shade I am." It was signed "Bart the Hun." She'd had to squint to read the minuscule printing, and her first thought was, It must have been hard for him to do that, with such big hands.

She stared at the earrings—they were the most delicate, the most beautiful piece of jewelry she'd ever seen, a simple pair of rich blue, oval sapphires, each surrounded by a lacy border of fragile white-gold filigree.

Melissa felt a strong temptation to try them on—then she realized with a pang she couldn't possibly accept them. To accept an expensive gift like this was a sign of accepting much more. And while at this moment she yearned for his closeness again, everything wary and logical in her told her it was impossible. She still didn't even know if he was single; if he were, and they came together, the difficulty of it would not be eased. In the last analysis he was dedicated to destroying all that she held so dear, that she had worked so long and hard to maintain.

With a little ache of regret, she replaced the smaller box in the larger one and put the box in her safe. She didn't know where he lived but she could return the package to his office. Tomorrow; she couldn't face that today.

She was still holding the card in her hand. She thought of throwing it away, but something made her put it in her purse.

When she kept her date with Peg the following noon, she arrived at the chophouse early. A few minutes later she sighted her friend, beaming, carrying two huge shopping bags. Melissa waved and Peg gestured with the bags to indicate that she was checking them.

"I've done it again," she bubbled when she got to the table. She sat down grinning at Melissa with a rueful, childlike air.

"Overdone on the plastic," Melissa said, feeling a giggle escape her. It was a statement, not a question; Peg was a generous, impulsive buyer.

"Of course. Well, it's Carl's birthday tomorrow . . . and after all, you only get born once a year." Peg chuckled and picked up the menu. "What are you having? After coping with all those mobs, I tell you, I want to *eat*."

"Oh, I haven't decided." Melissa was evasive. She didn't have much appetite at all; she hadn't really recuperated yet from the surprise of the day before and was struck by a poignant regret. The earrings would have been lovely with the blue sweater she was wearing. She studied Peg with affection; her small, slender friend had a very elfin look with her short, ruffled hair and uptilted dark eyes under winging brows. You almost expected her to disappear, like a leprechaun, Melissa thought.

Just then Peg glanced up from the menu and gave Melissa one of her oddly wistful smiles. The Pisces smile. It tugged at Melissa's heart because something about it reminded her of Bart Freeman. Really, if she could compare him with someone as petite and airy as her friend—the man had gotten to her, for sure.

To hide her expression, and to have something to occupy her hands, Melissa dug into her purse for one of her rare cigarettes. Her fingers brushed the small card from Bart Freeman.

She made an involuntary sound.

"What's up?" Peg asked her with concern. "You don't look very chipper today, kiddo."

"Oh, I'm just tired, I guess."

Peg looked skeptical. "I don't wonder. . . . Carl ran into Mark at the fights the other evening, and Mark told him about all the work you people are

doing. It must be exhausting. But I didn't mean
tired . . . you look kind of—sad, Melissa. Upset over
something."

If she couldn't tell Peg, to whom she'd always been
so close, who *could* she tell, Melissa decided.

And she poured the whole story out, pausing only
to give her order to the waiter, then for him to leave
after serving them.

Melissa picked at her mutton chops while Peg
ravenously devoured her kidney and bacon, on top of
four oysters, listening intently all the while without
once interrupting.

"I still don't know where you put all that food,
Peg," Melissa interjected, taking a small bite of
potato.

"Don't change the subject," Peg ordered good-
naturedly. "What are you going to do about Bart
Freeman?"

"I don't know," Melissa admitted unhappily. "I
thought I knew—I thought I had everything figured
out, but now I'm not so sure. I just can't . . . get him
out of my mind. And it's driving me up the wall."

She caught Peg's sympathetic and yet uncompre-
hending look. Peg always made lightning decisions,
never stopping to weigh and analyze things the way
Melissa invariably did.

"I know—typical Virgo. Right? Analyzing the life
out of everything. Cautious as an accountant . . .
don't say it!" Melissa made a face. She'd heard all this
from her mother since she could understand any
words at all.

Peg laughed. "Tell me about it. But that's the very
thing that makes you Virgos so attractive to the likes
of me. Carl does it until I could scream. He looks so
delightfully solemn. And then he turns right around

and . . . umm." Peg wiggled her brows up and down in a comical, suggestive way.

Melissa grinned. "Good old 'fatal opposites,' according to the gospel of Ria Draco."

"Or in plainer language—sexual dynamite," Peg said in her open manner. "From the sound of it, he does things to your metabolism. Have I got it right?"

"You've got it perfectly." Even with Peg she didn't usually open up much about things like this. Today she had to.

"It sounds to me like you two should get together. I'm sure you can work all the other things out." Peg was always overoptimistic, Melissa reflected, even more so in this case.

"I don't know about that," she protested.

"Oh, come on, now. Love will find a way, you know." Peg grinned and sipped her Chablis.

"I don't even know if that's what it is."

"Well, if it isn't, it ought to do until the real thing comes along." Peg set down her wineglass and twiddled thoughtfully with the stem. Then she said slowly and with care, as if eager not to offend Melissa, "You know, Carl and I have . . . talked about it a lot, Melissa. I mean, what a *waste* it is. For someone like you to be alone."

She looked up and smiled, half in apology. "I don't mean to crash into your private places. It's just that . . . what I have with Carl is so great . . . I want that for you, too. Oh, I know you have your work, and you love it. I feel the same way about mine. But that's our own, lonely thing, and the other . . ."

Melissa was touched by Peg's dreamy expression. It was impossible to resent anything she said; Peg had a way of being concerned without ever intruding.

"You're lucky," Melissa said.

"Sure I am. But I got that way by not letting the bad old days turn me off." Peg grinned and did her comical trick with her brows.

"And you think maybe I let Gavin turn me off to other people," Melissa said thoughtfully, without offense.

"Maybe. At least give Bart Freeman a chance . . . hear what he has to say. He might really *be* 'on your side.'"

"It's hard to imagine how," Melissa retorted.

"Well," the irrepressible Peg said, "he sounds like one of us to me . . . a Fish. That thing with the champagne—" She laughed. "One time, when Carl was very down about one of his projects and just couldn't get it right, I blew up about a million balloons and put them all over the house, and then hid in the closet when I heard him come in. It sure cleared up his head."

Melissa grinned, recalling what Ria had said that day.

"Believe me, when a Pisces clowns for you, it's love with a capital L," Peg said earnestly. "He sounds like one."

"You almost convince me."

"That's good, because I've got to get out of here . . . pick up the cake at that place on Eighth Street, and a lot of etceteras. It's just a party for two this year."

"Enjoy it. I know you will," Melissa told her warmly as they paid their checks and went out.

"You want to taxi down with me?"

"No, thanks. I think I'll walk a way." After Peg had found her cab, Melissa started to walk west. Maybe she'd even walk all the way—it was such a glorious autumn day, and there were no appointments that afternoon.

Besides, she was getting a little tired of people being able to set clocks by her. She smiled at the metaphor. Deep in thought, she was on Fifth Avenue before she knew it. Still full of restless energy, she continued walking east and headed downtown on Park.

Here and there she noticed smiling couples sauntering together in the golden light of the sparkling avenue with its green traffic islands; flocks of sailing pigeons, buff and white and gleaming abalone, echoing the quiet hues of the elegant buildings.

Melissa saw a man and woman crossing westward. They paused on an island for the traffic to go by; both looked up at the bright blue sky, then at each other, smiling with a very private happiness. A "party for two."

Obviously those two had no barrier between them. She looked away and began walking faster south.

Everything about his uncle's sanctum, Bart reflected, looked like the headquarters of Cotton Mather. Austere and oppressive, dun and white and charcoal. Even his prim secretary, the elderly Mrs. Cabot, was dressed like a pilgrim in a black dress with pristine cuffs and collar.

Now as he strode by her, Mrs. Cabot said, scandalized, "Oh, Mr. Freeman . . . sir . . . your uncle is in conference."

"Don't worry about it," Bart said over his shoulder and opened his uncle's door.

Ned Freeman, deep in conversation with the company attorneys, looked up, frowning. "Bart, I'm . . . tied up here."

Bart nodded to the lawyers and retorted, "I'd like to untie you for a spell, if these gentlemen will excuse us."

His uncle gave him a startled look; Bart didn't generally throw his weight around. This was foreign to his customary casual methods.

The attorneys were already getting to their feet; a president still outranked a chairman of the board who was only a vice-president, their gesture said. A faint flush of annoyance stained Edward's lean cheeks.

"Why, certainly," he said, with a face-saving gesture, as if he and not Bart had dismissed the others. "We'll take this up a little later," he said to the men in a majestic tone.

Closing the door on them, Bart demanded before his uncle could speak, "What's going on uptown? I understand that area is crawling with your representatives. I thought all this was going to wait for the next meeting of the board."

"Please sit down, Bart," his uncle said grumpily. "I refuse to talk when you're slanting above me like the Tower of Pisa."

Ignoring the remark, Bart continued leaning on the desk, supporting his weight with the flat of his palms. "I wish you'd answer my question."

"Will you sit *down?*" Edward demanded.

Bart kept on standing but took his hands from the desk. "Why are you proceeding as if we'd never even discussed the matter?"

"I told you before, we're totally at odds on this plan. You've always left these things to me; I'm just trying to do my job. Why is it different all of a sudden?"

"It isn't different. I'm still president of this company."

"With unusually limited power, if you recall." Edward smiled nastily.

That crazy provision in the will, Bart reflected. It hadn't been mentioned in quite a while. He himself

had almost forgotten it, because he was not going to
let it dictate his life.

"Limited as it may be, I'm going to hold up this
project until I'm satisfied."

"Hold it up?" Edward was flabbergasted.

"That's right. That's why I'm here now. You'll get a
formal memo this afternoon. I came here as a courte-
sy to talk it over first. But from the way you're
drawing in your hooves I don't think further discussion is going to help anything. I want all the files, the
plans, estimates, the whole megillah, sent over to my
office right away."

"That will take some time. The estimates, for
instance—"

"Whatever it takes. I want it all today."

There was a timid knock at the door. "Come in,
come in," Edward said sharply, still puffed with
anger. Mrs. Cabot poked her sleek, snowy head
around the edge of the door, her pallid blue eyes
perturbed, a tight look around her little pursed lips.
"I do apologize, Mr. Freeman," she said to Edward,
"but there's a messenger here who's *adamant* about
seeing your nephew in person." She raised white,
disapproving brows, as if to ask how he dared.

"Just send him to Roberta, Mrs. Cabot," Bart
intervened.

"I tried to do so, of *course*," she said with polite
reproach. "But apparently he has a package you must
sign for personally."

"Damn nuisance," Edward muttered.

"Okay, shoot him in." Bart was resigned.

The man handed him a familiar-looking package
and he signed for it and tipped the man. When he'd
left, Bart noticed the return address. His heart hammered against his ribs.

"What's the matter?" said Edward.

Hearing his uncle's curiosity, Bart knew his face had given him away. "You look like you've been hit with a wrecking ball."

"I have," said Bart.

Edward suddenly got up to pace and Bart saw him glance at the package. He knew his uncle's ability to lightning-read and memorize information and retrieved the parcel. "Look, I'm sorry I bellowed at you like that, Uncle Ned. I shouldn't have and I apologize. Nevertheless we've got to get this thing straight. There can't be two presidents of Freeman Company. I want full responsibility for the expansion project, given the reasonable limitations of my power by the board." He did his best to keep his voice level and calm, not to let his famous temper loose—as he had the other night, he reflected grimly. But he put that thought from his mind—it wasn't helping him right now.

"I see." Edward Freeman's answer was deliberately calm. "I'm glad you realize there are 'reasonable limitations,' as you put it. That's sensible. I'll tell you quite frankly right now that I intend to do everything in my power to bring the others to my side."

Bart leaned over and retrieved the package, then got up. "Fair enough. In the meantime I believe I'm within my rights to take over. So . . . I'd appreciate your sending the material to me as soon as possible."

"Very well. I'll take care of it immediately." As he left, Bart heard Ned Freeman buzzing Mrs. Cabot.

He walked slowly back to his office. Avoiding Roberta's speculative glance, he went in and shut the door. He depressed the button of the intercom. "No calls for about twenty minutes," he directed.

The package was still in his hand. He opened it and took out the small satin box, searching the packing tissue for some kind of note. There wasn't any.

Damn.

He discarded the larger box and put the small one in his jacket pocket. Leaning back he swiveled his chair and stared out over the sweeping panorama of the harbor. What a damned fool he'd been, storming out of her house like that. He might have alienated her for good.

Bart lit a cigarette and exhaled a cloud of wispy smoke, blinking. Through half-closed lids he surveyed the rhythmic patterns of the pumping gulls, the pompous little tugs making their way over the shining water. And his body was stabbed with longing. He thought of her exquisite face between the soft sheaves of dark gold hair; the changeable, innocent eyes that were almost purple on that first day, green the next and then a kind of greenish-gold from that funny-colored shirt she'd been wearing the other night.

The shirt . . . he remembered it sliding silkily under his fingers over skin that must be even silkier . . . where it was hidden, under the cloth.

Bart shifted restlessly, feeling an uncomfortable heat prickle his body. That face looked like a face from long ago . . . and the body was all woman.

Damn it, he'd have to find a way to convince her. He'd have to make her see that he wasn't out to get her—or anyone else, for that matter.

But how was he going to get to her? Bart leaned back and went over a number of possibilities. None of them seemed feasible.

Carefully he went back over all the things she'd told him about herself. There had to be a clue there, somewhere. Somewhere.

And then he remembered a certain thing. Full of new enthusiasm, he whirled his chair around and buzzed Roberta. He asked her to send out for special papers.

"Step on it, honey," he drawled in his old way, grinning to himself.

Chapter Four

*E*dward Freeman shifted in the Queen Anne chair, watching his sister-in-law across the small round table in her dining room of the Stuyvesant Oval townhouse. He was almost bursting with impatience.

Claudia Freeman had an ironclad rule: Difficult matters were never discussed during dinner but had to wait for after-dinner coffee and liqueurs. Edward had done his best to avoid having dinner there in the first place; how anyone as well fixed as Claudia could stay in this horrendous neighborhood was beyond his ken.

The house itself, of course, was a jewel, and then it had been there for a hundred years. But the area was an absurd patchwork of splendor and decay, some of the nearby blocks positively hazardous. Nevertheless there were always new "diehards," as Edward styled them, eager to invest in houses like this. Therefore the short block had been preserved, thus vindicating Claudia's stubbornness in retaining the house.

And Bart, of course, supported her, declaring in his overoptimistic fashion that the whole area would be going "up" again. He always scoffed at Edward's predilection for the neat safety of the Upper East Side.

The thought of Bart made Edward more impatient than ever. He drummed his immaculate fingers on the lace tablecloth.

Claudia grinned at him, and he was forced to admit that she was a mighty handsome woman, had kept herself well. They had always enjoyed a rather uneasy association. Edward Freeman had never quite approved of his brother's choice. Granted Claudia came from a very fine family; still, she was a little too plainspoken for his taste. And the ideas that she spouted were, it seemed to him, even more quixotic and maddening than other women's.

"Well, Edward," Claudia said in her rather husky voice, "let's get to it. What's got you riled?" She poured out their coffee from a graceful silver pot, sugaring and creaming his before she passed him his cup.

Watching the play of her long, slender fingers, the gleam of candlelight on her short auburn hair which was still apparently bright by nature and not artifice, Edward marveled that such an elegant woman could talk in this flippant, homespun way.

Her russet-brown eyes, exactly like Bart's, twinkled, their color enhanced by her vivid golden dress.

"Your son, Claudia," he said bluntly.

"Ah . . . not 'your nephew'?" She smiled. "Whenever Bart's crossed you, he's 'my son.'"

Edward detested this humorous parrying. "Be that as it may, he's suddenly undergone a dramatic sea change."

"Well, that's appropriate."

Oh, Lord, that astrology nonsense again, Edward grumbled to himself. "Water sign" was right, though —all wet.

"You mean the change of plan about Chicago," she said. "But that's marvelous. That's what we've wanted—for him to stay put and take hold. Isn't it?" Claudia was studying him curiously. She was a damned shrewd woman, for all her oddities, and he'd better watch his step.

"Of course, of course," he said hastily. "That's not what I'm referring to—I mean this sudden obsession with the expansion plan."

"'Obsession'?" Claudia's tone mocked him.

"Preoccupation, then." Really, Claudia could be such a nitpicker. "I didn't want to go into this at the office. Even my walls have ears. Are you aware that I've been fired by my own nephew from the building project?"

"No. Bart said there was something he wanted to go into with me tomorrow . . . maybe that's it. Exactly what happened?"

He told her. It annoyed him even more that she shared none of his indignation, remained totally noncommittal. "I see," was all she volunteered. That boy had her under his thumb.

"Frankly I am nonplussed by his sentimental attitude to that area, unless . . . ."

Too late he saw her hackles rise. "I wouldn't call it sentimental to have some regard for the city's most historic area," she snapped. "And 'unless' what?"

"Unless his infatuation for a certain young woman is affecting his judgment."

"What young woman?" Claudia was interested now.

"A completely unsuitable young woman with a dreadful shop in the area. When he was in my office he had a package addressed to her, obviously jewelry."

"How do you know?" Claudia demanded. "Did he actually tell you?"

"Come now, Claudia. It was the size of a jewelry box, and addressed to Ms. Darby Gillis, at Psychedelics on Eighteenth Street. I have been there, and I've seen Ms. Gillis. She looks like one of these pink rock singers, absolutely *non compos.*"

"Punk rock," Claudia corrected absently. "Oh, dear." Edward was gratified to notice a worried frown between her handsome brows. "But even so . . . that's not very serious. I daresay you sent trinkets yourself, in your salad days, to girls you were not going to marry."

"Well . . ." he said deprecatingly, unable to help preening himself a little. "But that has nothing to do with this. Apparently he is so besotted with this particular . . . young creature that he's canceled his Chicago trip and is spending time away from the office."

"You sound like a character from Jane Austen, Edward. Are you actually spying on my son?"

"Of course not. The idea! I'm merely putting two and two together. I don't want the boy to get into trouble."

Claudia's swooping brows went up again. "He's hardly a boy; he's thirty. Good heavens, Edward, he's dated innumerable women, ever since Elaine died. Why have you got him at the altar?"

"I'm warning you, Claudia. This is different. I really think he's serious about this questionable girl."

"Well, aside from the fact that she looks like that midnight horror show on Eighth Street . . . what do

you actually know that's 'questionable' about her?"
Claudia insisted.

"I've made certain . . . inquiries," Edward admitted with discomfort.

"Why, you *have* been spying. That's outrageous,"
Claudia protested. She was silent an instant, then she
asked abruptly, "Are you concerned about that special provision in the will?"

"What a way to put it, Claudia. How could you
think such a thing? Now, are you going to speak to
him or not?"

"Speak to him!" Claudia was miffed and Edward
wished he'd put it another way. "He's a grown man. If
he wants to tell me he will. Until then I'm not going to
mind his business. He's too smart to marry a girl like
that."

Noticing Claudia's angry look Edward was silent.
She had the most maddening way of provoking him
into awkward positions.

"What about the building?" she asked suddenly.

"What building?" he asked. Claudia was exasperating, he thought.

"The building that this . . . Psychedelics is in. Does
the Gillis girl own it?"

"Yes. But it's decidedly not a landmark."

"A potential landmark?" Claudia persisted.

"Why do you ask? Are you going to investigate,
after all?"

"No. I'll leave the spying to you, Edward." Claudia's brown eyes twinkled, reminding Edward of Bart.
He tried to conceal his frustration.

"More coffee?" Claudia offered with gracious calm.

"No, thank you. I'd better be going." Even now he
was anxious about his costly but unobtrusive Bentley
parked on East Tenth Street. He hadn't exactly succeeded, but he consoled himself that he might have

put a bug in Claudia's ear, and at least gotten things in motion.

"Antsy?" Melissa smiled at Ria over the remains of dinner in the Laines' pretty dining room. They'd had an early meal so they could get to the reading in good time.

"As usual." Her mother smiled back at her and made a nervous gesture. She was resplendent in a bright russet trouser ensemble with a soft, cowl-necked top that made her white skin and silvery hair glow, her dark eyes darker. Before her performances Ria was strung to high tension—like an acrobat, Melissa reflected, about to walk a narrow wire.

"Always antsy before and perfect during," Mark said in his deep, easy baritone, looking at Ria with affectionate admiration. He might assiduously avoid the house on the days of her poetry class, and he might relentlessly twit the poets, but he was always on hand for her readings. Melissa suspected he was more moved by Ria's lovely poetry than he revealed; under Mark's joking and matter-of-fact facade there was a sensitive and appreciative man.

"I've never seen it go otherwise," she agreed, patting Ria's shoulder. Melissa herself had dressed with care in honor of the occasion—Ria always hinted that she liked to "show off" her beautiful daughter. Melissa was wearing a simple but striking dress of cloud-gray with Ansel's silver and amethyst pendant.

"That's a delicious combination," Ria murmured. "You look like twilight." She took a sip of Chablis and made a face; she was not much of a drinker, but Mark had insisted a small glass of wine would settle her down. "Good heavens, I hope Karel shows up on time . . . and Antonio won't run over . . . and I hope

Marirose doesn't come see-through the way she did last summer," Ria said nervously.

". . . and that the taxis don't go on strike in the next half hour, and that a hurricane doesn't hit us, and . . ." Mark teased, smiling. He squeezed her hand, used to her fretting on these occasions.

"Oh, dear, let's change the subject." Ria smiled at them both apologetically. "At least we've got good news on the home front."

"We certainly do. Isn't it marvelous?" Melissa beamed at them. No one in the neighborhood had seen a sign of Freeman Company reps for nearly a week.

A week, Melissa thought, that had given her plenty of time to regret that last encounter with Bart. There had been no further phone calls, no more packages, no word at all. She had a swift, sinking sensation as she listened to Mark and Ria talk about it.

"Do you think they might have changed their minds?" Ria asked eagerly.

"Oh, I think that's jumping to conclusions, darling, but it is a very good sign." Mark was more cautious in his reaction. He glanced at his Freeman watch.

"It's about time to get started," he said. "Seven already."

"Good." Ria's confidence always increased as the hour approached. Her stormy temperament couldn't cope too well with waiting.

"Let me help you with this, Ma." Melissa began to clear away the dishes.

"All right, but be careful with that lovely dress." The three of them cleared the table and took things to the kitchen. Donning aprons, Melissa and Ria scraped dishes and put them in the dishwasher for later.

Within a half hour they were cabbing to the Greenwich House below Sheridan Square in the Village.

Peg, in her dependable fashion, was already there, looking cheerful and pretty in bright red, with Carl at her side. Mark and Carl went out to get a beer, promising to be back in good time.

Melissa and Peg, then a couple of other poets who soon arrived, checked out the lobby to see that all was well while Ria changed the position of the chairs on the stage and conferred with someone about lights.

It was almost time. Melissa was looking forward to this even more than she had in the past. It would be good, she decided, to lose herself in the excitement of the occasion, just drift off with the loveliness of the words for a while, and forget.

But later, listening to her mother's rich voice, and watching her dark, passionate eyes glow in the brilliant stage lights, Melissa realized that this loveliness had made her remember more sharply, rather than forget.

Ria was reading one of Melissa's favorites, and her mind silently anticipated the tempestuous and musical phrases; they were stately, burdened with overpowering emotion:

> I want you
> as I want tides.
> As I will never
> travel the apogee of the darkest moon . . .

Melissa recalled the relentless pull of his body, the amazing magnetism, the strength of him drawing her to him, into him, lost, like someone given to the rhythm of the waves, drifting . . .

> Wish
> that you could take from my breasts

an impeccable secret;
one which I have shared with no man.

That we might stand into each other
like surf.

That I could touch you.

Melissa took a shallow breath, hearing the dazzled
silence of the audience after the last word died away,
then the scattering of applause.

On the edge of her vision she saw someone quietly
moving down the aisle, someone tall, a man. She
repressed an annoyed exclamation, sensed a slight
disapproval in Ria's manner, although she was much
too poised to make it obvious to anyone who didn't
know her well. Why, oh, why did people have to come
in late and shatter the listeners' dreamy enjoyment?
Where in the world was the man who was supposed to
keep people out until the break between readings?
Melissa questioned in irritated silence.

Then she saw who it was—Bart Freeman. Suddenly
she was so excited to see him that there was no more
confusion of feeling, no ambiguity this time at all. She
was just glad, overjoyed.

Before he discreetly sat down, his quick scan of the
room found her, and their eyes met for a split second.
Her heart thudded and she felt a lightning warmth
strike her whole body, a dew of moisture in her palms.
Now she could see him only in half profile, but he
looked . . . wonderful.

He was immaculately turned out in a rich brown
corduroy suit and an open-collared shirt the color of
new cream. The tawny shades made his red hair
flame, and the light color of the shirt emphasized his
ruddy, outdoor look. His big shoulders more than
filled the space he had occupied, brushed the man

sitting next to him, and Melissa saw him move to the left with what seemed a whispered apology.

Melissa realized then, in her distraction, that she had missed most of Ria's next poem, hearing only the last stanza:

> Scarlet sleeps at your brow,
> beyond flamingo.
> I am sunless.
> From my shut wings, have fallen
> fern and hibiscus:
> on the lance of the north
> which brings me to your door.

It was painfully apt. Scarlet slept at *his* brow, Melissa thought. And I've been "sunless," with "shut wings." The phallic symbolism of the "lance of the north" pierced her senses as she recalled the power and virility of his splendid body. She felt her face grow hot with the foolish fear that everyone around her could read her expression or might follow her eyes as she looked at him again and again.

There would not be another intermission; he had arrived late. She would have to sit there in the unending tumult of emotion until the reading was over.

Absently she listened to the poems of Antonio Pavone, which she usually paid close attention to, and impatiently to the erotica of Marirose Acerbo. Marirose, as Ria had feared, was quite underdressed; the lights caressed the nipples of her breasts thrusting against the thin fabric of her shirt. Melissa couldn't help wondering what Bart was thinking; she shot a quick glance in his direction. She was delighted to find that he didn't seem to be reacting much at all, except possibly with restless boredom. He was looking up at the ceiling, then around the auditorium. At last he turned half toward her and grinned over his shoulder.

That smile undid her.

Then it was time for Ria to read her last poem.

Dividing her attention between Bart and her mother, Melissa saw him straighten in his seat. When Ria read certain lines, he shifted with apparent discomfort. This was one of her mother's most exciting poems, a phenomenon, Mark called it—a love poem written from a man's point of view, with astounding authenticity.

> She is clay and fire.
> In time before limit, beyond form
> she touched me . . .
>
> . . . Now, I crawl through mirrors,
> their stones.
> I cannot see her.
> I do not know how to walk
> upon this house of flame and blossom.
>
> I know heaven and hell.

She saw him clasp his hands on his knees, as if he were in the grip of a mighty feeling. Her pulses danced.

> I lose her
> in the name of something I do not remember.
> With seed and thunder
> I desire her.
> I crawl upon this room where she leads me,
> into a forest of petals,
> of faces;

walls running mirror and granite:
on her garments staining my eyes,
under the dumb beast who stares at me.

As Ria read the few remaining lines, Melissa saw
Bart shift in his seat again, evidently careless of his
neighbor, leaning sharply to his right so that he could
glimpse her out of the corner of his eye. It was almost
as if his whole body were straining toward Melissa,
and she was overcome with wild new emotion, feeling
her heart beat in her throat. Again she saw him in half
profile, and his entire expression was that of a man in
a feverish state of excitement.

Her mother had been able to say to him in the other
poems what she herself could not express in just that
way; to say for him in this poem, perhaps, what he
had wanted to say to Melissa without having the
words. How she knew all this, she could not have told.
She just did. She felt it in a way that was profound and
sure.

Then it was over and in a kind of haze Melissa was
applauding with the others. She saw Bart rise to his
towering height, clapping his big hands together repeatedly. A few people called out "Bravo," and
Melissa imagined he was one of them; she was delighted with his delight and very proud and happy that it
had all gone so well.

But when the audience started coming out, she felt
a sudden shyness. It would be hard to face him, in the
light of their last encounter, especially hard at this
moment when the turmoil of emotion must be plain
on her face. There was no way to avoid him, though,
and she realized she no longer wanted to.

She left her aisle seat and walked very slowly
toward the lobby, hearing him call out behind her,
"Melissa." She stopped and, standing aside to let

other people pass, waited until he had caught up with her in a few long strides.

"Melissa." He was standing there, staring down at her, totally unaware of the people milling around them. "It's so . . . good to see you," he said awkwardly, trying to gauge her reaction.

She thought for a minute that she wouldn't be able to speak, her excitement was so great, her confusion so total. But at last, she answered. "It's good to see you, too."

His face lit up and she could see points of brightness in his brown, eager eyes. "Let's get out of this," he suggested, gesturing to her to sit down again until the auditorium had emptied.

She moved back into a row of seats and sank down. He sat down beside her, hungrily taking in the sight of her, from her loose, softly waved hair to her eyes and mouth and dress. "How can you be more beautiful every time I see you? It's not possible." That rueful smile twitched at the corner of his sensuous mouth and her heart turned over. Right then it seemed that they had never been away from each other, that her bitter words had never been said or the anger that they had aroused had never existed.

She couldn't answer; she looked up at him, fearing and hoping at the same time that he could see her heart in her eyes. She couldn't believe how much she had missed him, how she had hoped for something like this.

"Your mother was wonderful," he said. "I never heard anything like that."

"Yes. Yes, she was, wasn't she?" Melissa murmured, bursting with pride for her lovely and talented mother. "I've never heard her read quite . . . like that before," she added, the perilous warmth stealing over her body again.

"It's a very special night," he said softly and with meaning.

The hall had almost emptied out, and they were still sitting there looking at each other as if they were the only people left in the city, she thought with elation. But she knew she must stir soon, must go backstage to congratulate Ria; anything else would be unthinkable. It wasn't long before the problem was solved for her.

She saw her mother emerging from backstage, with Mark, Peg and Carl and a half dozen chattering poets in her wake. With an exclamation Bart got up at once and stood in the aisle, waiting for Melissa to precede him. Then they walked toward Ria and the group.

Melissa felt almost hypnotized, sure that her face must be giving her away to all of them. But when she introduced Bart, she knew that only Peg and Ria really noticed her excitement. Mark was talking to Carl about boxing, and the other poets, jubilant and self-involved, didn't give Melissa's companion a second thought.

There was approval, however, in Ria's friendly look and Peg seemed so pleased she could hardly contain herself.

"Why don't you join us?" Ria asked Bart politely. "We're all going along to the Blue Mill for something to eat."

Bart glanced sidelong at Melissa. "Thank you very much," he said, "but there's something I've got to do. Perhaps I might join you a little later. Meanwhile, I wonder if I could borrow your daughter—just a short loan." He smiled his most charming smile and Ria responded.

"Why not?" she said lightly. "We'll look for you in a little while, then."

Melissa's heart was pounding like a drum when they said good-bye to the others and walked away in the opposite direction. "I lied," Bart murmured, looking down at her. "And then again I didn't—there is something I've got to do, Melissa. I've got to be alone with you, just for a little while. We've got to talk."

She nodded.

He smiled as if she'd given him the best present he'd ever gotten, and she was overcome with a new wave of tender excitement.

"Well, then," he said exuberantly, "what's your favorite place in these parts? Somewhere nice and quiet."

"On up the avenue," she said. She named a restaurant a few blocks north of Sheridan Square.

He said eagerly, "Let's go." All the way, on the crowded avenue, and crossing the busy street, she felt his look upon her, thrilled to the light contact of his fingertips on the small of her back, protective and strong.

When they went down the stairs into the restaurant Melissa felt as if she were floating down, not walking; it was impossible not to feel gratified when she noticed the stares of other women, admiring him; she radiated enormous pleasure when she noticed his commanding but easy way with the waiters, a manner that made her feel inordinately feminine, taken care of. At least tonight, she thought dryly.

Still, there was that floating feeling. She broke into soft, happy laughter.

"What is it?" he asked, smiling, after he had given their order and turned back to her.

"I was remembering a poem," she explained.

"One of your mother's?"

"No. One of my friend's—the girl in the red dress. You didn't hear her read tonight." He shook his head.

"She wrote a poem that goes 'How do I do? I am a red balloon this afternoon, I have no weight at all' . . . and there's some more. It doesn't matter. But I feel like that tonight."

"Do you mean that? Do you mean it, Melissa?" He was holding her gaze with his, speaking with deep seriousness, and once more his patent eagerness made her feel inexpressibly tender, open.

"Yes."

"Lady, so do I. So do I, ever." He reached across the table and took her hand. And just the way it had been before, she sensed a narrow web of fire spreading throughout her veins, and heard a faint desirous drum begin to beat in her pulses, in her heart, high in her very throat.

"Look, first of all," he went on hastily, "I want to say I'm sorry for what happened that night at your house. I was an utter barbarian."

"'Bart the Hun,'" she quoted from his card, smiling. "I wasn't so civilized myself, if I recall."

"You remembered that!" he marveled. "You remembered what I wrote on the card."

"Yes," she murmured. "I do. As a matter of fact I still have it."

He squeezed her hand hard and grinned from ear to ear. "That's so nice. That's nicer than you know, Melissa." Then his smile died and he said, "But you returned the earrings. I was sorry about that. They were an apology gift."

"I know. But I . . ."

Still holding her hand tightly, he reached into his jacket pocket with the other. "Would you accept them now?" he asked her very softly.

"Yes," she said after an instant. "Yes. Now . . . I think I would." She was very touched by his pleasure; his eyes darkened with strong new emotion and his breath grew short. He handed her the box and she took it, looking at him solemnly. She had a feeling that this acceptance of the gift was highly symbolic; that she was accepting and pledging much more.

She felt he knew it, too, because now his elation lit his whole face, and he clung to her fingers as if he could not bear to let them go.

When the waiter returned she withdrew her hand gently, with a slow smile. The waiter poured their wine and they raised their glasses. Bart touched Melissa's with his, and said in a low voice, "To the shining hour."

She repeated the toast and they drank, looking at each other over the rims of their glasses.

Then suddenly a new gaiety overtook them and they began to talk of a hundred things. She was dazzled at the unexpected depths in him, at all the things he'd done, the marvelous inconsistencies—on the one hand, he was an accomplished athlete, although he made light of his activities. Laughingly he told her that he had given up the "really dangerous stuff" such as racing and mountain climbing.

"Now," he said, "I'm content with old men's games."

"Golf, you mean?" she demanded, smiling. She could not imagine his being content with that.

"Oh, good Lord, no. A little tennis and surfing and karate, a little skydiving when I really get bored."

She broke into uncontrollable giggles. "Old men's games," she repeated, gasping. He was unbelievable, she reflected; on top of all that he had an amazing knowledge of poetry, theater and art, all revealed in a quiet, easy fashion with no sign of *braggadocio*.

"That last poem of your mother's . . ."

"Buffalo Waits in the Cave of Dragons," she said.

"Yes. It was amazing. It sounded like a man had written it. How did she *do* that?" His eyes took on a tender expression; they narrowed as he stared at

Melissa. "I don't mind telling you, lady . . . when I was listening to that, and there you were, just a few rows behind me. Well . . . it was all I could do not to get up and come to you and grab you."

There was so much yearning in his voice that she felt herself melting, warming again.

"In fact," he whispered, "what I want, in the worst way, right this minute, is to kiss you. And kiss you."

"I want that, too," she admitted, looking down, feeling her face take fire, unable to meet his eyes at that moment.

"Then let's get out of here. And find some nice shadowy street . . . on our way to the Blue Mill . . . so we can do just that."

Her heart was hammering almost painfully again. While he was taking care of the check, then pulling back her chair, Melissa felt as if every patron of the restaurant had to be staring, had to know what she was feeling. But she didn't care anymore; she felt as light as a petal, as giddy as a child on a merry-go-round, and she exchanged a conspiratorial smile with Bart before they went up the few stairs to the busy street.

She started to walk away in the downtown direction, but he caught her elbow gently in his big hand and asked her wistfully, "Do you really want to join the party?"

Melissa studied him. His brown eyes were pleading, his mouth expectant. She hesitated.

He put his arm around her waist. "Then let's find a shadow . . . a darker bistro, a more private place."

"All right."

"Where then? Wherever you choose."

"Eighteenth Street," she said. She was astonished at her own boldness.

"Eighteenth? . . ." He looked a little stunned, dis-believing. "Do you mean that?"

"Of course I mean it." Melissa looked into his widened eyes, and her face felt hot.

The words were hardly out of her mouth before he had stepped off the curb and was whistling shrilly to a taxi hurtling south.

The cab braked with squealing tires and Bart hand-ed Melissa in with great care.

"Where to?" the cabby snarled. Bart gave him the address.

"I don't go to Eighteenth Street in Brooklyn, buddy. It's too late at night."

Good-naturedly Bart chuckled. "No, no, Mr. Cost-anza," he protested, reading from the driver's medal-lion. "*Manhattan* Eighteenth Street."

"Oh, well, that's another *story*—whyn't you say so, pal? But it's gonna cost you. I'm going in the wrong direction."

"So be it, so be it, Mr. Costanza," Bart assured him and, as the snarling Benedetto Costanza slammed his mug-proof partition shut again, Bart moved close to Melissa and took her into his arms. She raised her face and their eager mouths came together, still half-trembling with laughter after the conference with their driver. In just an instant, however, the kiss was no longer laughing and playful; his hungry mouth closed over her lips and he made a little groaning sound, stroking her face as his lips clung and opened, learning again the quivering, soft contours of her own. The swerving taxi threw them even closer to-gether; she was nestled into his arms, inside that warm, protective circle that defined her world.

When their mouths parted she saw that his half-open eyes looked drugged and brilliant, glittering with wonder, and he gently urged her head down into the hollow of his neck, stroking her hair, kneading her arm and shoulder, squeezing her to him with such tender desperation that it seemed he was trying to absorb her into his flesh.

He whispered against her ear, "I don't believe this, Melissa. I'm afraid you'll run away again."

"No, no. Never," she answered softly, her answer muffled in the creamy shirt; she inhaled the clean male scent of him with wild delight.

She had completely lost track of time or distance, musing happily how strange that was for her . . . someone whose whole life and work had been the measuring, the order and direction of time itself. She chuckled against him, and he lifted her a little, smiling down into her eyes, demanding to know what she was thinking about.

"Time . . . maybe I'm beginning to get a glimmer of what time is, after all. It doesn't matter what time it is." She grinned.

He looked as if he were too happy to say a word; he just kept gazing at her and she watched the city lights play over his eager face, repeat themselves in the dark, piercing fire of his eyes, reflecting their whites and blues and greens and golds and scarlets like the dancing flames of a magical conflagration.

Melissa marveled over his comical interchange with the grim, indifferent Costanza, who had not glanced at them since their first exchange—it was wonderful, that odd anonymity of the city's night—some men she'd known would have reacted so differently to the driver's savage rudeness. Ansel would have snapped at him coldly; Gavin would have gotten into a rage and jerked her out of the taxi and they would have stood there having to wait for another one.

But Bart had seemed like a man who could not be

touched by any pettiness, someone so determined and so strong that he resolved to carry the spellbound hour steadily on, like a full cup of precious liquid, mastering it, so as not to spill a drop of this mystical liquor that was making them giddily drunk with love. Yes, someone apart, untouched, and yet determined; someone who knew the same earth-rending feeling that she knew.

She came back to reality long enough to see that they were almost there, speeding eastward on Fourteenth Street past the sadly graffiti'd statue of the mounted warrior in the pallid light of Union Square. She was almost astonished for an instant that the moments had been so few, and yet she'd experienced the insights and emotions of an hour.

The cab swerved and hurtled uptown blocks. Bart released her to dig into his trousers for the fare. The simple gesture was so moving and so beautiful, displaying the gentle force of his big, long body, the motion of his powerful hands, that she gave a little gasping moan.

Immediately he asked, "What is it? What's the matter?" And she soothed him, "Nothing. Oh, nothing. I'm just . . . so happy." One of his hands held his wallet, but with the other, he touched her face, and she felt as if her cheek were stained with fire.

"When is your birthday?" she asked with soft abruptness.

Puzzled and smiling, he said, "March eleventh." Then he added, "You are full of surprises. Why do you ask? Is there a planetary reason?"

"Well, perhaps." The cab was slowing near Time Was. As he absently took money from his wallet, Bart said lightly, "My mother taught me about women like you . . . women born in September, you know. But I never learned till now."

They were there. He thrust a bill into Costanza's tray without looking at it and got out, holding out his hand to Melissa. She put her hand in his, quivering at his very touch, and slid out quickly, stepping onto the street with that odd, floating feeling again, as if she were walking on foam rubber.

"Hey, buddy," Costanza was crying out with disbelief. "Do you know what you gave me here?"

"Whatever, whatever, Benedetto . . . *buon' fortuna.*" Bart laughed, putting his arm around Melissa's waist.

"Well, thank you very *much*. Good luck to *you*, pal." The taxi roared away.

"I've got all the luck I'm ever going to need." His voice was hollow now with excitement, shaking a little, as he urged her with the pressure of his hand toward the graceful house.

She was overtaken now with shyness and with trembling, and when they went up the outside stairs to the second floor she had a hard time making her key fit into the lock. At last she managed and they stepped into the harvest-colored living room, where she'd left one mellow light.

He shut the door softly and before she could make another move, stepped to her and enfolded her in his arms. Now they did not kiss each other, but just held on, held on for dear life, as if neither one could believe that finally they were alone together, free even of the eyes of the night.

It was so quiet that she could hear his quick, sharp breath and the drowsy tocking of the big grandfather clock by the stair. She could almost feel the anticipation in him, the hushed tension there is in waiting for a wondrous, longed-for event that any split second now would happen.

And she sensed in him, too, that amazing patience

and tenderness, as if he knew quite well how momentous a thing this was for her, and all the doubts she had.

"Come," he murmured, "sit down beside me, for a little." He led her toward the couch and they sat down close together. "Come here to me," he whispered. "Come here, Melissa." With his arm held out, he invited her into his embrace.

She could not say a word; all she could do was make a little sound of utter happiness and relax into his shoulder. "Now we have time. So much lovely time."

Melissa knew what he was saying—he knew that for her it had to be sweet and leisurely and slow.

"This is so peaceful and so beautiful. It's almost like living in another time, another place," he said softly. She murmured wordlessly again and, burrowing into his body, kissed the pulsating place under his warm ear, feeling the instant leap of his body, the whole of him brought to drumming attention by that small, single caress.

"Were you ever married, Melissa?"

She was able to translate that, too, in her mind, into an understanding of what he was asking her with carefulness and tender consideration. "No," she said against him. "But there was . . . someone, a few years ago. Someone who lied to me."

"I thought so." His deep rumbling voice vibrated against her cheek, exciting her unendurably. "And you were hurt. I felt it."

"Yes. I was. He was . . . married. For a while I thought you might be, too." She leaned back a little and looked at him. His whole face was transformed; it was like looking at another man. There was no mischief there now, or teasing or ironic humor. Every feature was marked by that unabashed tenderness; his eyes, under the level brows, were wistful, vulnerable.

"Oh, no. No. Not now. I was. Three years ago. She died." His words did not express grief, only a faint puzzled sadness.

"I'm sorry."

He drew her into his arms again and kissed her head. "No need. I know now I never really loved her at all; I was pretty young. She was someone my family knew; we were just . . . thrown together." He caressed her hair with both of his big hands and she began to tremble again with the joy of it. "I've never cared for anybody, until I saw you, Melissa Grey. Anything I knew before was . . . lukewarm. This is like a fire, a fever."

She sensed that his control was slipping away; his breath was becoming quick and shallow, his words so forced that it was hard for him to speak, it was clear.

The instant of letting go was upon them; there was no longer any need or sense in hesitation. Wisely, gently, he had waited, somehow knowing her need for this quiet prelude, for the talk between them.

But now she could feel her own body's heated responding; that sweet, lazy dissolution that made her feel no more substantial than vapor.

His hands were still lightly cupping her face. She raised her own hands from their resting place on his chest and slowly brought them up to stroke his fingers.

At once in his incredibly sensitive way he knew what she was asking with her touch; he took a swift, gasping breath and the light in his eyes blazed brighter as he slid his fingers down her face to stroke her neck and wander over her trembling shoulders and down her arms.

Then with savage exultation, the hands were no longer so gentle, but eagerly, wildly seeking; stroking her breasts under the soft-sliding fabric of cloudy gray-white, descending over her inward-curving waist to her quaking thighs while she cried out with a joyful pleading. He was kissing her, kissing her in a way that he never had before, hungry for her, his own mouth pleading with her, a sound of utter yearning torn from him, from the very depths of his hard and urgent body.

Now there were no more words, no thought, only their eager mouths devouring, hands exploring and he was drawing her upward to her feet, speaking to her with his fiery eyes. Melting and shaken she obeyed, going to him, into him, as they held each other so closely she no longer knew his flesh from hers, no longer could imagine another desire than to be nearer, ever nearer.

He let go of her mouth at last and holding her next to him like a vise began to walk slowly with her toward the stairs. She seemed to move upward as on air and when they reached the bedroom floor, and the threshold of the room where she had also left one rosy lamp alight, he swooped down and picked her up in his arms, carrying her over the threshold into that rose-colored haven.

Chapter Five

*H*e set her on her feet with cautious slowness like something infinitely precious and took her hands. He gave one lightning glance at the surroundings, murmuring, "So beautiful." Then his eyes were all for her, leisurely examining her again from her head to her feet.

Suddenly from somewhere she heard the faint, thrilling sound of a passionate tenor; the moment was so enchanting, of such perfection that she felt tears of pleasure gathering in her eyes.

"Melissa. My Melissa," he whispered. With deft hands he unclasped the medallion from around her neck and laid it aside. He undid the fastenings of her soft dress, watching it slide off her shoulders to reveal her breasts under the lacy white chemise, the breasts that rose and fell swiftly now with her accelerated breath. His fascinated gaze followed the soundless descent of the dress to the carpet.

She stepped out of it, thrusting it away with a quick movement of her foot; he inhaled sharply, devouring the sight of her, not even touching her now, but just gazing, gazing. And then he was close to her again, holding her, stroking her, leaning to kiss the fragrant lace that barely veiled her, teasing her budding nipples to full bloom; sliding down, as he still held her, to kiss her lower body wildly, caress the slender length of her trembling legs in their frail hose.

She closed her eyes, swaying; he held her legs firmly, still caressing her without ceasing, a groan of pleasure escaping from his throat. She put her hands on his hair, thrilling to its vital, springing fire, almost faint with the pleasure of his mouth upon her body.

She dimly knew in a dizzying sequence that he was on his feet again, undressing her completely; the mild air kissed her naked skin, and she was lying on the rosy bed, her languorous eyelids shuttering her sight.

"This can't be happening," she heard him say. She felt his tall presence above her and knew his stare without even seeing him; they had become so close already.

"Yes. Oh, yes, it is." Her eyes fluttered half-open. She watched him take off his clothes, revealing first his long, tanned, muscular legs; legs of amazing strength for such a lean-looking man. Then he whipped off his shirt and his bare virile chest stunned her with its symmetry and beauty; her glance followed the trail of reddish-brown hair, pleasingly scant, yet rich and vital, that disappeared under his brief bikini.

He knelt down by the bed and with an excruciatingly tender, moving gesture, stroked her hips with his hands and laid his face against the satiny skin of her upper legs. She could feel his hot breath on her as he spoke in a shuddering whisper, "Melissa, Melissa, if this isn't real, don't tell me. Don't wake me up, Melissa."

That heated, explosive tickle, and the slow movement of his mouth against her, aroused her to a desire that was climbing to a frenzy; her flesh burned, and she moaned faintly, leaping under his caress. "It is real, it is," she gasped, and then he was on the bed, kneeling above her, kissing her everywhere with his opened mouth.

The nibbling lips wandered over her breasts as her nipples thrust outward with joy; she felt his tongue, quaked as his eager mouth took one breast, then the other, into its fevered cavern, and small ripples of aching fire rayed out into every inch of her body as his mouth journeyed lower to explore her.

Her body arched to the ecstatic contact of his tongue, a pleasure so sharp and exquisite that for an instant it was almost unendurable; she cried out in savage pleasure. But then, with the steady rhythm of the strong caress, her joy began to build, to climb, and she was soaring like a bird of fire, riding the heights on phoenix wings; she grasped his lean, beloved head, holding it tightly, moaning out her pleasure, making high, wordless sounds, lost utterly in that unbelievable happiness.

She drew a sobbing breath, her eyes still tightly closed, feeling a dewy moisture below her lids, aware that he had moved away for one lightning instant to remove the last of his clothes. He pressed his long, hard body against hers, and then they were wholly together. She marveled that there could be more delight for her; she hadn't believed it possible, but now in that dancing closeness, with wonder, she recognized her body's new awakening and this delirium was deep and full, much more complete than the one before. She held him close, wrapping herself around him with an abandon utterly alien, running her hands tenderly over his back and shoulders, savoring his haunches and the muscle-play under that burnished skin that was smooth as polished wood warm from the sun.

Now their wild, sweet closeness was the only world remaining; beyond imagining, past belief, she climbed with him to the swift, brilliant peaks of pleasure, totally consumed. Their outcries were almost in unison, wordless, marveling, and she felt the thrilled convulsion of his flesh before his deep, incredulous murmurs died away.

With gasping breath he lowered himself and lay beside her, lifting her head with great gentleness so he wouldn't pull her hair. "Come here, come close, Melissa."

She moved to his body, lay silent and dazzled, stroking the big arm relaxed lightly upon her.

He traced her hip. "I still can't . . . believe this, Melissa." She smiled to hear his drowsy whisper and moved her face caressingly against his chest. "I can't believe it either," she confessed. "No emotion, no feeling in my whole life ever happened so quickly." Heat suffused her face.

She could feel him bend his head to study her. His arm tightened around her, and he asked with teasing softness, "Are you actually blushing . . . or is it the light?"

"It's not just the light." She was conscious of the strangeness of it, the wonderful strangeness, and yet mirth rose in her. It was a fine time to be feeling suddenly shy.

"I think that's great," he said, smiling. "I think everything about you is . . ." He stopped, and added with chagrin, " 'Great.' I wish I had the words—words pretty enough for a poet's daughter. But I don't. I can't say all the . . . amazing things I feel."

"Oh, Bart, I can't, either. . . . I can't . . . tell you what this has been for me." She slid upward in his embrace, leaning over him, stroking his head and cheek, finding the resonant hollow at the base of his neck, kissing it.

He moaned with pleasure and grabbed her more tightly.

She leaned against him, glorying in the strength of him, the magnificent tenderness. "Anyway," she remarked, chuckling, "you remember what Dorothy Parker said about poets, 'and such.' She said she preferred a man who solicits insurance. Maybe I'm looking for the same relief. Strong, silent, athletic; I'm fond of Ria's following, but oh, how they do talk and talk . . . and talk."

His laughter growled in his chest and escaped; deep, hearty male laughter that was most endearing. "I feel more adequate already." His big fingers played gently with her hair.

"Adequate!" Melissa leaned to him more closely and ran her lips down his chest. He shivered pleasurably.

"You'd better watch it," he warned. "I don't think you have the slightest notion what you do to me." All of a sudden his tone became less light. "Darling, darling," he whispered, as his touch strayed from her hair to her face. He traced the shape of her nose and cheeks and chin with a feathery touch. "You are so beautiful, so wonderful you're just unreal. You said nothing ever happened to you so quickly. It didn't seem quick to me," he confessed, his thumb caressing her mouth. "I wanted this almost the minute I laid eyes on you. The only thing that was instant was the way I felt—that first morning, seeing you there in the sun . . . in those soft, kind of misty whatevers. . . ."

She smiled at this masculine version of the gauzy cotton gray and lavender.

". . . like a little slender puff of smoke," he concluded dreamily.

"And you said you didn't know any pretty words," she teased him. He hugged her and they lay in silence for a time. Once more in the quiet night she heard the faint, lovely sound of a recorded tenor singing the ecstatic aria from *Turandot* that always moved her to near crying.

"'. . . the topaz cry of tenors,'" she quoted under her breath and realized it had been aloud, because he answered.

"That's beautiful," he said.

"It's from one of Ria's poems."

"That's exactly what it's like," he marveled. He shifted her in his embrace so he could see her better, his bright gaze adoring all of her. "Everything about you, everything about this is so . . . beautiful. From the start it's all been like something I used to just imagine."

"And for me," she answered softly, kissing him with swift, renewing passion. Suddenly they were coming together again, forgetfully, with quickened breath, kissing each other with even greater longing, flowing into each other's bodies like moving clouds. And again to her utter astonishment, they found another height of joy, this time so shattering that she ached with its lingering, widening, ebbing waves of delight.

His eyelids had grown heavy; he was drifting off to sleep. When his hold upon her slackened, and he breathed a peaceful, deep and rhythmic breath, Melissa slipped out of bed, showered and put on a

nightgown. She padded back to the bedroom. Before
she turned out the rosy light, she took another look at
the painting of the clown, and then at his sleeping
face. The resemblance, she thought, was remarkable.
Asleep his face was almost childlike, all traces of
arrogance and mischief gentled away.

She snapped out the light and lay down beside him.
At once, instinctively, he murmured and moved to
her, circling her with his arms. In their strength and
warmth she cuddled close, trying not to think of the
future, drifting into sweet darkness as soon as she
closed her eyes.

Melissa woke up quite suddenly, feeling vital and
alive. The sun must be high, was her first thought—
the light through the gauzy rose-colored curtains was
so brilliant that the whole room was glowing. It
bloomed with the freshness of a new rose.

"Good morning." Bart was sitting on the other side
of the bed, fully dressed, grinning at her. His tanned
face, his red hair were vivid in the lively gleam of the
room. A steaming cup of coffee awaited her on the
side table.

"Good morning. Oh, how wonderful! Look what
you've done." She leaned over to kiss him, then
eagerly sipped the coffee. "Now my heart can start to
beat," she quipped, like the comedian who'd made
that saying famous.

"Great," said Bart. "And that's not all I've done—
I've used your unicorn. . . ." She giggled; her shower
curtain was decorated with a giant unicorn. "And I'm
thinking about two hundred things you might like to
do today."

Blessed Saturday, she reflected. And what a fine
day it was going to be. She realized all of a sudden
that the coffee had just the right amount of sugar.

"You remembered how I take my coffee, even," she murmured.

"I remember everything." Gently he took the cup from her fingers and set it on the table so he could kiss her. His fingers played with the ruffles of the gown over her breast. "And when I see you in that, I know what I want to do first today."

She melted into his embrace with sweet surprise. There seemed to be no end, no slackening to their wanting each other. In a moment he was naked to the skin, caressing her urgently through the frail fabric of her gown.

Afterward they lay lazily side by side, holding hands and staring into space. "That painting," he remarked, "is something else. I'll be damned if it doesn't remind me of something."

"It should." Smiling, she waited for him to make his own discovery. He squinted at it, then recognition broke out over his face.

"Well, what do you know? I don't believe it." He turned to smile at her, bright-eyed.

"Spooky, isn't it?" Her comment was half-humorous, but her voice shook.

He looked sober. "Fated, lady. Fated. Something I never believed in before, but now I'm not so sure." He leaned over her and took her face in his hands for another lingering kiss.

Vibrant from his mouth, overwhelmed with happiness, she thought, My "fatal opposite."

She almost wondered if she'd said it out loud, because he said in the same half-laughing tone as hers, "Chalk one up for our starry friends."

"It maddens me when they make sense. My mother's convinced that it almost never fails."

"Yours, too?" He laughed, picking up her hand to kiss it. "You know, that's funny—you and my mother have the same birthday . . . remember? And she and I have always gotten along like wildfire."

He was suddenly silent, regarding Melissa from under half-lowered lids. "And would she love *you*. . . ."

The direction of their talk had gotten very serious, Melissa realized. The idea of meeting families was pretty premature. That was commitment talk and even with all that had happened it was still too soon for that; the fate of Time Was still divided them.

She'd had an impulse to say, "I'd like to meet her." Instead she answered lightly, "Well, as Ria would say, we're cut from the same cloth."

Sensitive to his reactions she had the feeling he'd suspected her tone. He looked a little taken aback, for some reason. Quickly she changed the subject. "How about some breakfast? You must be starving."

He stared at her for an instant, then said, "Oh, I can last."

"Why don't I go downstairs and get it started?"

"No way. I want *you* waited on today, not me. Let's have it out."

"All right," she said easily, thinking how sweet he was.

She sent him off to shower first, and he agreed, admitting he'd be quicker. After she'd bathed and was slipping on a robe, he called to her, "How'd you like to go sailing?"

"I'd love it. I never have."

She returned to the bedroom to find him lounging in a chair, smoking. One of Maria's cats, the beautiful gray-striped tabby, Daisy, was sleeping on his lap.

Melissa had to laugh; the cat's smug, matter-of-fact possession of her perch, and his care not to disturb her, were so comical and charming.

"Who's your friend?" he demanded. "I didn't know you had cats."

"I don't, really." She explained that the cats were her neighbor's. "She did the paintings, and the ones downstairs."

"No kidding? She sounds like somebody I'd like to meet."

"Well, that can be arranged." There it was again—the assumption that they would be spending a lot of time together. It warmed her heart, and yet she could not help the sudden, nagging doubt that assailed her as she recalled once again the problem that still loomed over them, the future of Time Was and her house.

But she didn't want to think of that now, at all; didn't want to spoil this bright, happy day. To cover her uncertainty she said, "Meanwhile, meet Daisy."

"Hi, Daisy." He stroked the rumbling, drowsy cat. "So . . . have you got any sailing clothes?"

"Sure."

"The whole world practically is in dry dock except me; I'm a diehard who doesn't pack it in until nearly October. Sorry, Daisy," he said softly, persuading the cat awake and urging it from his knees to the floor. Grumpily she jumped down and arched her plump back, looking up at Bart with reproach.

"Hey, don't look at me like that," he protested. "You make me feel like a real louse."

Melissa grinned, touched that he didn't even notice the trail of grayish hairs on the front of his corduroy trousers.

"Okay, get yourself in your gear and let's go. I'll take my friend downstairs." Bart made a sound between a whistle and a kiss to the cat, and it followed him out of the room.

Melissa threw some things in a canvas shoulder bag and got into some slate-blue sailcloth trousers and a long-sleeved harmonizing T-shirt. She threw a matching jacket over her arm and went downstairs.

Bart was on the couch, smoking and looking around with enjoyment, with Daisy cuddled up against his thigh.

He got up, remarking to the cat, "Well, this is good-bye, sweetheart. It was great while it lasted." Daisy opened one green eye and looked at him with feline scorn.

He laughed and threw his jacket over his shoulder. "Ready?"

"Oh, yes." She nodded happily, melting again with his infectious charm, even more aware of his tall, lean strength as he towered above her, walking out with her into the sun.

That day and the next were the most pleasurable she'd ever known in all her life, beginning with their leisurely brunch at an outdoor café and the taxi ride to his place downtown for his gear. He lived in a modern monolithic apartment complex overlooking the harbor, on a high floor.

"Not as nice as your place . . . but it's good to be near the water," he remarked. While he made a quick change into ducks, T-shirt and sneakers, slinging a sweater around his neck, she wandered around his living room, looking at his trophies and souvenirs. She couldn't help noticing the almost monastic quality of the place, as if it were somewhere he used only to sleep and store things. There was no sign at all of frequent female visitors—she began to believe what he had said about not being involved until he met her.

They went down to the garage to get his car and drove to the marina. She was a little skittish at first to step on the unstable deck of the sailboat, but after

they had cast off and were sailing on the Long Island
Sound she began to relax into a state of dreamy
pleasure.

"It's like flying," she told him, and saw his face light
up as he beheld her delight. He was really the most
giving man she had ever known, constantly watchful
of her ease and pleasure, touchingly anxious to make
her smile.

They docked at about sunset and drove to a com-
fortable, quiet harborside restaurant on Long Island,
white-walled, with booths and tables in dark, weathered wood.

Coming in from the sharp air to the warm coziness
of the place was very agreeable, and her sense of
pleasant ease deepened and grew. She looked into his
eyes across the table that glowed with a candle in a
hurricane lamp. They spoke little, content to enjoy
just being together, savoring the plain, well-cooked
food with enormous appetite and later feeling fine
brandy radiate in their relaxed, replete bodies.

"Where to?" he asked her as they headed back to
the city.

"Anywhere," she murmured lazily, leaning back
against the leather cushion. He drove with moderate
speed and total command; she'd never felt so taken
care of, so complete.

They went back to his place and made slow, sweet
love; napped, and later drove uptown for the last
performance of a movie. It seemed a foregone conclusion that they would spend that night together, too.
They went back to her house.

Sunday was cool and misty, grayed with drizzle;
after she had made a large breakfast, they decided to
drive down to Greenwich Village to take in an off-
Broadway play where casual dress could be gotten
away with, to save another trip to his apartment.

After the matinee, they wandered the rain-washed streets to find an equally casual restaurant. The area abounded with them; they settled on an Italian restaurant on MacDougal Street, an easy, family kind of place where the food was plentiful and tasty, and the atmosphere jovial. There, as everywhere they'd been that weekend, Melissa was conscious of Bart's benign effect on everyone he dealt with. He was a man for all places, she thought happily. But what about all times? she questioned in uneasy silence.

"And? . . ." he asked her smiling, studying her. "What conclusion have you come to?" There was a peculiar seriousness in the teasing query.

"That all this is . . . just delightful," she murmured, feeling the inadequacy of it, sensing her own evasion.

Something flickered deep in his eyes. "Yes. Oh, yes." He seemed to be repressing something else. "Melissa . . . may I have tonight, too?"

She nodded yes, thinking that it was already difficult to imagine a night without him. And that thrilled and frightened her. It was just too soon to feel like this.

Later, when she was close in his embrace again, he said, "This night . . . and tomorrow night. And the nights after?"

She did not answer; she couldn't, not yet. But she took his face between her hands and kissed him deeply, wishing fervently she could stop being afraid of the future, stop thinking of the real barrier that lay between them. Maybe she'd been foolish to avoid a discussion of it during this magic interval; he seemed literally to have forgotten. But somehow, as vital as it was, she hadn't had the heart to bring it up. There had to be something, *something* uncomplicated and right, even for a little while; even if it was based on a kind of lie. Melissa felt she'd missed so much, and she deserved that at least. She wouldn't think about tomorrow.

Putting his arms around her, Bart fell into a deep and easy sleep. She drowsed restlessly and some time later was awakened by a scratching sound, a bump from far below in the house. It sounded like someone was trying to break in. More likely it was one of the cats who'd gotten into the shop, because the sounds were so slight.

A robbery was really unlikely; her security system was one of the best. So it didn't even occur to her to wake Bart. She got quietly out of bed and slipped into scuffs and a robe and stole downstairs. There was a light outside the inner entrance from the house to the shop and she switched it on.

She made a sound between exasperation and a gurgle of laughter. Philo, the mischievous black-and-white cat, was staring at her from her desk with a mixture of triumph and chagrin at being caught out. Apparently he had been playing with the phone cord and pulled the receiver off; furthermore he'd knocked two of the credit card machines on the floor and several other things.

Melissa unlocked the two locks on the door—she made an awful racket—and went in. "Philo, Philo." Now she was giggling, not annoyed at all, because the cat's expression was so comical she couldn't help it. She went to the desk and put the phone back. She picked up the things from the floor, tapping Philo lightly on his haunch.

His dignity was so offended she picked him up to console him and he rubbed his face against hers.

Melissa heard a light tapping at the inner door. Bart was standing there with a questioning look, blinking with sleep. She let him in.

"What's going on here?" he demanded drowsily. He was wearing only his raffish duck pants and he looked piratical towering over her. She recalled what she'd been thinking before she fell asleep and felt a quick blend of guilt and tenderness.

"I heard something," she said, "and came down. But as you can see, it was only Philo, another neighbor."

Philo was crawling up his trousers, obviously very attracted. Bart laughed, and ordered, "Whoa. The rest is *skin,* pal." He retrieved the cat and held him against his chest.

"Wait a minute," he remarked. "Wait . . . a . . . *minute.* You *heard* something and didn't wake me up? Good Lord, you don't know who it might have been, Melissa. You need a keeper."

"I've done it before," she said airily. "It's always been one of the cats."

"You still need a keeper," he repeated. "And I'm it." He put Philo down and went to Melissa, taking her in his arms.

"What's going to happen," Melissa protested, on the edge of laughter again, "if the police come by and see a light?"

"They'll see this." Bart lowered his head to her mouth. His kiss erased everything in her mind but him.

"Melissa. What am I going to do with you?" He looked around the dim-lit area, gleaming with its many clocks and rhythmic with steady ticking. With his arm still around her, he murmured, "I love this place. The historic site." He grinned down at her. "Where Bart Freeman met Melissa Grey."

She smiled back, enchanted with him, trying not to think of what else that implied.

"Why don't we check it out to see if your visitor did any damage?"

"I don't think that's likely."

"I'll do it anyway," he insisted. "All of a sudden I have a strong desire to check your security system." She was touched by the protective note in his voice. He carefully inspected all the locks, alarms and other devices.

"You win, lady. I'm happy to report you have a fine system here, one of the best." He was sauntering back to her when something in a glass case caught his eye.

"Oh . . . this is pretty." He leaned over, examining it. She went to join him and realized it was "her" watch he was looking at—an exquisite timepiece at least eighty years old. At first glance it seemed simple, a band of delicate white gold links, an enameled face set in a plain white gold case. But the hour marks were tiny, intricate symbols of the astrological signs, from the Ram at the nine o'clock position proceeding to the Goat at noon, the Scales at three, the Crab at six and so on.

"It *shines,*" he said. It was true—the enameled face, as one moved to look at it, had a little "moon" that sailed across the narrow expanse of silver-gray glazed enamel. "This is wonderful."

"Yes." Melissa had often thought of keeping it for herself, or for Ria. But it was so exorbitant she'd always felt she couldn't afford to, concluding that the watch would have to find a richer wrist. "The 'star watch.' Or the 'moon watch,' I should say."

"Mmmm." Bart looked up at her, speculation in his dark eyes. Then he straightened. He glanced at one of the clocks, whose hands pointed to two. "It's late. And I've got a rough day tomorrow. Shall we?"

She nodded. Her heart sank. Tomorrow they would

both return to that "other world," the real place of problems and opposition.

He must have read her expression, because he said, "Melissa, why did you look like that . . . when I said that about tomorrow?"

"No reason, really." But she could see he was far from satisfied. However, he scooped up the now-drowsy Philo and followed Melissa from the shop, watching her as she locked up again.

"What do I do with the package?"

She grinned. "Put him down. He'll follow us upstairs and I'll scoot him out through the hall door."

When they had gone back to bed, Bart said out of the dark, "You still didn't answer my question, you know."

"What question?"

"About tomorrow." He tightened his arm around her. "You're thinking about the thing we didn't talk about," he added astutely. "Trust me, Melissa. I'm working on it."

His voice was so sleepy now that he could hardly form the words. "It's late," she said softly, burrowing closer to him. "No more talk tonight."

He seemed content with that and soon sleep descended on both of them.

The next morning Melissa was the one to greet him with coffee. She was already dressed. He awoke with a groan of protest, reaching for her.

When he saw the coffee he said, sounding drugged, "You're something else. Fold back your wings so I can kiss you; an angel's fallen into the bed."

He suited the action to the word and then took grateful gulps of coffee. "And you remembered how *I* take it. Bless you and thank you. This waking up is like a birth trauma. And a *Monday*."

Melissa's heart turned over. From Ria's astrological

lore she recalled that Pisces people wake up slowly and painfully. She herself was an undiscouraged morning person, and never felt threatened by Mondays. After a lonely weekend Mondays could be a positive joy. But that was before.

Now she was absolutely dismayed by her unwillingness to face a day of business, the fact that they hadn't discussed the property.

Revived by the coffee, Bart jumped out of bed and, kissing her on the top of her head, said again, "Thank you, thank you, lovely lady." He picked up his clothes and headed for the shower.

He declined breakfast. Looking harried, he said, "I'd better get down to the waterfront and put on my polite gear. I have an early appointment and I've got to sell some respectable people."

"Sell them?" she queried, smiling. "To whom? Is there a market for respectable people?"

He laughed, some of the lines in his face smoothed away. "Very good." His vitality and good humor seemed restored. "You are very wonderful," he said, sobering. "So was this whole weekend, Melissa. And it's just the beginning."

When he held her for a good-bye kiss, she thought, I hope it is. Oh, how I hope it is. It was almost painful for their little time together to come to an end like this.

"Just the beginning," he repeated firmly and he looked down solemnly into her eyes. Once more he bent to take her mouth.

Then he said, "If I don't leave now, I'll stay forever. So long, darling. I'll call you."

After he had gone she wished he'd said what time he would call. She realized, annoyed, that the old wound left by Gavin still wasn't healed; it had left her with a deep sense of insecurity. She still knew Bart

Freeman so little. All morning, sleep-deprived and absentminded, she wavered between remembered delight and a sense of anxious disbelief.

In fact the whole day was full of problems. First there was a call from Ansel, which she didn't quite know how to take. He was as casual as if there'd never been a good-bye, chatting about inconsequential things. Finally he asked if Freeman Company had approached her yet. They'd seen two others.

She was dismayed. If Bart was working on something, then why were these people still on the job?

Later Ria called, too. She rarely dropped in or called, saying she didn't want to be a pest. However, since the development threat had come up, she and Melissa had been talking to each other every day. Melissa blurted out what Ansel had told her.

"Yes," Ria said, "we heard that. They approached the other two on Friday. I can't understand why they're holding off on seeing you, Melissa. It could be a good sign—maybe they feel the house is landmark material. I don't know. In any case, we're having a special committee meeting tonight." Ria hesitated. "Unless you're otherwise engaged . . ."

Oh, dear. She and Bart had failed to show up at the Blue Mill Friday night . . . and then, over the weekend, she'd ignored the ringing phone a couple of times.

"I tried to get you Saturday, but you were out." Melissa could hear her mother's catlike curiosity. She couldn't, she just couldn't tell her anything. Not now. Not yet. It was just too new, too uncertain.

"Yes, I was," she answered calmly. "It was such a marvelous day I couldn't stay in."

"I liked your beau," Ria remarked. "What was his name again? I was in such a state I didn't catch it."

What a break, Melissa thought. Now there was no need to worry her mother with all the complications.

"Bart," she said hastily. "I'm sorry we didn't make it to the Mill, but we ran into some friends of his and before we knew it, it was awfully late. He's not a 'beau.'"

"Don't worry about it," Ria said easily. It was evident that Melissa's casual tone reassured her. "So can you come to the meeting tonight?"

"Let me get back to you," Melissa hedged. "I've got a lot of things piled up here and I may have to work a little late," she added mendaciously.

There was a brief silence, then her mother answered, "Of course. Talk to you later."

When they had hung up, Melissa regretted having to lie to Ria. Now she might assume Melissa was getting involved in another disaster, like Gavin, and was hesitant to confess it. But Melissa realized why she had—this whole thing was just too complex to go into right now. As perfect, as magical as the weekend had been, she was still left with a feeling of uncertainty.

She wanted to talk to Bart before she attended another meeting, have the whole thing out with him.

And in the last analysis, she finally admitted, she would rather be with him that night than with anyone in the world. The man who was a threat—it was crazy.

But he still hadn't called. Melissa felt that nagging doubt again. To make it worse she was confronted with two very demanding customers, one after the other; a delivery she was expecting wasn't made and she was late getting on with the repair of the delicate Waterbury Lady L.

Finally she took care of the latter. But at noon Bart still hadn't called. She decided she'd make lunch in the house, in case he did. By one-thirty he still hadn't phoned.

Worst of all, about three, she was reluctantly forced to sell the "moon watch." Her watch. A prosperous-looking older man came in, asking for something very special for his anniversary.

He chose the watch. Feeling foolish, Melissa sold it to him with a sinking heart. He paid in cash, to her surprise; that was an awful lot of cash to walk around with, she reflected. And when she asked him if he'd like to sign a card before she gift wrapped it, he flushed.

"I'll . . . er, wrap it myself," he stammered. "Just give me a blank card. You see, I have some . . . special paper," he explained. She wondered why he felt he had to justify himself to her; the whole thing was quite odd.

After he'd gone she was assailed with self-doubt and self-reproach in addition to the other doubts. If she loved the watch so blasted much, why on earth had she offered it for sale in the first place? Why hadn't she just kept it, or given it to Ria, even if Ria did in fact prefer yellow gold?

Melissa thought somberly, I've never been generous enough with myself. And it's stupid. But since the thing was done, she tried to dismiss it from her mind. Irritated, she realized also that it was too late to go to the bank and she was stuck with that enormous amount of cash. What a day.

Her head began to ache with fatigue, and unwelcome thoughts whirled in her tired brain.

It was nearly five when Bart phoned. He sounded slightly frantic. "You can't imagine what a hellish day it's been," he explained. "I'm sorry, darling . . . I'm so sorry I couldn't get to you before."

He sounded like it was the end of the world, she

reflected, and answered calmly, "It's all right. Really it is. I've had a . . . hectic day, too."

"Anything in particular happen?" There was a strangely urgent curiosity in the question, and for one awful instant she wondered if he could be referring to the information she'd gotten from Ria. How could he know? Her dormant suspicions stirred and snuffed out her pleasure in hearing his voice again. "New cat burglars?" he teased. She couldn't even laugh at that.

"Oh, no," she said deliberately. "Nothing particular, just a lot of general headache."

She listened to a beat of silence. Something *was* going on, she concluded gloomily. Then he said hastily, "Darling, please . . . can you forgive me? Just a second? I'll get right back to you. All right?"

"All right," she said dolefully, hearing him whisper "Damn," and there was a click. After what seemed a long interval, which she endured with rising impatience, she heard the click again and his voice.

This time, mysteriously, he sounded brighter, almost elated. "Well." The word fairly exuded satisfaction. "That's *that*. Now for more important matters: dinner?"

Melissa hesitated. Even with all that had happened between them, as much as she longed to see him, she felt a peculiar reluctance. Something about that interruption still bothered her. "I'm very . . . tired," she began slowly.

"Melissa? Is something wrong? Please tell me," he urged her and she was touched in spite of herself by the anxiety in his voice. "Please, my darling. Are you really 'just tired' . . . or is it something else?"

"Really," she assured him. "I'm just horribly tired. It was . . . quite a weekend," she said in a softer tone.

"That it was." His comment was tender, reminiscing. "I miss you already. But look here, you get some rest. I'll call you in the morning."

"Good-bye, Bart."

"Oh, no, not that!" he protested with mock horror. "*À tout à l'heure*'s nicer. Presently, lady, any hour."

"All right, then," she conceded. "Any hour now." All of a sudden she was charmed, warmed again as she always was by his presence and his voice.

"I'll be counting them, Melissa," he said softly.

After she put down the phone, she regretted her decision not to have dinner with him. It had been silly, when she wanted so much, needed so much to see him. And there was the other thing, she realized too late: She'd wanted to confront him openly about the company expansion before she went to another meeting. Well, it was too late now. Resigned, she called Ria and told her she'd be there.

What she learned there later was disquieting; from all the signs, Freeman Company was apparently pushing ahead with its plans. Over the weekend a number of owners had been approached. The committee that had organized the evening's meeting was drawing up tentative outlines to be presented to the Landmarks Commission. Another committee was meeting with attorneys to discuss a possible court suit.

By the time it was over and Ria and Mark were walking home with her, Melissa's eyelids were at half-mast. "Get some sleep," Mark ordered affectionately. "It's going to be all right, I promise you."

But Melissa still wasn't so sure.

And the bed was so empty when she managed to fall asleep.

It was just ten the next morning when the phone rang in the shop. "That was a long, long night."

The soft, suggestive words in his deep, resonant voice made her heart flutter. "Yes," she admitted.

"Yes." She hadn't meant to start it like this, hadn't had the intention of revealing herself to him so completely. But as usual, when the time came to carry out her plans, they never worked.

"I missed you like hell," he said. "It's crazy. But I missed you. Dinner tonight?"

Someone was at her door. "I'm not hedging," she answered, "but there's somebody at the door. May I call you back?"

"I'll call you . . . about fifteen minutes."

Melissa went to the door to admit the caller. It was a messenger with a long narrow package in his hand. When he'd gone she ripped it open. There was no return address. She unwrapped the box and opened it. The moon watch gleamed up at her. One of her own cards was in the box.

She read that familiar black handwriting: "A surprise to make the hours shine." It was unsigned.

Touched almost to the point of tears, Melissa took the lovely watch from the box, removed her grandmother's watch from her wrist and put the moon watch on. The frail white gold hour hand was pointing to the tiny symbol of the double fish, Pisces, the symbol marking his season of birth. She turned her wrist, watching the play of light make the masterfully captured "moon" sail across the face.

The phone rang again. "What news?" he asked eagerly.

"Bart. Oh, Bart, it's beautiful. It's very dear of you."

She heard a sigh of relief. "At last. In good time, too, it seems—at the hour of your fishy friend."

Melissa smiled at the double entendre. "You don't seem so fishy now; is that what that interruption was about yesterday?"

"Bingo. I was bawling out my henchman on another phone. About to have his hide for not completing his mission."

It was all falling into place now—his eager questioning, and then his elation when he came back on the line. The man's embarrassment about the wrapping; they must not have worked that part out, she thought, amused.

"Melissa . . . will you keep this present?"

She hesitated a second and then almost laughed out loud. If she didn't, he'd return it to her stock. The whole idea was so absurd that she was helpless. "Yes," she said in a low voice. "Yes, I will. And thank you."

"It's my thank-you to you," he said soberly. "For giving me the best two days—and three nights—of my life."

She melted. And she was overcome with shame for thinking that he'd been maneuvering again.

"Dinner?" he persisted. "Six?"

"Wonderful."

She was almost childishly pleased that she happened to be wearing a rose print dress that looked lovely with the watch.

The interim fairly flew. Before she'd hardly gotten started it was dusk.

Almost to the moment she saw him standing at the door, beaming, holding a bunch of vivid red roses.

Going to let him in, she thought, It's time to stop the suspicion and the doubting.

And when he took her in his arms again, utterly indifferent to the interested passersby, Melissa knew just how much he always made her hours shine.

Chapter Six

$\mathscr{B}$art turned onto the East River Drive. "I found a very special place. I think you'll like it," he said mysteriously.

"On the waterfront?" she asked, putting her hand lightly on his knee.

"In a way." He responded at once to her touch. He was looking straight ahead, but she felt a quick, excited, side-glance flicker. "You really know how to shake a fellow up, don't you, lady? There's no place to pull off here. You're making me forget dinner, and I've got to remember driving right now, if we want to get there at all."

She laughed softly, feeling more carefree, happier, than she ever had in all her life. "By all means, then, let's stick to the plan."

He was being very cagey; she was filled with anticipation. They sped by the Williamsburg and

Manhattan bridges, still heading toward the lower tip of the island. The downtown skyline loomed up ahead, a pile of fairy castles in the gathering dark. Then they were leaving the highway near the Brooklyn Bridge; the car turned into Water Street.

"What on earth? . . ." she asked.

"You'll see." He parked and went around to open her door and hand her out. She could see no restaurants anywhere.

"This way." To her amazement and delight, he led her onto a barge tethered below the Brooklyn Bridge. It was a continental dining place with a splendid view of the harbor.

They were shown to a table with the finest panoramic vista, and when he'd ordered their cocktails, he reached across the table for her hand. She said softly, "I'm enchanted . . . just enchanted."

"I'm glad," he murmured, "because that makes two of us." His glance dropped to her wrist, and his eyes lit up when he saw that she was wearing the watch. He turned her hand this way and that, dreamily observing the little moon move across the face of the delicate timepiece.

"I want everything to be special for you. Because you are." Their eyes met and held. "And we have a lot to talk about, Melissa—things we didn't talk about before."

She was touched by his tenderness, gladdened by his serious air. They did have to talk—about that thing that was still so troubling. And she was delighted that he had been the one to mention it first.

"Yes. But not right now. I want to . . . float some more for a while." She was surprised at herself; she was being infected with his own romantic ways, and she smiled broadly, both in amusement at herself and in answer to his own wide smile.

"Much, much later," he agreed, squeezing her hand. "That's the way I like to hear you talk."

They enjoyed a long and leisurely dinner accompanied by a fine Chablis that made her feel pleasantly giddy and languorous; their conversation touched on many things—their pleasure in the City, all the things she most liked to do and, little by little, his random tale of his experiences. He had been so many places, done so many things, that she was dazzled by them.

"But this is home," he said, with a symbolic nod toward the dark, shining waters, the lights of the passing vessels. "Now more than ever. You've made everything I love even more lovely, Melissa."

She reached across the table and touched his hand this time, and he grasped it with eager feeling, kneading it in his strong fingers as new waves of warm emotion swept her body. She recalled what Ria had said about Pisceans: "They glorify the simplest things." That's what Bart did for her.

The waiter had returned, asking if they would like dessert. "Melissa?"

"No," she murmured. "No, thank you."

Bart caught something in her tone, for when the man had gone away, he said, "Shall we go?"

She looked steadily into his eyes, almost sure that he could read the feelings there. "Yes, oh, yes."

"Like to explore the waterfront?" he asked softly, a smile twitching at the corners of his sensuous mouth.

"That sounds lovely."

Hastily he asked for the check and they were leaving, stepping back on shore.

In the shadow of the car, he took her close in his arms and lowered his mouth to hers. Their kiss had a new hunger, a sweet wildness deeper and stronger than anything before. Her hands were stroking his hair, his neck, with swift and urgent longing, tracing the wide span of his shoulders, creeping below his jacket to caress his hard and muscular torso.

"Melissa, Melissa," he whispered, gasping, "I don't know what's gotten into you. But whatever it is, don't ever change it—it's wonderful."

He was starting the car, turning onto the highway again, heading south. She saw his harborside apartment building come into view and she was buoyed on excitement, losing track of time again as he pulled into the garage.

In moments the elevator deposited them on his floor, and they were entering his monastic living room with its wide, brilliant view of the harbor.

Once more she came into his arms, and with half-closed eyes that dimmed the twinkling harbor lights numerous and bright as fallen stars, she raised her eager mouth for an achingly sweet and long and shattering caress.

Then he was throwing off his jacket, turning out the lamps in the spacious room. "I'd be jealous if a gull saw this, even." Now there was only the faintest illumination from the twinkling night; bolder in the shadows she began to divest herself of her clothes, as Bart did of his. They were standing naked in the semidarkness. He ran his hands down her pulsating body.

Then in an instant he had picked her up in his arms, and she felt with a throbbing quiver his hairy chest against her side, his hard muscles against the bare softness of her skin. As he carried her into the room beyond, he bent his head again and kissed her deeply; the muscles in his big arms felt shaky from excitement.

He set her down slowly on her feet in the darkness of the bedroom; there was only a shaft of dim light streaming in through the open door. His back was to the light, and she delighted in the tall, lean, muscular outline of him as he stood with his legs slightly apart before he pulled her close again to take her quivering mouth relentlessly with his.

The scent of him, his nearness, and the feel of his sleek, smooth skin pressing against her vibrant nakedness made her feel almost faint with longing; then, in the flick of an eye, she felt herself possessed of an alien recklessness, a whole new daring that she had never known with anyone before. Her hands were caressing him everywhere, playing with the rippling muscles of his chest and arms, straying downward to his hard, lean middle, feeling the shape of his hard legs.

All the while his own exploring fingers caressed her, discovering her curves and valleys. They were past words, beyond any awareness except for the sensation of each other's throbbing flesh and fevered skin.

With a groan he scooped her up in his arms and lay her on his bed. And this delirious meeting of their bodies was, for both of them, the most astounding, the most shattering of them all.

At that very hour, two guests were being entertained at Edward Freeman's Park Avenue apartment. It had not changed a whit in the fifteen years since his wife's death. It was still the stiff, traditional place it had been during her lifetime, with the look of being barely lived in at all. His puzzled and uneasy guests, Harvey Brill and Ferris Paradine, were oppressed without knowing why, as they perched stiffly in the living room. Brill, the attorney, knew nothing of such things, but his wife or any other woman would have sensed that every vase was in the place it had always been and only the flowers had been renewed. Even the flowers were arranged rigidly without imagination by a meticulous but joyless housekeeper.

Brill's own Georgian house on West Eleventh Street, thanks to his wife, combined warmth and elegance in an enviable fashion, or so he had often been told. Edward's quarters were typical of him, Brill thought.

He was as surprised as Ferris Paradine, the banker, by this unexpected invitation. Even with all that had happened, Edward had never invited either man to his apartment; their meetings had taken place after-hours at the office or at various clubs.

When they were seated in the living room and a grizzled, unhappy-looking maid had ministered to them with their choice of coffee, tea or highballs, Brill looked at Paradine. The banker was in the same position as he, not especially chummy with Edward Freeman.

"I realize," Edward began pompously when the maid had gone, "that this is a rather unusual place and time for a conference. But there are things to be taken up that are too . . . classified even for the office."

Paradine set down his Scotch with a blunt hand. "Something gone wrong . . . has somebody been tipped off?"

"No, no," Edward assured him. "I'll get to it if I'm given the opportunity," he added in a scolding tone.

Paradine bristled; he hated the man's ways. Brill was merely amused, although he wondered just how much boredom he should have to endure in this otherwise profitable venture.

"This is an unprecedented matter," Edward began delicately. "A . . . family matter of some complexity."

Would the stuffy ass never get to the point? Brill agonized.

"It involves my sister-in-law, our boy president"—

Edward smiled unpleasantly—"and a certain young woman." He seemed to relish his listeners' suspense and the drawing out of his story.

"Bart being blackmailed or something?" Paradine asked curtly.

"Please." Edward held up his hand. "Nothing so crude as that. Bart is getting too deeply involved in the building project."

"Thought he was jetting all over the place, keeping his nose out of things," Paradine growled.

"Please, Ferris." Brill put his hand on the banker's arm. If Paradine didn't keep quiet they'd never find out what this period-piece was trying to tell them. "Go on, Edward."

"Thank you, Harvey." Edward sounded snappish. "Now both of you know that Claudia's always on his side, and she has certain allies on the board."

That Sloan woman, Brill reflected, for one. And she lived somewhere in this area.

"But you don't know the full story behind the stock distribution," Edward went on more quickly. He detailed his late brother's eccentric testamentary provisions regarding Bart Freeman. Brill was shocked.

Generally articulate and cool, rarely at a loss for words, he found himself stammering, "Why . . . why, that's absolutely bizarre."

"I couldn't agree more," Edward rejoined. "But there it is. And that's where this young woman comes in. Her name is Melissa Grey and she owns one of those ramshackle buildings in the area, on Eighteenth Street."

"So offer her a special price," Ferris Paradine growled.

"Oh, no. That was tried several years ago and she laughed at the developer. She'll never sell the ordi-

nary way. I've kept my people away from her for that
reason. She'll need special handling, not a special
price alone."

"And Bart's sweet on her?" Edward nodded. "You
didn't get that from Bart," Paradine deduced. "How
do you know?"

"I have an excellent man . . . but I got that from a
resident down there, Ansel Harper, also in my em-
ploy."

"I don't care much for that, Ned." Paradine
frowned.

Edward, who detested being called Ned, winced.
He shot back, "Even for the considerations you're
enjoying, Ferris?"

Brill smiled. For a businessman Ferris Paradine
could be awfully naive. "Or in English, for all that
money?" Brill put in.

Paradine gave him an uncertain look. He poured
himself another finger of Scotch. Brill was thoughtfully silent.

The more impatient Paradine pressed Edward,
"Well, what do you want from us? Are we supposed
to put out a contract on this Grey girl?" he asked with
dark and heavy humor.

"Really, Ferris." Edward made a sound of disgust.
"Hardly."

"With the money involved we could certainly afford
it." Paradine seemed to be enjoying his joke, Brill
decided with distaste. These were apparently not his
first drinks of the evening.

"Be serious," Brill snapped at the banker. "Do you
want me to check over this will, Edward, to see if
there are any loopholes in that absurd provision?"

"That would be very helpful. Failing that we've got
to come up with more immediate solutions. If Bart
fulfills the proviso of that part of his father's will, he'll

have total power. And heaven only knows where that will take us."

"To the pokey, is my guess," said Paradine. Worried as he was, Brill could not help his amusement at Edward's prissy disapproval of Paradine, who delighted in revealing his simple origins.

"I really didn't bargain for anything like this," Brill said gruffly. "Maybe if we can get something on her . . . the girl, I mean. Have your people come up with anything?"

"No," Edward said regretfully. "But I know you have resources, Harvey, that are unavailable even to my people."

"True enough," Brill admitted. He had friends, or at least people who owed him something, in many different places. "I'll try to come up with something. Let me sleep on it, Edward."

When he and Paradine were leaving the apartment house, they hardly noticed the plainly dressed, middle-aged woman walking her dog on the other side of the avenue.

Hannah Sloan saw Harvey Brill and Ferris Paradine emerging from Edward's apartment house. That's odd, she thought. They were thick as thieves at the board meetings, but as far as she could gather Edward wasn't the social type who mixed professional relations with pleasure. It could be just a coincidence, she thought. But still . . .

Hannah and Claudia Freeman had become fast friends in recent years, allied not only by their common passion for the preservation of city landmarks, but also by the awareness that as women they were *personae non grata* to the male members of the board, who really only tolerated them.

She wondered if she should give Claudia a call. And say what, you idiot? she immediately questioned.

What did it mean, after all? And yet, when Hannah
went back to her house on East Eightieth Street, the
expression "thick as thieves" kept haunting her.

Melissa stirred from a half drowse, covered with a
striped sheet, blinking in soft light. Bart reclined with
his chin propped on his fist, staring at her.

"Hello, sleepyhead." He moved close to her on the
bed, kissing her cheek, then her neck.

"Ummm . . . what happened to me?"

He smiled, ruffling her hair. "Cocktails, wine,
dinner and love. Wonderful love. Then you took a
little nap."

She saw her moon watch on the table. "It's nearly
midnight. I don't believe it."

He grinned. "Time flies when you're having fun."
He slid down and put his head in her lap. "Are you
hungry? Believe it or not, I am. Why don't I have
something sent in?"

She stroked his face and hair. "All right." Lazily
she lay back as he got up, enjoying the sight of his
magnificent body as he strode to a closet, slid open the
door and got out a brown robe.

"Don't even dress," he said easily. "Just stay as
sweet as you are."

She giggled when he leered; the sheet just covered
the tops of her breasts.

"They can send us whatever we like from the
restaurant downstairs, table and all."

"How nice. Just something very light for me—a
fruit salad or whatever. And lots and lots of coffee."

"Whatever you say." He picked up the bedroom
extension and ordered a substantial meal for himself,
salad and coffee for her.

Feeling very naked, she said, "How about a loan?
A robe . . . or something?"

He went to the closet and returned with a short Japanese kimono of heavy cotton. "Not exactly your style"—he grinned—"but any port in a storm."

"It's fine." She peeled back the sheet, conscious of his look, and tried to put the robe on in a sitting position. It was a little difficult.

"You amaze me," he said softly. "You delight me, Melissa. One minute you're an absolute firebrand, the next you're a modest lady. You keep a man guessing. Here, let me do that." He urged her upward and tenderly put the robe on her, belting the sash snugly.

Then he rolled up the sleeves. "Look at yourself," he said, gently teasing. He turned her toward the mirror. The robe swallowed her, the tied sash's ends hung down past her knees. "You're the sweetest thing I've ever seen in my life." He hugged her from behind and kissed the top of her head.

She closed her eyes, leaning back against him. He felt as hard and strong as a tree; his body exuded security and warmth and peace.

Melissa opened her eyes and smiled at him in the mirror. "I'll be sweeter," she teased him, "if you let me take a shower."

He released her, patting her on a charmingly curved spot. "Sure thing. It's a far cry from gardens and unicorns, but be my guest. Right in there."

The big, efficient bathroom was much like the rest of the apartment—austerely luxurious, neat and plain, almost without character, all steel and glass. The only note of color was in the giant, fluffy towels striped in orange and gold and brown.

She stepped into the shower and soaped herself with his titanic bar of soap that smelled like cedar, noticing again that there was absolutely no sign of feminine soaps or bubble bath for guests. And that delighted her.

When she returned to the living room, dressed in the oversized robe, she felt refreshed and contented.

A wheeled table was already there, set with their late supper. Bart gave her a hug. "Umm . . . even when you smell like me, you smell better. I'm afraid my collection doesn't run to flowery stuff."

"That's nice. You don't know how nice," she added, looking up into his foxy eyes. "Your stock has gone way up."

"Finally." He grinned at her and ate his dinner ravenously. When he was pouring coffee for them, he said, "Time to talk. Past time. Let's have our coffee over there."

He took their cups to a table in front of the couch. "I told you what it was like for me, from the start, Melissa. I was hit so hard with you I didn't think of anything else, not at first. And then, last weekend . . ."

She melted at the sight of his slow, rueful smile and put her hand on his knee. ". . . was no time for business talk," she finished for him.

"Right. But you see, the funny thing is, even before I knew you I had my doubts about the project, for several reasons. I'd been working on an alternate plan, a plan that will exclude the whole street, much less your block. But somehow you've given me a kind of extra impetus."

He sketched out his plan for her.

"I love it. It sounds wonderful. You said your board will have to approve it. Do you think they will?"

"I'll make them buy it." She saw the stubborn set of his jaw.

"Meanwhile I have a selling job to do," he added.

"What do you mean?"

He set down his cup and put his arm around her. She laid her head against his shoulder. "I've been the

wild boy president too long, not holding tight enough.
Running all over the country and half the world . . .
like Japan, to check out their production methods in
electronics, things like that. Sometimes things that
weren't so practical. I'm not really sure what my exact
standing is with the board right now."

"I see."

"And I have another reason now not to run," he
said, bending down to kiss her. That warmed her
heart, and yet they really hadn't talked that much
about the project or about their relationship. There
were still so many things she wanted to ask, needed to
know. But when he was near her backbone melted,
questions evaporated.

"The main thing is," he asserted, "we've brought it
all out in the open."

Not quite all, she thought. Gavin had said, "Let's
don't spoil this with talking. . . ." Talking about an
unmentioned wife, in Gavin's case. Were there things
that Bart was keeping from her? Involvements with
other women? She shook off the unwelcome thought.
"I'm glad you told me. Now . . ."

"Now," he said in his buoyant, optimistic way,
"we'll have no more problems, no more doubts." He
squeezed her close, melting her. "Okay," he added
briskly, "if I'm going to get going in the morning . . .
and get you back to Timeland on time, we'd better get
some sleep. I'll take this debris to the kitchen."

She helped him.

Before they fell asleep she kissed him good night,
caressing his face, wanting so much to believe in
him.

"Happy?" he murmured.

"Very happy," she whispered, ordering herself in
secret silence: Repeat after me—Bart is *not* Gavin.

* * *

Early the next morning Bart dressed for the office, delivered her to Eighteenth Street and sped off downtown. It was only a quarter to nine when her apartment phone rang. She was warmed to hear his deep voice again so soon. But it wasn't a purely sentimental call.

"Something's come up, honey. Pretty heavy, in Milwaukee. I've got to fly there this morning. But I'll be back in a couple of days. I'll be calling you regularly."

It was the worst possible time, Melissa thought with gloom as they said good-bye. When she was away from him, she felt so unsure of things . . . just the way she had with Gavin.

But soon her crowded day began to distract her; a short time after Bart's call she got another from Ria. "Our campaign is starting to move." Her mother sounded elated. "We have an appointment with the landmarks people the day after tomorrow. You must come."

Melissa promised that of course she would.

Then things got quite busy; she was wholly diverted when a client brought in a round gold Ingersoll pocket watch that she recognized as a design made in 1892. It dangled around her neck on a heavy gold chain. The woman took the watch off its chain almost hesitantly. Melissa noticed that she swiftly and shrewdly gauged the shop's evident security devices. She seemed reassured then.

"There was a man I used to take it to in Connecticut, but he's retired. I just moved into the City."

Melissa smiled, mentioning the year of its manufacture. The woman was impressed by her knowledge.

"That's also the year this business was founded," Melissa remarked.

"I see I'm leaving it in good hands." The woman laid it carefully in its case and left satisfied.

Melissa delicately opened the antique case and read the legend inside: "This watch is guaranteed to keep good time for a year." It had kept good time for nearer a hundred, she reflected. It was a special pleasure to work on this old timepiece that was so treasured, that had been "born" the same year as Time Was.

And Bart had said he had a plan that would help her keep her store. She had to believe that. When she heard his voice again things would fall into place.

That hope and the prospect of the auction she was going to that afternoon combined to lift her spirits high.

By the time she left to walk to the auction rooms, only blocks away, Melissa's world had brightened to match the gold-and-blue afternoon with its crisp winds prefiguring her favorite month, October.

That same afternoon, Claudia Freeman walked into the auction rooms on East Twenty-fourth Street, still chagrined at what she'd done a little while before—making that sneaky visit to the psychedelic boutique for a survey of Darby Gillis. It was embarrassing to have spied, like Edward, especially when she'd been so superior about that. But at least she'd eased her mind on one point: The girl was pathetic and certainly not a threat. It was the other point that disturbed her. Edward must have cooked up the story. Why?

Her attention was distracted when she saw several people she knew. Even in New York the auction world was comparatively small. Fortunately she didn't know any of the group well. She needed some time to sort out her thoughts and impressions.

Claudia took a chair near the front and looked

around the crowded room, three-quarters full even at this early hour. Sotheby's it wasn't, she judged wryly, but there were some very attractive items up for bidding. She opened her catalog. But instead of the listings, she kept seeing the scene she'd witnessed earlier.

Entering the psychedelic boutique like a wandering tourist, Claudia had found it apparently empty, although she heard murmuring and laughter from the rear. The place was dim as twilight, with garish hot-pink and orange lights, and there was a sickening smell of cheap incense and other sinister aromas she couldn't immediately identify.

On the littered shelves were small jars of powder and mysterious objects labeled *Erotica;* books on black magic rubbed covers with the more sensational treatments of astrology, which made Claudia's gorge rise. She particularly detested books that classed witchcraft with that subject.

Still no one appeared. Claudia saw a metal bell on the counter and tapped it gently, bringing forth a clamoring ting. There was a rustling movement behind the beaded curtain at the rear. "Ah, Darby," a man's voice muttered.

Claudia's heart hammered. Thank heavens Bart was away.

Finally a young woman appeared just behind the beaded curtain. Parting the strands, she undulated into the front of the shop. This was apparently Ms. Darby Gillis. Claudia had to admit that Edward's description had been brilliant—the girl looked as if she'd just rolled out of an illicit bed. She was scantily dressed, even by contemporary standards, and her hair was so frizzed she reminded Claudia of the bride of Frankenstein.

Even in the dim light the heaviness of her makeup

was apparent; unwillingly Claudia conceded that she had a lovely face, small featured under the deforming paint, with sultry, heavy-lidded eyes. And her body was very shapely.

"Hi," she said with sullen casualness to Claudia.

"Hello," Claudia replied with a terrible false brightness. "You have a very . . . unusual place here."

Darby didn't answer. She stood where she was, leaning against a shelf with a cynical expression. Claudia almost felt like apologizing for coming in.

Nevertheless she was determined to get the girl talking. So she asked for some astrology books of a very scholarly nature, that couldn't possibly be on sale there.

"I dunno," the helpful Ms. Gillis said, yawning. "The astrology's there, with the witchcraft stuff."

By then Claudia was feeling slightly giddy from the garish dimness, the heavy incense smell, the whole picture. She noticed that Darby Gillis had a small tattoo on her slender white forearm. How could Edward have made such a ridiculous assumption . . . or have assumed that Claudia was stupid enough to fall for a lie about it?

"Thanks," she managed, and pretended to study the astrology titles. "I'll just look around," she volunteered. Again Darby Gillis didn't bother to answer.

The beaded curtains clicked and an enormous young man strolled through them. He was heavily bearded, with shaggy brows over small dark eyes that glittered as he examined Claudia. She wondered when his clothes had last been washed; it must have been a landmark occasion.

Speaking of landmarks—the building that housed this shop was a very interesting one.

"This is quite an old building," Claudia remarked. "Who owns it?"

"I do," Darby said, and her jaws began to champ. Claudia realized she was chewing gum. "Are you buying, too?" The grimy young man had come to attention.

"No," Claudia said firmly. "Well, thank you," she added, although she didn't know for what, and escaped.

The whole incident had been ludicrous and depressing, Claudia reflected as she gazed unseeing at the now full auction room. Edward couldn't be fool enough to think that Bart was romancing that girl. It was an insult to him. Suddenly Claudia saw heads turn and automatically turned, too.

An incredibly beautiful young woman was hurrying in to take an empty chair ahead of Claudia. A man's voice called out softly, "Melissa." The newcomer greeted the man coolly.

Claudia repeated silently, Melissa. She'd always liked that name; it had a kind of old-fashioned fragrance, like a bouquet of small white flowers. Queen Anne's lace or lilies of the valley. Unbidden, a memory came to Claudia: her birthday present from Bart had been tied with a bow of silk lilies of the valley.

This girl looked like a Melissa, she thought, with that shining, dark gold hair, the exquisite features and the clear blue-gray eyes. Her clothes neither masked nor flaunted her beautiful figure, and she was meticulously turned out. At that moment the girl named Melissa turned to speak to someone and caught Claudia's eye. There was an odd look on her face, almost a sign of recognition. It was strange; Claudia certainly didn't know her.

If Bart chose someone like that . . . oh, well. Claudia picked up her catalog again and tried to concentrate. She found the clock she'd come to bid for. She'd better pay attention; it was a low number and might come up at any moment. The bidding began.

She heard the auctioneer announce the number. It interested Claudia that the beautiful Melissa was also bidding. She wondered idly if this girl were also a Virgo—Virgos liked clocks so much.

Claudia signaled and the price rose. Melissa bid again. When Claudia made her second bid, she noticed that Melissa was trying to look calm but was hiding nervousness. Maybe she was afraid of being outbid. Something made Claudia withdraw; the clock went to the lovely blond girl.

The auctioneer evidently knew her well. He smiled in a friendly way and said, "Sold, to Ms. Grey of Time Was."

Time Was. That's where her swan clock had come from. Bart had chosen it himself. He must have met this lovely creature. He'd have to be brain damaged to prefer a Darby Gillis to Melissa Grey. There was something very fishy about Edward's story.

Claudia recalled all the times Edward had encouraged Bart to travel, to stay heart-free. He distinctly didn't want Bart to get married. Suddenly it came to her. The provision in the will, that required Bart to marry before he could take over Freeman's. That was it. That was why Edward had chosen this Darby as the "threat," counting on Claudia's habit of noninterference. He had been sure that Claudia would never stoop to investigating. Now it began to make some sense.

She got up and hurried out.

Maybe . . . maybe it was Melissa Grey Bart was after. Claudia's heart lifted with that hope.

The rest of the afternoon was frustrating for Melissa. She had made good purchases at the auction and hurried back to the shop, and then no one else came in at all. And the vague familiarity of the smart red-haired woman at the auction teased Melissa. She had Bart's coloring; Bart's mother was a "clock freak." The woman had stared at Melissa, and yet she hadn't approached her or acknowledged her.

Obviously Bart hadn't told his mother anything. Or maybe he had, Melissa thought uneasily, and his mother disapproved, for some reason. Blast it. Why was she thinking all these gloomy thoughts—why did she always think negatively when he was away? That was a bad sign. Maybe it was a bad sign that he'd gone away, when he probably could have sent someone else. Sudden tension gripped her.

Melissa ridiculed herself for writing such a depressing script, and yet when she was lowering the window gate for the night there was a chill edge to the dark that was more than physical cold.

"Hi, there!" It was a pleasant distraction to hear Maria's voice and see her impish grin. She was huddled into an oversized jacket, her fine hair in disarray. A grocery bag was in her arms.

"Hello! What have you got there—cat food and peanut butter?"

Maria let out her hearty laugh. "Twenty cans of cat food, a loaf of bread and a jar of peanut butter. You're psychic."

"Just experienced." Melissa grinned and walked over to kiss Maria. "How about a *dinner* . . . out . . . my treat?"

"It sounds wonderful. Did you empty the store today?"

"Just the opposite. I did some buying. Can I help with that?" Melissa nodded at the sack.

"Not on your life. Just let me nourish the beasts and get out of this plumber's gear and then we'll go gallivanting."

Companionably they went up the inside stairs. Melissa discarded her dress and jacket for a pants suit and light sweater; she was chilled. She thought, Bart might call while I'm out. He hadn't said what time he'd phone. Well, she wasn't going to sit and wait. She'd done too much of that for Gavin.

While she was combing her hair and freshening her makeup Melissa was assailed with unhappy memories. She'd become deeply dependent on Gavin, and he'd been about as stable as a funhouse floor. Never, never would she put herself in that position again. Maybe Bart wasn't Gavin; on the other hand, she wondered if their lovemaking had committed him to anything. When Maria came downstairs Melissa felt new confusion. Maybe she herself was the one who wasn't committed; maybe she was still frightened of that. Bart had almost hypnotized her into that wild submission, swept her too fast into love before she knew her own mind, before she was ready to trust wholly again.

Melissa shook off her roiling thoughts and asked Maria, "How about the Old Arbor?"

"That would be lovely, I haven't been there in ages."

They walked the few blocks to the pleasant restaurant, Melissa sensing Maria's unasked questions, unspoken comments. She knew she wasn't her own calm, open self, and Maria could surely feel it.

When they went into the candlelit restaurant, with its old brick walls and exposed beams, Maria said,

"This is a treat. And they've got a fire going already."
Orange light danced from the flames in the main
room's big fireplace.

Melissa couldn't help thinking how it would be to
dine here with Bart; the fire was almost the color of
his hair.

"I'm glad," she said to Maria when she heard the
old woman's pleasure, and she was reminded of
Maria's rather straitened budget, and her rare enjoyment of places like this. She decided not to spoil
Maria's dinner with any more woolgathering.

They had a choice of several rooms. "That one?"

"Anywhere you like," Maria said agreeably.

As they passed the second room, Melissa glimpsed
a table of eight and exclaimed.

"Well, well." Maria waved. At the table Ansel
Harper was sitting next to a sexy, frizzy-haired
woman. His expression was chagrined when he saw
Maria and Melissa. At the table were six other shop
and homeowners, mostly newer residents.

"Should we go in and say hello?" Maria asked
casually, a puzzled look in her eyes.

"Let's not," said Melissa. Maria gave her a quick
glance. Melissa raised her hand to the party and she
and Maria went on to the next room.

"That's interesting." Maria sat holding her open
menu without looking at it.

"Yes. An interesting get-together."

"That's no get-together; that's a meeting." Maria
studied Melissa over the tops of her eyeglasses.

"I think you're right. But what kind of meeting?"

The waiter interrupted them. When they'd given
him their order, and he'd gone off, Maria said,
"Maybe Ansel Harper's talking them around."

"To sell out, you mean."

Maria shrugged. "Well, he looked like a sheep-killing dog when he saw you." She chuckled. "And I'll bet it's not because he's with a hot date. You've broken off with him, haven't you?" she asked shrewdly.

"Yes."

"About time. I thought so; otherwise he wouldn't be courting anybody else . . . especially not that one. Unless he'd been lobotomized," Maria added.

Melissa laughed. "My greatest fan."

Suddenly in the pause they heard Ansel's voice, very clearly, all the way from the other room, loud and tipsy.

"Drink up. I insist. This is my party and I say it's time to get partier."

Maria raised her brows. "Well, I declare. Ansel's party. Since when is he doing that well?"

"Since never, as far as I know. That was one reason I could never get . . . involved," Melissa murmured. "I mean the *reason* he never did well—a kind of not caring."

"I can understand that. But he seems to be doing better now. Maybe . . . he's got some kind of deal with Freeman Company." Maria sounded thoughtful.

"What kind of deal?"

"Taking a . . . cut of some kind to sell out and get the others to follow suit." There was anxiety in Maria's comment.

Melissa hated feeding her friend's anxiety but it made sense. "You might have something there," she said slowly, thinking about it.

"There's something crazy about all this. Why haven't they approached you yet, Melissa?"

She felt a flush creeping over her face.

"I think I know why." She decided she might as well tell Maria everything. And did. But not quite all.

Maria looked skeptical. "Are you sure you can trust

this young man? Maybe it's all part of an attempt to . . ." Her face got pink. "Er, impress you."

"Delicately put," Melissa retorted with a lightness she didn't feel. "But he's not like that, Maria."

"Neither was Gavin, Melissa. If you'll forgive me for bringing it up. Was there ever anyone more plausible?"

No, Melissa conceded silently. Never. Except Bart Freeman.

Maria seemed guilt-stricken, full of remorse. "Look, I'm sorry I ever brought that up."

"It's all right. It really is." Melissa reached across the table and patted the old woman's hand.

Hastily Maria changed the subject, as if to atone for her indiscretion. But all the time she was talking to her friend, Melissa was thinking of Bart, and like a cold undercurrent, she felt the intrusion of new uncertainty in herself. "I was sure for a while," she blurted, "but now . . ." She thought of the eager light in his eyes, the deep sincerity in his voice. At the same instant she began to wonder if her body had betrayed her into belief.

"And now," she concluded frankly, "I'm getting confused again."

It was true. And it was a disturbing, subduing realization.

When she and Maria parted for the evening, the old woman patted her arm and said, "Maybe you'd better forget what I said, Melissa. I'm just a cynical old buzzard and I don't want to stand in the path of true love."

If that's what it was, Melissa reflected. She hadn't even stopped to examine her true feelings for Bart Freeman—maybe his physical attraction was so over-powering she'd misread that, too.

"Don't look glum, my dear. Maybe Time Was will

end up like that famous bar in the forties. It remained standing despite all the builder's millions . . . and still does. Saying 'in your eye' to that enormous complex up there."

Melissa had to laugh at her friend's triumphant expression.

But she didn't feel much like laughing when she was alone again. If the other owners backed out, where would that leave the association . . . and Time Was? If she and Mark and Ria had to do battle alone, what would it be like? She wondered if they could even afford it.

The ring of her phone aroused all-new, conflicting feelings. It had to be Bart. And yet here she was about to answer with the same ambiguous emotions she'd experienced after they'd first met each other.

"At last." His first eager words in that resonant, sexy voice erased everything else for a moment.

"Oh, Bart, it's good to hear from you."

"Darling, good's not the word. I know it's crazy but I miss you like hell already." She heard an edge of anxiety in his voice.

"I know. I miss you, too. Things aren't going well, I take it?"

"How did you know?" he demanded.

"Just the way you sound."

"You *are* wonderful." The warmth was very real and still she could hear that underlying tension. "Things are pretty tangled. I've got to be here two more days, at least, and it couldn't happen at a worse time, when I need to be back in New York."

She wondered why he'd put it that way instead of "be back with you." But she was always too analytical, too picky about things, and this was no time to let him know that, when he was so obviously pressured. And yet she couldn't help thinking of all the things that were going on. If someone was paying Ansel off, who was it?

"Melissa?" Bart prompted. She hadn't realized how long she'd been silent.

"Is everything all right?" he asked her anxiously.

"Of course it is." She tried to sound reassuring. He rushed on, telling her something of what he'd been doing, how achingly he missed her.

When they hung up she still did not feel the glow she usually felt after they'd spoken.

And she had the gloomy feeling that she'd left him as anxious as he had left her. Maybe . . . maybe when he was back with her it would all come right.

It had to.

Chapter Seven

$\mathcal{W}$ell, that's it, I'm afraid." The executive at the landmarks office studied Melissa, Ria and Mark with friendly regret.

"I guess we had to get it from the source," Melissa admitted. "We knew there'd be delay, that there were several entities involved. But you were the only one who could tell us about the Commission's priorities." Her heart was in the soles of her shoes; it sounded so unpromising.

"I *am* sorry. As to the Board of Estimate calendar, that's like a municipal delicatessen; just take a number."

Melissa was in no mood to appreciate the woman's little joke. They'd known all the rest—that Melissa and Ria, as co-owners of the building, were perfectly within their rights to nominate the house for landmark status; that the Commission held its meeting the very next week. Also that the Board of Estimate had

ninety days to veto or modify the Commission's
decision, and didn't reach their decision until after the
City Planning Commission had sent them an advisory
report. They'd researched all that. What they hadn't
foreseen was the crowded calendar of the landmarks
agency itself.

"So you don't think it could get to the Board of
Estimate before December?" Mark asked.

"Oh, no, not possibly. Nearer January. I prefer to
be conservative; I don't want to build false hope for
you. Now, if your neighborhood group could get
moving . . ."

"They're moving like a glacier," Melissa said dryly.
"As a matter of fact there's some internal . . .
disagreement right now which is delaying us further."

"That's too bad. Swift movement by them would
obviate any need for speed on the city's side. You
could just sit back and wait at your leisure for that."

"Don't remind us," Ria said, smiling sadly.

"There's only one bright spot in all this," the
woman asserted.

"And what is that?" Mark asked a bit dryly.

"Ponderous as the process is, once it's done, the
landmark owner has the full power of the city behind
him. That's it, for good—no more question. The
building can be demolished only with the owner's full
consent."

They all knew this, of course, and Melissa had a
feeling that it was being repeated just to console
them. Cold comfort at the moment, she thought as
they thanked the woman for her time and went out.

The elevator ride down was silent, but Melissa saw
anxiety in Ria. They parted on Vesey Street before
going their separate ways, Mark to a subway to take
him back to 116th Street, Ria to a cab. Melissa

declined to share it with her, inventing an errand in the neighborhood.

She didn't feel like talking about Time Was anymore today; she'd had it up to here with worry about that. What's more, she wanted to avoid a private conference with Ria; she was coming nearer and nearer to telling her all about Bart Freeman, and that wouldn't do at all. It was still too new, too tentative. And knowing her mother, she would practically have Melissa in a white veil if she learned how far it had gone. Or alternatively she might react even more strongly than Maria had, believing it was too problematic altogether, considering their respective positions and concluding that a Freeman was the last thing the family needed.

Melissa was so deep in thought she hardly realized what direction she'd taken. She was getting a headache about the whole blasted thing—they should have nominated the house years ago, when she'd first been approached by a developer. But she supposed glumly that they'd assumed this was something that "happened to someone else," like an airplane crash or a fire.

The question of Bart and his role in all this plagued her, too. He'd seemed so tired and preoccupied she hadn't wanted to press him about the plan. What could he do about it there, anyway?

Then she thought, Tired and preoccupied. Just from business? How they could become such strangers again in just a few days? . . . It really dismayed her.

She woke up and realized where she was. She'd walked so far and fast that now she was almost in front of the beautiful old Trinity Church on Broadway. She stopped. This was one of her favorite sights, typical of

the patchwork splendor of New York. Behind the
dark, ancient church with its seventeenth-century
burial ground, the glittering facade of the Trade
Center loomed in dazzling contrast, like a poster
depicting the past and future blended in the present.

She could say one thing for the past—she knew
what it had been. But the present, with all its puzzles
and problems, and the uncertain future, were something else again.

Right now she didn't even know how things were
going to be between her and Bart when he returned.

But she began to get a clue the moment he phoned
her, telling her the day and hour of his arrival. He'd
insisted that she shouldn't go to the trouble of meeting
him, and she gave in. But underlying his disclaimer
was a very real desire that she should; she'd heard it in
his voice.

So when the time came she decided to surprise him.
Even when she was dressing she began to feel a high
excitement, an enormous anticipation. It was a brisk,
invigorating evening, so she chose a suit and sweater
in shades of blue, to match the sapphire earrings.
Putting them in her ears, and slipping the moon watch
on her wrist again, she thought, In for a penny, in for
a pound. I might as well go sentimental all the way.

She cabbed to the airport far too early and had to
kill a great deal of time. Her nervousness grew and
grew until she was in an absolute swivet. When she
heard the first announcement of his arriving flight, her
heart gave such a leap that she could feel its almost
painful thudding high in her throat. Then came quiv-
ers of anticipation all along her body.

Slowly she got up from her chair in the waiting
room and started to walk toward the arch of the

echoing passage, already sensing the quickened tempo, the excitement of arrival.

Deliberately she stood staring through the great wall of glass, trying not to peer down the long walkway where passengers were beginning to come out. Then she caught sight of his flame-red hair, his tall lean body in dark brown, with a raincoat slung over his shoulder, towering over the people ahead of him, and her reserve was gone.

She was smiling now, and waving wildly, as he held up his own arm in return. As he came nearer she could see that he was absolutely beaming, his white grin a wide slash on his ruddy face, and he was striding faster and faster toward her.

Melissa started walking toward the metal barrier as he hurried forward, turning his lithe body this way and that to avoid other, slower passengers. Before they'd reached each other he'd tossed his bag and raincoat to the concrete and was holding out his arms.

When she came into those arms, Melissa knew there was one thing that was sure—everything else would have to be put on hold, at least for a little while.

He'd left his car at the airport; hurriedly they got in. And he was kissing her, kissing her hungrily and long. She was on the sliding board of sensation once again, out of control, swooping and sliding downward to that familiar forgetfulness; lost again in the feel and taste and smell of him, in the wordless sounds he was making; rejoicing in the sight, when she opened her eyes, of his blazing eyes and parted mouth and happy face.

All senses, every sense assaulted sweetly, wildly at once. She should have known all along. It had been like that since the first time he'd kissed her. All she'd ever had to do was come within the radius of his appeal and her thinking mechanisms failed, leaving her all sensation, wafted along on feeling in one inevitable direction.

His foxy eyes glinted in the lights of passing cars as he gazed down at her face, framing it with trembling hands. The hard feel of them lit a fire in her cheeks; she felt warmed in skin and sinew, flesh and bone. "Oh, my darling," he said, "I missed you." He kissed her again. "You're here, at last you're here. You sounded so far away, at times, on the phone that it scared me, Melissa. Tell me there's nothing wrong."

"Oh, not now. There's nothing wrong now," she answered with a small, breathless gasping. It's always "not now" with us, she thought, always tomorrow. And she felt a perverted, fierce gladness that that was so; this was the one perfect, all-consuming thing that brought her forgetfulness.

"Let's get out of here. As the fellow said, 'Your place or mine?'" He started the car and eased it toward an exit.

"There are nearer places," he said, grinning sideways at her as they took the highway. "But I can't see you in a motel . . . that's not your style at all."

"I've never been to one," she admitted, "unless I was traveling."

"We are traveling; we're miles from New York." He laughed with a happy sound.

She hesitated. Then she said shyly, "You're right."

"Are you sure?" he asked her seriously. "I'd hate it if you didn't . . . like it after all."

"That couldn't happen. Anywhere we're together has to be beautiful."

"Come here," he ordered, and put his arm around her. They drove slower now, looking. "Eureka," he said, sighting a nice-looking place.

When he parked outside, he said, "And I have luggage, too. I think I had a great idea."

She watched him write Mr. & Mrs. Freeman, San Francisco, on the register, and stifled a giggly feeling when the man sent a bellboy with them to their room.

Bart closed the door; Melissa dimmed the lights. "I've got a couple of pairs of pajamas in here," he said, nodding at his suitcase on the rack at the foot of the bed. "We can split the difference, and *vive* the difference," he added, his voice subtly changing as he came to her, started caressing her. "Oh, this is so nice, so nice."

He slipped off her jacket, surveying her curved body in the light, soft sweater and side-slit skirt. His hands traced the outlines of her; his breath quickened, his eyes grew bright. She accepted with a sharpened pleasure the touch of his stroking fingers and reached out her hands to run them down the sides of his head, over his warm ears and strong, sinewy neck. There was a deep tremor, a leashed eagerness in his whole frame; swiftly, suddenly, he was holding her to his body, pressing her to him. Her quivering softness melted to the urgent hardness of him; at every point of her flesh she could perceive the absoluteness of his male desire—from the magnetizing pull of his seeking mouth to the wall of his broad chest to the muscular strength of his strong thighs.

In tacit haste they undressed, their clothes scattered all about them, and this time their throbbing bodies met in a hot smoothness of skin; they stood fitted to each other, delirious, in the irreversible rhythms of a newer, deeper, utterly total desire.

He was saying her name again and again deep in his throat, with tender desperation, while she was feeling, more than ever before in all her life, savage abandon.

He made a slight backward movement, urging her

with him, and they moved like dancers slowly to the bed; he laid her down beneath him. His hands were awakening her breasts, stroking her body, caressing her most secret places as she cried out with excitement; then, in another hazy instant, his lips were hungrily caressing the hardened tips of her breasts, arousing her to the point of frenzied madness.

But now, with a teasing, seductive sound, she was slipping out of his grasp, motioning him to lie back on the bed. In the dark he made a sound of puzzlement and question, until she was lying against him, caressing his breasts as he had been igniting hers, and his body leaped with the force of his need and his excitement.

He said her name, once, hoarsely, in wonder, and then she was running her hands over his body, bringing him to greater and greater arousal.

Protesting, he grabbed her by the shoulders and pulled her upward, and she cried out with deeper, wilder desire. Their bodies met wholly again and they moved with abandon like dancers in a savage ceremony of yearning.

All that had been empty in her was filled; she could feel him quiver in every sinew and they both cried out almost in unison as they reached the flaming height.

Afterward, gasping, she lay upon him, her parted lips finding the fast-drumming hollow beneath his ear, pressing kisses on his skin as his arms held her closer and closer, hands kneading her shoulders and her back, tracing the curve at her waist that swelled gradually into arcing softness on her hips.

"My love, my love," he whispered, and the hot words riffled her hair veiling his face. She brushed her hair aside and touched his cheeks and lips and nose with her mouth. She could feel moisture under his eyes.

She thought, marveling, It meant that much to him . . . he was touched that deeply. "Oh, Bart," she whispered, and repeated her quick, light, tender kisses.

He seemed unable to say a word. Then, at last, when they had regained their breath and senses a little, he very gently maneuvered her down to his side and held her close to him, stroking her still-thrilled, vibrant skin.

"Melissa, do you know something? All the way back on the plane, this was . . . starting. Do you know what I'm saying?"

"Yes, oh, yes." She kissed his chest. "It was that way for me. I think it started even when you phoned, and were so sweet about my not 'bothering' to meet you."

He made a chuckling sound of delight. "Oh, that was so *great*, to see you standing there. Like a present. So unexpected. When all I was expecting was to race through that terminal and jump in the car and drive to you like a bat out of hell. Wasting all that precious time. And *then* . . . when you agreed to this . . . well, I could hardly believe it. I wanted to, but I was afraid you'd think . . ." He stopped, searching for words.

". . . think that your interest in me was not that pure," she teased him, running her fingers down his chest, savoring the hard flatness of his stomach.

"Watch it, lady. I'm a ravening beast."

". . . think that your intentions were not honorable," she went on, teasing him in a melodramatic voice.

There was an abrupt silence between them. Oh, Lord, I shouldn't have said that, even in teasing.

"Melissa," he said soberly. She wondered what was coming. Maybe she'd gone too far, struck some kind of nerve. He was half sitting, looking down at her, and in the near-dark relieved only by an outside light streaming in through an opening in the blind, she could see that his expression was very serious.

"Melissa, you were kidding. But I think it's time to *talk* about 'honorable intentions.'"

Somehow the way he said it was not wholly mocking; the nineteenth-century phrase sounded at home on his mouth.

"We shouldn't have to lie when we register at a place like this," he said. "We should make it true. You must know I want us to be married. Don't you?"

If she had expected anything it hadn't been that. They were still practically strangers to each other; they had met only a few weeks ago. Apparently disturbed by her continuing silence, he repeated, "Don't you?"

"I couldn't know, Bart, until you told me."

"Of course, you couldn't. What a damned fool I am; I just assumed so much . . . assumed, because you always read me so well, that you must know. I'm asking you now, darling. Marry me, please. There's no other way for us to go." He squeezed her to his side and kissed her head.

"Bart . . ." She turned her head away a little, thrilled, touched, yet somehow still uncertain.

She had never known such conflict in herself; things had always been black and white, one way or the other. But this—this was a thousand shades of color. On the one hand, he was offering her the answer to all her hopes and dreams, the filling of emptiness, the banishment of that long loneliness. The sweet magic of their times together suffused her being. He was there, before her. The man she thought she might never find, the perfect man for her. Her heart cried out, "Yes, oh, yes."

And still her cautious, wary mind braked her wild emotions. From the first moment he had been less than open. That described Gavin, too. And in so many ways Bart and Gavin were just alike— charming, overwhelming, sweeping her along on a reckless wave of desire that drowned her deepest self. She couldn't forget that unendurable pain from the past; it had been so wracking it had nearly torn her asunder. What if this bubble burst, too? She couldn't bear it. But Bart isn't Gavin, she debated. Then she realized how long she'd been silent.

"Melissa?" His voice was gruff with anxiety.

"Bart, I . . . don't know yet. I don't know."

"Don't *know?*" He sat up and took her by the arms, turning her to face him. She still kept her face turned away at an angle. "Melissa."

He took her chin in one of his big hands and gently forced her face into direct line with his. His foxy eyes were full of hurt, pleading in the semidark. "Let's have some light on this. I want to look at you."

He leaned over and snapped on a soft bedside lamp, and then he stared into her face. "What are you saying? Are you saying you don't love me . . . after all that's happened? After all . . . this?"

"Oh, I do love you," she blurted, knowing for the first time how deeply true it was. "Yes, I love you." She smiled. "Something you haven't even said to me."

"Oh, Melissa, you must have known from the first that I love you. Everything I said and did was meant to say it. . . ."

That couldn't be denied: every word and gesture of his, every tenderness and gift, his consideration and care, his eagerness and passion, all had said the words without saying them in fact.

"Of course I'll say it," he rushed on. "I love you,

love you so much, Melissa, that it's had me crazy from the very beginning. I think I must have felt it the first day, without even knowing it then."

She leaned into him and took his face between her hands, lowering her mouth to his for a lingering and sweet and very thrilling kiss.

"But you haven't answered," he said, when their mouths parted. "You haven't said yes."

"Don't you see? I can't yet. We've only known each other for a few weeks, and even in those weeks we've spent only a short time together."

"But the nights, Melissa. Can you honestly say you spent nights like that with me without even thinking of getting married?"

"No. I did think of it, I suppose. But I'm afraid, Bart. I'm still afraid." Afraid for Time Was, she thought.

"Of what? Of *me*? How could you be, Melissa?" He grabbed her and kissed her savagely, as if the very caress could convince her. "How could you be afraid of that?" he demanded softly.

This was what she'd longed for, dreamed about. She couldn't understand her doubts, but she still had them.

"There's been too much in the way . . ." she said, thinking of all her doubts and suspicions, thinking of how that other love had almost destroyed her. "I just think it's too soon for you to . . . commit yourself like this."

"That I don't know my own mind. I'm not some kid, Melissa. I've never been more sure of anything." She was silent. He added gloomily, "I think it's you who don't know your own mind. You're still operating in the old way, acting on old emotions. Someone hurt you and you believe you can never fully trust a man again. That's it, isn't it?"

"Yes, that's part of it. I was hurt. So deeply that I made up my mind I'd never put myself in that position again. I was made an utter fool of by a married man who successfully hid that fact from me for a long time. He was so very, very plausible. When I found out the truth the shock was . . . horrible. It just blew my trusting mechanism apart.

"You asked me to take a lot on faith, too. And we haven't been together long enough really to know each other, Bart. I can't help being afraid your feelings might just . . . blow up, too. It's all gone so fast, so much has happened. There have been so many unanswered questions in my mind."

There was an uneasy silence now between them. He let go of her and with a muffled oath leaned over and retrieved his jacket from the floor, pulling cigarettes and lighter out of a pocket.

This should have been the happiest moment of her life. Now this had happened.

He offered the pack to her. She shook her head. Coolly, she thought, like a stranger. He lit a cigarette and, inhaling deeply, lay back against the pillows, staring upward. His neutral expression chilled her.

"I think . . ." she began timidly. "I think you'd better take me home."

He wheeled about and stared at her. "Take you *home?*" There was pain and anger in his voice. Then he calmed down and, putting out his cigarette, reached for her. "No, darling. Please . . . I'm sorry if I said something that—"

"It isn't that," she said miserably. "But all the same, right now, I think it would be better."

She could feel him still staring. But he made no further protest. "I'll dress in there," he said curtly, indicating the bathroom, "and leave you some privacy."

"Thank you," she murmured, thinking, Why are we talking to each other like this, with this horrible, cold politeness, like two people who've just met on a train? But somehow it was too late now to reverse the order of things.

When he returned from the bathroom she was dressed again. She almost felt like crying when she remembered how he'd talked about the pajamas. But at this moment his face was shut and bland and she didn't have the courage to say anything to try to change it.

They walked out to the car and when he started it she noticed the night clerk inside looking out with a cynical expression. So much for the myth of Mr. and Mrs. Freeman. Their leaving like this, in the middle of the night, made the whole encounter seem cheap and sordid, like a dirty joke. And it had begun so sweetly; it had been so beautiful.

As they drove away, she said, "Bart . . . I'm sorry. I didn't mean to . . . spoil it."

"It's all right, Melissa. I guess you just couldn't help it." He no longer sounded angry, merely sad.

He concentrated grimly on his driving and they sped back to Manhattan. In an amazingly short time they were turning off the highway and he was pulling up before Time Was on Eighteenth Street.

"I guess . . . it wasn't so far after all," she said uneasily, trying to smile, attempting to put things back on their earlier footing. But he didn't smile; she could see now that she had hurt him too deeply, confused him. He looked tired and depressed.

"Bart . . ." She must make one more try.

"Oh, Melissa." His face melted and he moved to her, taking her tightly in his arms. "Forgive me. For being such a sulky fool. Let's give this a little time, love. Please. Don't give up on me yet. I love you so much. You've got to think about it. I don't care how much time it takes."

Her heart was singing again; she almost wept with her relief. "I'll never give up on you, Bart Freeman."

He hugged her, whispering, "Thank you. Thank you, Melissa. Just let me keep trying." He let her go and smiled. "Maybe this is better, anyway. I've got a whale of a day tomorrow . . . today, that is. And I want you to know a lot of it has to do with *that.*"

Bart gestured toward the house.

"Oh, Bart, that's wonderful." She kissed him. "Don't give up on me, either. Give me a little time . . . will you?"

"I told you. All the time you need. But that doesn't mean I'm not going to bring it up again tonight. As for giving up on you, lady, that's never going to happen. Not while I'm still breathing."

Bart watched her walk away, admiring the slender, round lines of her beautiful body, her luxuriant golden hair, her gorgeous legs. How he loved that woman.

As usual, he'd jumped the gun with her, as he'd done with things all his life, and he'd known she was still skittish because of that other man, that damn fool who had hurt her so badly. Well, he was only starting. And he'd get a ring today, just in case. The prettiest diamond Tiffany's had in stock.

Elated at the thought, he gunned the Jag, delighted that she turned to wave, and practically flew down East River Drive, where there was little traffic at this time of the morning.

He got a couple of hours' sleep, showered, shaved and changed, amazed at how refreshed he felt. It was only a little after eight when he walked through the empty outer offices of Freeman Company.

There was plenty on his desk to clear away, and he

was itching to get back to the building file. And it was
far too early to call Melissa; she'd probably be fast
asleep. The thought of her made him ache with new
desire. But it was so distracting he turned off the
lovely pictures of the night before and raced through
the mail and messages.

He was so deep in his study of some structural plans
that he hardly heard the others come in.

"Well, welcome home."

He looked up, expecting to see Roberta there with
coffee, but it was his mother. He had been out of it,
not even to recognize her voice at first.

"Thanks. Welcome to Chaos," he retorted, indicating the jumbled desk. He got up and went to her,
grabbing her for a quick, affectionate kiss.

"You smell nice," he commented. "And you look
even nicer."

She flushed with pleasure. His compliment had
been sincere; she looked about thirty-five years old
this morning with her gold-colored dress and her neat,
bright hair. But there was a look on her face he'd
seldom seen. She was always so poised and self-
confident; this morning she looked tentative, almost
shy.

"How did it go?" she asked. "When did you get
back?" He leaned out the door and said good morning
to Roberta, asking her to bring them some coffee.

"It went fine," he answered. "And I came back on
the red-eye special this morning." The first part was
true, anyway. After the secretary had brought them
coffee, he shut the door.

"I've got something very special to tell you," he
said. He was surprised to see an agitated expression
come over her smooth face.

"Come on, Ma, it's good," he protested, laughing.
"I'm thinking about getting married."

He'd expected her to react very differently. It was something she'd seemed to want for quite a while. But she only said, "Are you sure?" There was a tentative, tight smile on her lips.

"What kind of reception is that?" he demanded. "I thought you'd be jumping for joy."

"But who is she, Bart?"

"Somebody you'll love. You'll just go crazy over her the way I have."

Her attitude surprised him. She didn't have that look of unconditional happiness and approval that he'd somehow expected; her expression was still tentative, almost anxious.

"What's the matter?" he asked her gently. "What's going on? I meant it—she's someone you'd really love. She's beautiful and bright and what people used to call a 'lady.'" He grinned. "Not that I need anybody's approval—I'm going to marry her anyway, no matter what anybody thinks. When she says yes." The conclusion was rueful.

"She hasn't accepted you yet?"

"Not yet. But she will."

"Bart . . . you haven't even told me her name," Claudia protested.

"Grey. Melissa Grey." He felt tender all over again just saying the name. "She runs the shop where your clock came from."

He was amazed at the effect of his announcement. Claudia's eyes lit up and her trembling smile widened and widened. She might be ready to cry at any moment, from the look of her. "Bart. Melissa Grey?" Claudia clasped her hands together. "Oh, good heavens."

Bart just went on staring at her.

"But that's . . . marvelous. Marvelous. Wonderful." Claudia was absolutely delighted, like a child

who'd been told she could go to the circus after all.
She made Bart feel almost paternal, in that odd role
reversal that sometimes happens.

"You know her?" he demanded, grinning from ear
to ear.

"Not exactly. I've seen her."

"Where?" Claudia told him about the auction.

"Well, I'll be damned." He was feeling wonderful.
What he'd said was true—he intended to marry
Melissa if the whole of America opposed it. And he
would; he'd chip away at her resistance until she gave
in. All the same, this was a bonus. It was gratifying to
see that he could make his mother as happy as
himself.

"I knew it all along," she said. She rubbed the
corners of her eyes with her fingers to capture small
escaping tears.

"Knew what?"

She flushed. "Oh, for heaven's sake. It's just some
insanity of Edward's." She told him what Edward had
said about Darby Gillis.

"Who in hell is Darby Gillis? Sounds like a girl
jockey. Where am I supposed to have met her, at the
track?"

Claudia laughed. "You know, the one who runs
that psychedelic place on Eighteenth Street." Bart
recalled it.

"Oh . . . *that* one. Uncle Ned had me matched up
with *that* one? He must be losing his marbles. When I
saw her I thought it was Hallowe'en."

Claudia answered his laughter with her own. "I
knew it. I knew it. I told him you couldn't be that far
gone."

"Now what in hell made him say a thing like that?"

She sobered. "I don't know. I'm beginning to
wonder about a lot of things. As a matter of fact,

that's why I'm here in the first place—to talk to you about it, before we got diverted. I think something very peculiar's going on." She told him, then, about Edward's visit; about a call she'd gotten from Hannah Sloan, who said she'd seen Brill and Paradine coming out of Edward's apartment building late that evening.

"I think so, too," Bart said grimly. "As a matter of fact, I've been going over these plans. Look here. Look at these figures." She walked over to the desk and followed the direction of his guiding finger. "These figures are theirs," he explained. "These are mine." He pointed to some scribbled figures on a yellow sheet.

"That's quite a discrepancy," she murmured. "What exactly does it mean?"

He straightened and looked into her eyes. "I'm not sure yet. I've only started. But I'm going to find out very soon."

"I hope it is soon," Claudia said anxiously. "You know, the next board meeting is the day after tomorrow."

"Too well. If I have to camp out here and sleep on the couch for the next two days I'm going to get to the bottom of it before then."

"Good." Claudia got up to leave. "I'll leave you to it. And if there's anything I can do—camp out with you, anything"—Claudia grinned—"give me the word."

He got up and hugged her to him. "Will do."

"Bart . . . you said she hasn't accepted you yet. Why not?"

"She thinks it's too soon," Bart said wearily.

"She'll come around. Give her time. After all, how *could* she turn down my wonderful son?"

Bart wished he could share his mother's confidence. But he'd have to get his mind off that for the moment;

there was a hell of a lot to do. And he had to begin
doing it.

He made several calls, one to the city's department
of buildings, one to a man who specialized in discreet
and private services. Then, after searching the Yellow
Pages, he made a couple more.

Before he got back to the structural plans again,
Bart sat back and went over his conversation with
Claudia. He was sure now he knew what his uncle was
trying to pull; he could almost follow it, step by step.
He was desperate to keep Bart Freeman from exercising that option. First, he'd produced Darby Gillis to
get Claudia into a swivet. His mother would be too
proud, too ethical to snoop into his private affairs.
From the first mention of a threat, to Edward's
suggestion that she be "paid off," would be a hop,
skip and a jump for Edward Freeman. Then he would
have gone to Melissa and offered to pay *her* off,
blowing all Bart's chances with her forever.

The old buzzard must have had a private eye on
them . . . or someone else in his pay. At any other
time Bart would have laughed at this cloak-and-
dagger tale, but not now. Because now, he decided,
his uncle had something to hide. And with luck he
might have railroaded his plan through, with Bart's
present stock options.

But he wasn't going to. Not now. Suspicions didn't
hold up in court, but evidence did. And Bart was
going to get that evidence.

He jumped back into his perusal of the estimates
and plans. It was all very, very subtle, he discovered;
some of it was so cleverly masked that it was fairly
impossible to prove at this stage. Laboriously he
began to check the whole thing again with a calculator.

Red-eyed with fatigue and strain, he looked up at

the precision clock on his desk. Two o'clock already, and he'd completely forgotten that he'd had little breakfast and no lunch. He buzzed the curious Roberta and asked her to have something sent in.

He wolfed his food as he worked and then began to make some more calls, to friends in the construction trade, to architects, realtors and attorneys. It would hardly do, he thought dryly, to consult the house lawyers on this one. A pattern began to emerge.

So did another. It would take at least a week to get together what he needed. Meanwhile the board was sitting the day after tomorrow. Bart rubbed his eyes, feeling momentarily downcast.

But there was another chance, just an off-chance, maybe. He called back the fellow who offered discreet services, who as luck would have it had gone out; Bart left a message.

When he noticed the passage of time again, dusk was falling. He got up and switched on some lights and checked the clock, unable to credit that it was five.

And he thought: Melissa. What must she be thinking? She'd be thinking he was a self-pitying, sullen jerk who had purposely neglected to call her. And he also had to get uptown to Tiffany's. Damn it all to hell.

Quickly he dialed her number.

By ten to five Melissa was getting very anxious. Why hadn't he called? Maybe she'd made the worst mistake of her life last night.

She couldn't help feeling doubt, even after their talk of marriage. Maybe there was some reason he wanted to marry her besides the simple fact of loving her. She reviewed all of their time together, from that first day, when he'd just happened to come in and buy a clock, scrutinizing the building, asking her questions about the business. That first lunch date, when he'd managed to get her to tell him all about herself without volunteering much about himself.

His appearance at the community meeting, the way he kept the talk away from business on their first wonderful weekend together: the company still pushing its expansion plans even after Bart had told her he had an alternate plan. And then, when they finally *had* talked about the fate of Time Was, Bart's vague and unsatisfactory answers. Worst of all, that night she'd seen Ansel plotting with the locals at the restaurant; the idea that Bart's attraction was so powerful that it had clouded her mind and judgment. Bart had never gone into his plan with her fully, never given her real proof that he meant to save Time Was.

But what kind of paranoia was this? Melissa mocked herself. Surely a man would not offer a commitment like marriage as part of some maneuver.

She couldn't believe now that she'd said no.

What an utter fool she'd been—thinking the old disaster had anything to do with this, with now. Just because that instant thing with Gavin had turned into a nightmare was no reason to believe it couldn't work with Bart. All the wonder and the glory of their nights together returned to haunt her; she melted to remember his tenderness, his generosity, the stunning magnetism of his tall, lean body, the warmth of his foxy eyes, the touch of his hands on her. She knew now just how much she loved him, and always would.

But he'd said he'd give her time; that good-bye kiss had been so promising, so sweet. Only an adolescent could jump to such gloomy conclusions in just a day. But that's just what she felt like.

Aggravated by lack of sleep, her imagination was

running wild. She hadn't been able to take a nap; the whole day had gone wrong.

The clocks were pointing to five after five when the phone chimed.

"Darling . . . had you given up on me?" His voice sounded wonderful and she felt that instant warmth and reassurance from his resonant question.

"Not at all," she lied softly.

"What a day." He let out a long breath.

"You sound exhausted. I had an awful day, too."

"I am a bit wasted," he admitted. "Sorry your day was bad. But there's still the night. Is it too late to ask you to dinner?"

"No. No, not a bit." Now she was terribly eager to see him.

"Would seven, seven-thirty be too fashionable? I have a very important errand to run . . . for you . . . and that's the earliest I can make it. I'll take you someplace special."

"How about here?" she suggested. "I'll buy *your* dinner, for a change."

"Oh, that sounds just . . . perfect. Are you sure?"

"Very sure indeed. And seven-thirty's wonderful. It'll give me time."

"See you then, with bells all over me."

She smiled as she hung up. She closed the shop early and got busy. The house, fortunately, was at its shining best; the cleaning woman had come in that morning. She rushed out and shopped for filet mignon, which she would put on at the last minute, remembering he liked rare steaks, with perfect vegetables and an extravagant dessert. The filet would call for just the right red wine, and she lingered long over its choice.

Back home she put the foods away and devoted

herself to setting a very special table. She used her most fragile china and prettiest silver, arranging them on a bright yellow-orange cloth almost the color of the dining room wall, glad that that very morning she'd bought some bittersweet and asters for the pottery vase in the center of the table. The vivid colors made the cozy space even warmer, most inviting.

That done, she took a long, leisurely bath, washed and blew-dry her hair, took care with perfume and makeup. Then she slipped into an aster-blue pajama suit faced in gold at the neckline and cuffs and put the sapphire earrings in her ears. She was delighted with the result.

The easy dinner preparations took hardly any time at all, and everything was ready when the bell rang at precisely seven-thirty.

Going to answer, she remembered that first day, when he'd implied that he was always late. For her, he had always been on time.

What kind of a fool, she thought, could fail to trust a man who tried so hard to please her, even in these small ways?

When she opened the door and saw him standing there, tall and appealing, with his heart in his eyes, smiling his rueful smile, she was unable at first to say a word. But she answered her own silent question: Not this one, not anymore. And that's a promise.

"Oh, lady, lady." He took her slowly and gently in his arms the moment he had closed the door. Raising her face to his, she kissed him with tender welcoming.

He stepped back then, and his big hands slid down her soft sleeves to grasp her hands in his fingers. "Everything, stop," he ordered softly. "First I just want to look and look." And his foxy gaze savored all of her, from her free, shining hair to her smiling face, as he lightly swept back the waves of hair to look at the sapphires in her ears. Then his look descended to her drifting blue and gold clothes, all the way to the blue sandals on her feet.

"Pinch me." He grinned. "From head to toe you're unreal. This isn't true." He glanced around the autumn-colored, peaceful room.

"Oh, yes it is. Would a drink help convince you?"

"I doubt it. But I'd love one. I could use it." He sat down on the couch and she noticed the pleasing likeness of his bright hair to its color.

"You look so tired," she murmured, bringing him his drink.

"That doesn't begin to describe it." He sipped his highball, and added, "This is just what the doctor ordered for tonight. It's so sweet of you to do this for me."

She made a gesture of dismissal. "Are you hungry?"

"Ravenously."

"Then bring your drink downstairs. I'll put dinner on the table." He followed her down to the dining area, remarking, "So pretty," before he collapsed into one of the chairs.

She was very curious about his day, but resolved not to ask, certainly not now. He ate hungrily and with great appreciation, praising each dish and exclaiming over the wine. When they were sitting over coffee, the candles burning low, she asked, "Did today have anything to do with . . . the building project?"

"Absolutely everything." A shadow had fallen on his face and she almost regretted the question, although it had been burning in her mind. "Believe me, Melissa, there's more to this—" He stopped abruptly.

Chapter Eight

$\mathcal{M}$eeting her clear, curious gaze over the candlelit table, Bart was stymied. How in hell was he going to tell her all of it—that he suspected his own uncle was a thief; the whole rotten mess? If she was hesitant to accept him already, he could imagine how she'd feel if she knew she'd be entering a nest of snakes like that.

Now he saw a momentary uncertainty shade her beautiful eyes and he cursed himself for his own ineptitude. He'd have to try to fix it, some way.

"There's more to this than meets the eye," he temporized, desperately trying to find a way out of it, to decide just how much to tell her.

"In what way?" she asked quietly. He could see that she was getting uneasy. Damn it, she'd been so sweet, so lovely, so welcoming . . . forgiving him for his impatience and temper. If he blew it now—

"All kinds of technical problems, my darling, that

would bore the life out of you." He reached into his pocket and took the ring box out. "Maybe we could talk about this, instead."

Her glance went to the box, then back to his face. He knew it had been a weak, evasive answer and prayed that in his muddled fatigue he hadn't sounded condescending, belittling. She was the kind of woman who would never put up with that; he'd said it almost like an exasperated parent who wanted to still a fractious child with a toy.

But he'd miscalculated again—there was no predicting women! Because now she was smiling, receptive-looking. Eagerly he opened the box. The dying candles glittered on the beautiful ring—a water-pure Brazilian aquamarine surrounded by an oval pattern of fiery, twinkling diamonds that pulsed like minute stars.

"Will you wear this, for now?" he asked her. "Until you decide to wear the one that goes with it?"

To his joy and amazement, she nodded. "Yes, I will, Bart. I will."

It was the loveliest night, he thought, that they had ever spent together, even if, as he wryly recalled afterward, they hadn't even made love. They were both so tired they just fell asleep together in each other's arms.

He had to rush off in the morning, which he greatly regretted, and wondered if he imagined a slight withdrawal in her manner, a certain hesitancy, as he left. But no, it couldn't be. She was probably just preoccupied with her day, too, as he had been with his. At least she'd accepted the ring, and that would make everything all right.

Bart plunged into the day, reassured.

* * *

Things moved so fast at Time Was that morning that it was almost two before Melissa got her breath. She sold three clocks in the morning, one to a man who was able to carry it away himself, then two to women, for whose purchases delivery had to be arranged.

On top of that a grandfather clock was brought in by professional handlers for cleaning and repair. Getting started on the clock, Melissa discovered that it was going to be quite a job; it apparently hadn't had a cleaning for years. She finished one phase of it and decided to take a breather. She washed up, enjoying the sight of the lovely aquamarine on her left hand. It was the perfect size and shape, exquisite in every way; it typified Bart's perfect taste and she loved it more than anything she'd ever owned.

Even if, for an instant, he'd hurt her a bit last night by passing over her interest in his activities, everything that had come after had canceled that brief moment out. After all, he'd obviously worked himself into exhaustion on the plan that would ultimately save Time Was. She was determined to content herself with that.

In her dreaminess she was startled by the sudden appearance of Ansel Harper at the door. Surprised, she went to let him in.

"Hi, there," he said, with a rather forced casualness. "I haven't seen you in so long I just wanted to stop by and say hello."

She wondered why, all of a sudden. His gray glance dropped to the ring on her left hand.

"Does that mean what I think it does?" Now she was really surprised. This curtness was totally unlike the usual slow Ansel who got around to things in the most circuitous fashion.

"Yes. Yes, it does."

"Well . . . I guess the best man's won." It seemed even odder that he didn't ask who it was, but Melissa was struck with another thought, so distracting that she could hardly pay attention to what Ansel was saying. Ria. She hadn't even told her mother yet, and she must. How could she have been so remiss? So much had happened, she supposed, that her head had been in a whirl. But she would have to tell Ria. Tonight. She'd invite herself for dinner.

"Melissa?" said Ansel. She drifted back to him, aware that he'd been saying something else.

"I beg your pardon," she said.

"I said, There are no hard feelings now, are there?" He had a disproportionately guilty look, she decided. What did *he* have to be guilty about? She was the one who'd broken off with him.

"Of course not. How could there be, Ansel?"

"I mean about . . . everything." She realized now he'd had a bit to drink. And she recalled the scene in the restaurant, his party of property owners.

"No. I have no hard feelings, Ansel. You just did what you had to do. I realize you and I aren't in the same boat, when it comes to the real estate thing." And it was true; Ansel had no reason not to sell out. It was no more his fault than the other owners' that the campaign had fallen through. As for any conspiracy—she couldn't imagine the careless, easy-going Ansel being involved in anything like that. She thought, with compassion, He's not even smart enough. She and Maria had let their imaginations run away with them that night.

"No, Ansel, of course there are no hard feelings." She was still a bit puzzled that he hadn't asked who the "lucky man" was. Maybe he was still infatuated with her; maybe that was why he'd rather not know. Anyway, she was too preoccupied with the phone call to Ria to care much right now.

When he left he seemed to be in an awful rush. But she dismissed the idea. Right this minute she was going to call her mother.

"I have something to tell you. Can I come over tonight?"

"Of course, darling," Ria said easily. "Come for dinner, about seven."

That was that. It was certainly not something she was going to blurt out on the phone.

She went back to the grandfather clock project, keeping an ear out for the bell at the door. When it did ring, a glance at her moon watch revealed that it was after four.

A stately gray-haired man in a homburg was at the entrance.

She went out to make a "be right with you" gesture, hurried back to wash her hands and came out again still in her coverall.

She admitted the man with a smile, excusing her work-stained appearance.

"Why, that's all right, Ms. Grey." He was extremely dignified, almost stiff, dressed in very conservative clothes. His features were regular and august, but there was something a bit artificial in his smile, she noticed vaguely.

He held out his well-tended hand. She shook it a little uncertainly. "I've come to do you a favor, Ms. Grey. But let me introduce myself. My name is Edward Freeman."

Her face must have expressed her emotion, because he said with that rather unpleasant smile, "I see it is a name that's not unknown to you. To put it bluntly,

I've come to make you an offer—a kind of double offer, as it were."

"But what are you talking about, exactly?" She felt caution assert itself. Who was this man—not Bart's father? No, he'd said his father was dead.

"I'm Bart Freeman's uncle. I'd like to discuss your property."

Melissa couldn't speak for a long moment. What on earth did this mean? Bart had assured her that the other plan was not going to go through. Yet here was his own uncle, asking to talk to her about her property. This didn't make any sense at all.

"I think there must be some mistake," she managed at last, weakly. "My property is not for sale."

"Come now, Ms. Grey." Edward Freeman made a deprecating gesture. "You haven't heard the offer." And he named a figure, a figure so outrageous that she couldn't believe it.

But she asserted, "In the first place, Mr. Freeman, I have asked for landmark status for this building. Its personal value to me, and to my family, is beyond price . . . even one like that. Apart from that, I am at a loss to understand why you're offering me at least four times its market value."

"Well, let's say I'm offering a little more than the price of your house."

"Now I *don't* understand, in the least." She was almost dizzy with confusion and dismay. What in the world was going on?

"Then I'll be blunt, if I may." Freeman smiled that awful smile again.

"Please do."

"This 'engagement' of yours and my nephew's . . ." The way he said the word made her blood boil. "It just won't do, you know, Ms. Grey."

Won't do, she said to herself, enraged to silence. Then she spoke. "How do you know about it, Mr. Freeman?"

"Well, really, Ms. Grey. The boy told me and his mother just this afternoon. How else could I know? I am here to tell you frankly that his family does not approve of you, for obvious reasons. What's more, you'll be doing yourself a kindness if you break it off."

"Why?" she demanded.

He seemed taken aback at her self-possession, her cool query. But he went on, "Because Bart is using you, Ms. Grey. You're a personable young woman, so it is no hardship on him, certainly . . . but all the same he's using you to gain the power he needs to run our company into the ground. And his mother and I are not going to allow that to happen."

She was dumbfounded.

"The fact is," he continued, "after the death of his wife the boy ran quite wild. His father, in order to put some kind of . . . brake on his rashness and impulsiveness, specified in his will that only on remarriage would Bart gain control of the necessary number of stocks to give him full power. We thought the provision quixotic at the time, but after observing Bart for the last few years we now realize its wisdom." He studied her keenly; she could almost feel her doubts beginning to resurface, and she was aware that Freeman could somehow sense that. There was a triumphant little flare in his cold gray eyes.

"So you see, if you think about it, Ms. Grey, everybody will be better off if you send my nephew packing . . . his family, the company. And you. This building"—he looked about him with disdain—"has no chance at all of being declared a landmark. I can tell you that. My sister is very versed in these matters and she agrees with me completely."

Trying to hide her dismay, Melissa turned from Edward Freeman and pretended to adjust one of the clocks on a shelf. "I see," she answered in a deceptively level voice.

"You agree with me, then, I hope?"

"I don't agree at all, Mr. Freeman. Not yet. Certainly not with your evaluation of this building." She willed her voice not to shake.

"But I feel I've given you some food for thought. Am I not right?"

"Oh, yes, Mr. Freeman. That you have done." This time to her annoyance her voice was trembling.

"Then think about it, Ms. Grey. That's all I ask."

"Perhaps I will, Mr. Freeman." Melissa was afraid she'd scream if he didn't leave at once. She was thankful when he said, "I'll be leaving, then. But I'll be in touch. Or rather, I'll wait for you to get in touch with me . . . if and when you decide to do the sensible thing." He touched the tip of his homburg and strolled out.

Melissa stared after his departing figure in utter confusion; for long minutes she hardly knew how she felt, whether it was pain, insult or bewilderment—probably all three. Then in the midst of it all her sense of humor came bubbling to the surface: it had been like a scene right out of an old 1930's movie, with Roland Young or somebody white-haired and dignified offering the mercenary chorus girl a small fortune to leave the scion alone. It was unbelievable.

She shook her head and went back to the job on the grandfather clock. If she didn't keep busy, she knew, she'd either cry or scream or giggle in hysteria.

But when her whirligig thoughts started to still, the situation didn't look so amusing. There was too much Bart hadn't told her, from the very beginning. And now she didn't know whom to believe. Her picture of

Bart was so utterly different from that presented by
Edward Freeman, it was amazing. The man she knew
loved her, and was on her side. The man Edward
Freeman had talked about was an irresponsible liar.

What if he were using her to gain control? Yet she
couldn't accept that. She just couldn't. But why
hadn't he told her about it?

And to think that the Freeman family found her
"not quite right" was a bare-faced insult; it was
driving her into a fury. It would be a cold day in hell
before any Grey begged to be admitted into any
blasted family.

Melissa was almost tempted to cancel her dinner
date with her mother. What she had to tell her now
was a far cry from the earlier news. But she decided
that was just silly; she'd really like to talk this over
with her. And as for "upsetting" her—that was nonsense, too. Her mother was about as fragile as shining, resilient Damascus steel. And then, Melissa
couldn't wait.

Bart Freeman looked at his desk calendar again and
thought, Looking at it's not going to change the date.
The damned board still meets tomorrow. And he was
nowhere near the end of his investigation. The whole
thing had played hell with his schedule—one man
being on vacation, another in the hospital and the
hired investigator, so far, coming up with zilch.

His personal schedule was shot to hell, too, he
judged with gloom. This was no hour to ask Melissa to
go to dinner, but he must call.

The other call had to come first, though—it was his
last hope. He dialed his mother's house on Stuyvesant
Oval.

When she answered, he asked abruptly, "How's it
going?"

"I've reached three of them . . . there's just one more. The three agreed," Claudia told him elatedly.

"Great. Who's the fourth?"

"Cutler."

"Oh, boy." The toughest one because he was always straddling fences. You never knew where you stood with Cutler.

"Hang in," Claudia said brightly. "I'll give it my best try. I was just going to call him again when you phoned."

"Okay. Then I'll let you get to it."

Bart rubbed his eyes. He hung up and dialed Melissa. "Honey, how are you?" She sounded strange. But maybe it was just his anxiety, in general, working on him.

"I wanted to take you to dinner," he said, "but I'm swamped here. I'm still at the office."

She explained, still in that odd tone, that she was having dinner with her mother.

"Well, that's good . . . considering. How late do you think you'll be? Maybe we can get together later."

There was a long hesitation.

"Melissa?"

She was still silent.

"Melissa," he said more urgently. "Is something wrong, darling?"

Instead of answering directly, she said, "I really don't know how late I'll be. Maybe we'd better make it . . . tomorrow, Bart."

Now he was speechless, stumped. It was a pretty cold answer for a woman you'd just gotten engaged to. He didn't like it . . . at all.

"Something's the matter," he insisted. "Tell me what it is."

"I'll talk to you tomorrow," she repeated.

"No. I'll call you later," he persisted.

"All right. Until later, then."

After they'd hung up, he swore. He really didn't know what to make of women . . . particularly that one. It was like trying to take a butterfly's blood pressure, getting through to her. Damn it, he loved her so much it made him nuts.

He waited with hope for Claudia's call, but the phone was silent for a half hour as he plowed on through the sheets of figures, cost estimates and commissions beginning to dance in front of his eyes.

At last the phone jangled.

"I've got him," Claudia said triumphantly. "Cutler. I practically had to promise him one of my clocks," she joked, "but he's agreed. With us and Hannah that's enough to get a postponement, but the others insisted on one more week."

"That's great," Bart exulted. "If I couldn't get it together in another week, it would be no good anyway. *You're* great, lady."

"Nothing to it," she responded lightly, but he could hear her pleasure in his praise. "Shall I call Edward . . . and Brill and Paradine?"

"I wish you would. In fact, you'd better." Bart laughed grimly. "The way I'm feeling now I wouldn't be as polite as you are."

"I know what you mean. I'm not feeling ultracivil myself. It *still* boggles the mind." Bart was relieved she hadn't asked him if anything else was bothering him besides the investigation. He certainly didn't want to go into that right now. "Well, I'll hang up now and call them. They'll be fit to be tied." She chuckled.

Bart wished fervently he could get as much enjoyment out of this as Claudia had. She'd said it made her feel like Mata Hari.

His smile faded. He took out his calculator and

went to work, double- and triple-checking himself on the last estimates.

They were getting there now.

But his victory would be pretty hollow . . . if something were wrong between him and Melissa.

"I really can't believe it," Ria said for the third time as she poured out their coffee in the Laine living room.

She'd made the remark twice before, once when Melissa first told her and Mark the whole story, and again during dinner.

"It's a hell of a tangle," Mark agreed, settling himself into his wingback chair and tamping tobacco into his pipe. "And that thing with Ansel—who did you say was with him at the Old Arbor?"

Melissa told him again.

He looked thoughtful. "Do you think Maria could have been right—that Ansel was being paid off by Freeman's?"

"It sounds logical," Ria offered, taking Mark his coffee. She came back and sat down beside Melissa on the sofa.

"Maybe somebody got to a lot of owners," Ria added.

"But the big owners . . ." Melissa began.

". . . can't be bought," Mark finished for her. "Sure. But why should they help us with this thing, when the smaller owners are so damned wishy-washy and uncertain they're not following through? I wouldn't either. After all, the big guys' property isn't being actually threatened."

A subdued silence fell over them.

"Never mind that. Right now it's Melissa I'm concerned about," Ria said. "Even if Bart's not involved in the hanky-panky—and I don't see how he couldn't be, as president of the company—how could his family have the nerve to pull something like that? Who could object to Melissa?"

"Nobody outside a funny farm." Mark gave Melissa an affectionate look. "It doesn't make me too happy about this guy as a son-in-law, I'll tell you. I wonder, though . . ." He paused thoughtfully. "No, that's too farfetched."

"Don't *do* that, Mark Laine. You always do that—drop a hint and get me curious and shut up like a clam." Ria was irritated.

"I was wondering if all this were part of some kind of ploy," Mark offered.

Melissa smiled. "You've been reading too many industrial spy novels, Mark."

"Too right. I think you should give that ring back, Melissa, and forget this Bart Freeman, once and for all. If that's the kind of family he's from . . ." Ria was fuming.

"That's exactly what I'm going to do," Melissa said calmly.

Mark studied her. "Don't you think you're being a little hasty?"

"No. I've had it with the Freeman Company and the Freemans—with all the uncertainty and maneuvering, and worrying and wondering. I've just had it."

"That's tiredness talking right now, honey," Mark commented.

"You've got that right. But I've made up my mind."

"Good," Ria said enthusiastically.

"I'll walk you home." Mark stood up. "Whatever you do, you know, I'm with you . . . every step of the way."

A little later when she'd said good night to Mark and unlocked the door, Melissa heard the phone ringing; it had the insistent sound of a phone that had been ringing repeatedly for a long, long time. It was Bart, asking her in a rush if he could come over. She told him yes. Better to get it over with, she thought, as soon as possible.

But as soon as he stepped through the door her resentment softened; he looked tired and grim, with deep lines between his brows and around his mouth. Nevertheless, he took her in his arms with vitality and strength.

"Oh, honey, it's so good to see you," he said. "I couldn't really *reach* you when we were on the phone . . . where were you? Why wouldn't you talk to me? What's the matter?"

"Sit down, Bart," she evaded. "Let me fix you a drink."

"No. No, thanks," he amended. "I want an answer."

"Your uncle came to see me today." She could not keep the edge of anger from her voice, although she was trying to be calm.

"My uncle? What did *he* want?" Bart was still standing, staring at her.

Melissa sat down. "He wanted to buy Time Was. . . and me."

"What do you mean?" he demanded. A spark of distant anger lit his worried brown eyes. He threw himself down on the couch beside her and grabbed her arm.

"You're hurting me," she said in a low voice.

He looked offended, but he loosened his grip, repeating, "What do you mean, Melissa? What did he say to you?"

She told him coolly, word for word, what Edward Freeman had said to her that afternoon.

"Why, that . . . that . . ." Bart spluttered. He took a deep, jagged breath. "I can explain the whole thing to you, if you'll listen."

"I don't see how you can, Bart. All I understand is that you promised me my house would not be threatened . . . then your uncle made me an offer. You told me he is chairman of the board at Freeman's. And all I know is that he offered me money not to marry you." She heard her voice shaking. She had begun to relive the anger and humiliation of the afternoon all over again.

He started to speak but she said, "No. Let me finish. The worst thing of all was your never even mentioning that provision in the will. I can't help thinking that was a very good reason for you to press me to marry you."

"I can't believe I'm hearing this. I can't believe this is *you.*" He sounded stricken. "The reason I didn't tell you about the will was very simple . . . I'd just plain forgotten about it."

"Forgotten! How could you? How could you possibly forget something that important?" It just *wasn't* possible, she reflected.

"It wasn't that important. Not to me. I'm not about to have my actions dictated by someone else's ideas."

Melissa studied him; he seemed so open, so plausible. But Gavin had been plausible, too. Her heart sank at the thought. And if that was the way his family reacted to the news of his engagement, what kind of life could they have together?

"It just won't work, Bart," she said miserably.

"Don't say that to me, Melissa. Don't say that *this* can't work." He put his arms around her abruptly and pulled her toward him, then with one of his big hands he forced her face up to his for a hard and brutal kiss.

This time there was no tenderness in it, no delight;

he was trying to force his will on her with the pressure of that demanding mouth. She writhed and struggled, resisting.

Finally he let her go, his eyes bright with pain and anger.

"It's really very simple," he said wearily. "You don't love me, Melissa. You never have. If you did, none of this would make any difference. You'd listen to what I have to say. But you won't listen. You're still too enslaved by your past to have any trust left at all. It's all so simple."

"Nothing is that simple," she protested, turning her head away.

"Anything important is." She turned back to look at him. He met her eyes levelly, and continued. "The fact is, you're afraid of commitment. One guy did you in, and that's turned you off to all other possibilities. I thought there was more to you than that. I still think there is. I see qualities in you you don't even know yourself. But now you're acting like you're afraid of your shadow."

The truth in that stung her, but she was aroused to a new, defensive anger. First his own uncle humiliated her, and now he himself was daring to criticize her in this horrible way.

"You've said enough." She wrenched the beautiful ring from her finger and put it into his hand. "I can't keep this any longer."

"Don't do this, Melissa," he pleaded. "Let me talk to you, dammit." He held out his hand, still offering the ring to her with the gesture.

"We have talked, Bart, and it did no more good than it ever does. You really think you can erase everything, solve every problem, by kissing me and treating me like a retarded child. Well, you can't."

He stared at her sadly. Then she could see that his

sorrow was leaving him, frustrated ire replacing it. "I see that you won't listen to reason at all, that it's no damned use. All right, Melissa, if that's the way you want it."

He got up, holding the ring loosely in his hand, and stalked to the front door without another word.

The phone by Bart's bed shrilled just as he was drifting off into uneasy sleep. He fumbled for the lamp switch in the dark; when it flooded the table, the first thing he saw was the beautiful ring, its circle of diamonds winking at him mockingly in the lamplight. The clock read 3:00 A.M.

"Melissa?" he mumbled. He was really ready to eat crow.

There was a brief silence at the other end. Then a rough male voice answered. "Afraid not. It's Brower."

Bart was instantly alert. "What have you got?" It must be something, he judged, for the man to call at this hour.

"Plenty. And quite a tab." There was a growling chuckle. "The subject hangs out in some very costly gin mills. And he was really putting it away tonight. I got the sweetest little tape, enough to hang him. Too bad it's not admissible."

"What I expected?"

"Just what you expected. Mr. Freeman, you're a corker. It's almost like you staged it." Brower laughed. All this verbiage was unusual for him; till now he had always been so tight-lipped and business-like. He sounded as though he'd had a few himself before switching to his on-the-job tonic water.

"What time shall I drop off the tape?" Brower asked in a more businesslike manner.

"As long as you're still navigating, how about now? Where are you, by the way?"

"Not far from you, Mr. Freeman. He ended up downtown. I can be there in, say, fifteen, twenty minutes?"

"Fine." Bart replaced the receiver and sat on the side of the bed, lighting a cigarette. He couldn't wait to get the tape on his deck. As Brower had mentioned, it was a shame it wasn't admissible. But it would be admissible in the only place it needed to be. As far as that went, Bart still hadn't figured out yet exactly which way to go. There was the company to consider . . . and Claudia. And up until tonight, he thought bitterly, there had also been Melissa.

What would she have felt like, marrying into a family with a thief so prominent in the family tree? The thought of her cut him like a knife. Somewhere along the line, in the middle of all this mess, he was going to have to convince her, too. If he lost her—but he couldn't even consider that. Especially not now.

One thing at a time. Right now he had to get some clothes on, make some coffee. It was going to be a very long night.

He got up, threw clothes on and made a pot of coffee.

Brower was as good as his word. In exactly twenty minutes he was there with the tape, declining coffee or a drink, saying he was up to his eyebrows in alcohol already and wanted only his bed.

When he'd gone, Bart inserted the tape into his machine. It was amazing that anyone could be so indiscreet. Evidently "the subject," as Brower unfailingly called him, had been spilling it all to a woman, because Bart could hear feminine responses faintly in the background. All kinds of plans when "the deal" went through, mumbled details of the deal itself. With this and the other stuff he had, Bart was just about ready to proceed.

Just a few more items, he reflected, to wrap it up.

He snapped off the machine. He should have felt victorious, but his head was swimming with exhaustion and the prospect of all that was still left to do. And he was haunted by the memory of that frustrating, disastrous interview with Melissa; the outrageous move of Edward Freeman.

Well, that was his own damned fault. He'd predicted almost to the word what his uncle might do, and he hadn't let Melissa in on it. If he had, then she would have understood.

He'd do things differently this time around. First, he'd let the old buzzard have it—would he ever let him have it.

Or maybe he wouldn't. No, that would tip his hand altogether. Better to wait and hand it all to him in one sweet, ticking package like a bomb.

And Melissa? Bart glanced at the ring on his bedtable. He almost ached remembering how right it had looked on her long-fingered, delicate hand.

He wasn't finished, he decided, not by a long way. He'd get to her again, some way, if he had to start from scratch, like the beginning. It was a song he'd sung before, but the melody was still valid.

He'd made a dent once with roses and wine, had reached her by following her to a meeting, a poetry reading. There would be other times, other places. He recalled her friend upstairs, who was a painter. If poets had helped him once, maybe another artist could help him out again.

Bart's father had told him about the old-time boxing great, John L. Sullivan, who said he'd gotten to be champion by getting knocked down and getting up, getting knocked down again and still getting up, *ad infinitum*.

Well, the great John L. had nothing on Bart Freeman. Some of the ache had eased; he was almost smiling when he plummeted without warning into a heavy sleep.

"It doesn't compute," Peg Linden murmured.

The sudden remark, out of nowhere, puzzled Melissa. She was sitting next to Peg on a padded bench under one of Maria Deres's most striking paintings. The exhibition crowd was at its height; over the exclamations, shrieks, squeals and laughter, it was hard to hear. "What doesn't?"

"That nineteenth-century soap opera, starring Bart Freeman's family." Melissa gave her friend a side glance. Peg was flushing. "Oh, dear, I promised myself I wouldn't mention that today."

"Keep your promise, would you?" Melissa pleaded. "I'd like to lay last week's ghosts to rest and enjoy myself."

"Gotcha." They made no more attempts to talk for a while; the noise was almost deafening in the small art gallery on Hudson Street, with its wide facade of glass. Melissa stared at the painting on the opposite wall—a vivid and stormy sea painted in *bravura* shades of blue-green. Two minuscule dark figures stood on the shore near a small orange boat.

Melissa was inevitably, painfully reminded of Bart. The orange boat recalled the fiery color of his hair; the tempestuous, overpowering waves were like a symbol of his personality, and had the tempo of the wild emotions he had always aroused in her body. Every now and then, without meaning to, she found herself remembering that last awful scene with him. The pain and emptiness of the last few days had been acute, almost overwhelming. And yet somehow she could not quite believe that things could be right again between them; with such a horrible abruptness her slowly building trust had begun to totter.

"Are you revived a bit?" Peg asked her.

"I think so." This bright and beautiful Sunday afternoon, both she and Peg had made it a point to dress up to honor the occasion; Peg was in her usual vivid red and Melissa was wearing a blue-green dress that echoed the seascape tones. Unfortunately they'd both made the mistake of wearing high heels, and the standing around had gotten to them; they had collapsed on the vacated bench. "Are you about ready?" Melissa asked Peg. She herself had been on hand when the doors had opened.

Peg nodded and they began to make their way among the well-wishers, prospective buyers and others gathered around Maria. The painter was resplendent in a velvet jacket and a flowing tie; her face lit up when Melissa stooped to kiss her and congratulate her again.

Melissa straightened and stood by, waiting for Peg to say her farewells. When she glanced through the glass wall Melissa stiffened. Bart was coming through the door.

The sun made a bright aureole of his vital hair, and he looked more appealing than ever, casually immaculate in a suede jacket that almost matched his hair, a soft brown turtleneck sweater and matching trousers. The jacket made his shoulders seem almost as wide as the door, gave his weathered features an even more rugged look.

"Hello, again," he said to Melissa in a friendly, easy tone. She was aware that women were staring at him, that Peg and Maria, too, were suddenly all eyes.

Trapped, but determined to carry it off, Melissa just as calmly said hello.

"You remember Peg Linden," she said coolly. He nodded politely and Peg acknowledged him with a wide smile.

"And this is Maria Deres," Melissa said, introducing him, "by whom we're surrounded." She indicated the paintings.

"What a wonderful way to be surrounded." Bart grinned at Maria, glancing at the paintings. "I've admired your work often at Melissa's house."

Melissa was deeply annoyed at him for showing up here. But of course—that was exactly why he had. He banked on her good manners. She couldn't run away from him here.

But she murmured to Peg, "We'd better be going."

"You can't leave *now!*" Maria insisted, regarding Bart and Melissa with a mischievous glitter in her eyes. "You've got to give your friend the tour, or at least let me. I don't run into a fan like this every day."

The old woman beamed up at Bart. "I don't run into a *man* like this every day, either, even if you're fifty years too late."

He bent down and kissed her cheek. "Too bad. We would have been the toast of the Depression." His eyes lit on the ocean painting. "Oh, that's a beauty."

Melissa really felt trapped now. She couldn't possibly rush off rudely when this avowed "friend" of hers was so enthusiastic about Maria's work. This could lead to a sale for Maria, to look at the thing from a practical angle. Peg's here-to-stay manner implicitly agreed.

While Bart and Maria wandered from painting to painting, chattering as if they'd known each other forever, Melissa looked on. Then she saw Bart con-

sulting with the gallery manager, handing him cash
and a card. They came back to Melissa and Peg, and
Maria was fairly glowing.

"This young rascal won't listen to reason. He
doesn't understand discounts for friends," she scolded
amiably.

"Don't understand them at all," Bart said lightly.
"I can't wait to see that one on our—" He gave
Melissa a look and amended, "On my wall."

"I think it's the best," Peg agreed. Then she
glanced at her watch. "Uh-oh! Carl's going to think
I've been abducted. I've got to get back to Brooklyn."

"If you have trouble with a cab," Maria advised,
"just whistle for us . . . or the law."

"That won't do at all," Bart declared. "My car's
right outside. Why don't I drop you . . . and Melissa?"

Trapped again, she decided. How could she possibly object to that, and inconvenience Peg?

They said good-bye to Maria and hurried to the
sidestreet where Bart's Jag was parked.

Opening the passenger door, Bart suggested casually, "You get in first, Melissa. Peg'll be getting out
before you do. You won't mind if we drop her first,
will you . . . since she's in a hurry?"

Melissa murmured that of course she wouldn't.
How could she? She had to admire his smooth maneu-
vers, as uncomfortable as she was feeling.

When they were crowded into the narrow front seat
together, with Melissa's hip snug against his hard
thigh, she could not help the shiver of excitement that
ran over her body. At the same time she realized how
doubly convenient this arrangement was for Bart. He
knew too well what his nearness could do to her.

As they sped downtown Bart and Peg chatted

companionably across Melissa, who was hard put to join in. The feel of his body so close to hers was a not unwelcome distraction; already that closeness was exercising the old magnetism.

When they reached the entrance to the Brooklyn Bridge, Melissa looked in the direction of the barge restaurant below the bridge, where he had taken her that night. She met his eyes for a fleeting instant; they were warm and pleading.

Melissa said little for the rest of the drive. They dropped off Peg in Brooklyn Heights and Melissa declined her invitation to come in.

As soon as Peg disappeared she wished she hadn't, because Bart said, "Your friend gave me a very good idea."

"About what?"

"Abduction." He gave her a sidelong glance. "Would you come for a drive before I take you home?"

"No, Bart. I'm sorry. I really didn't want to stay at the gallery . . . and I didn't even want to come over here. But you very conveniently managed both."

"Please, Melissa." He put out his hand and covered hers with it. "All I want is a chance to talk to you."

"We've talked. It's always ended up the same way," she said. "What you consider conversation is always another . . . form of endeavor," she added dryly.

He withdrew his hand and sighed. "You know, there was never a kidnapper who consulted the victim's wishes. Why should I be different? I've been acting out of character."

He started the engine and they shot off.

"What are you doing? This isn't the way to Manhattan."

"Right you are. I am going to kidnap you, after all,

Melissa. And the only ransom I'm asking is that you listen."

"But where are you taking me?" she protested.

"You'll see."

She was really exasperated now, but there was no way out of it, for the moment.

The Jaguar was heading for Staten Island.

Chapter Nine

After they had been driving for a time in silence, she snapped, "This is ridiculous. It's . . . outrageous. First you trap me in a social situation, then you try to buy yourself back into my good graces by buying Maria's painting. . . ."

"Such conceit, Melissa," he teased her. "Surely the painting is worth it, in itself?"

"Of *course* it is, damn it." She fumed, because the accusation had been conceited. And illogical. "But now," she persisted, "you're forcing me to go with you. How could you do such a thing?"

"Desperate times call for desperate measures, lady. I'm taking you to a place where nobody can even hear you scream—with vexation, that is, since I'm not exactly Jack the Ripper."

His comment ridiculed her reaction and she quelled her anger. She supposed she was making a lot of out of nothing, if it came down to it. All the same she wished fervently she were anywhere else right now; she had never failed to succumb to his charm, once she was within that dangerous perimeter of his appeal.

"It certainly looks it," she remarked. They were deep into Staten Island now, and the random houses were becoming few and far between.

"We're nearly there." The sun was sinking and its last fiery rays reflected in the Gothic windows of a brown, wood-shingled house set far back from the road. "That's it. Welcome to Freeman House."

He turned and guided them slowly up a winding drive. Melissa was charmed in spite of herself. The house had deeply overhanging eaves, gables and dormers, oriel and bay windows.

Bart pulled up and got out, opening her door. "Come into my parlor, Ms. Grey." She saw no lights behind the diamond-paned windows.

"There doesn't seem to be anyone at home," she remarked.

He opened a keycase and selected a key, unlocking the front door. "Ah, but there is now. Come in."

As he switched on lights by the door, she stepped into the quaint and charming house. "Why, it's lovely," she exclaimed involuntarily. "It looks so old."

"About 1855, to be exact," he said casually. "This is where I lived when I was a kid."

"Who lives here now?"

"No one, at present. A caretaker. I gave him warning, though; he won't shoot us." Bart grinned. "We keep it because we can't quite let it go."

"I can see why," she admitted, forgetting for the moment the awkwardness of their situation; her interest in the house took all her attention.

"But the nearest neighbors," he leered, "are very far away." He went to a cabinet and rummaged in its interior. "A small libation? Sherry?"

"Sherry, thank you." She wandered around the room, looking at things. He brought her the sherry in a delicate glass. She murmured thanks.

"Sit down, Melissa." She obeyed, taking a sip of her wine and setting the glass on the table. She wondered what was coming next; she thought she knew.

"Now," he said briskly, sitting down beside her with his own drink. "See? No hands." With a comical face, he put both hands around his glass and held it up for her to witness. "No hands on you, no hanky-panky. Just talk."

"That's a switch," she commented dryly. But she picked up her own glass again in a defensive way and sipped.

"But you're still nervous, Melissa. Why are you so nervous?" he demanded. "Are you afraid of what will happen if I kiss you?"

She grasped the delicate goblet with both of her hands. "Don't be silly." But to her dismay the answer sounded shaky.

"You're not so sure, are you?" His voice was triumphant.

She saw, looking up at him, that his brown eyes were bright and eager and victorious.

"You're not . . . are you, Melissa?"

"Of course I am." But she wasn't. She wasn't at all. It was history repeating itself, over and over. Again, his physical presence was enough to confuse her, deprive her of her very will and reason.

"I don't believe you." He set down his glass and with gentle caution, loosened her fingers from around the stem of the goblet and placed it next to his untouched tumbler on the table.

Then with the lightest, tenderest motion, he lifted her hands from her lap and drew them both to his mouth, kissing each finger with excruciating slowness, a lingering winglike caress that thrilled and touched her almost beyond endurance. She could feel the ice in her heart beginning to melt with the heat of his lips, and her resistance beginning to slip away in that traitorous fashion it had so often before.

Nevertheless she tried to control her runaway feelings. She said, as if the caresses had hardly affected her at all, "You told me all the ransom you'd ask would be an ear."

"I'm sorry I neglected them," he murmured, smiling, and sweeping back the hair on both sides of her head, he caressed one of her ears and then the other.

She drew back. "There's just no way to win with you, is there?" she asked as steadily as she could; that caress had been even more arousing than the first.

"No. Why keep trying, Melissa? I told you I'm never going to give up on you." He was holding her face between his hands now with a bruising grasp, staring down into her eyes, and there was naked pleading and desire in their bright brown depths.

"Please stop this, Bart. There's still too much between us that's unsolved; there are too many things you've kept from me, things you've left dangling."

He let go of her with an exasperated breath and reached into a cigarette box on the table. Taking out a cigarette he lit it with a table lighter shaped like the helmet of a knight in armor.

Bart made a face. "I'm very near the end of the mission—saving Time Was and a good many other, smaller items," he interjected ironically, "like Freeman Company. I've been hard at work slaying the dragons, Melissa. And all the time I get the feeling you look on me as Don Quixote, rather than a real knight in armor."

"There are no knights in shining armor, Bart. With

us there are just a lot of big problems. Your family isn't the least of them. I'm not going to marry someone whose family looks on me as a kind of . . . liability," she finished miserably.

"Damn it, Melissa, I told you that isn't the way it is."

"Then what way *is* it?" she demanded. "Even now—right this minute, it seems just exactly that way . . . oh, yes, you've brought me to your family house. When it's empty, like some kind of shady little secret. The 'knight' dallying with the scullery maid, if we're going to talk medieval."

She hadn't meant to put it quite like that, to let her hurt show, her temper fly out of control. But now it was done; the unpleasant words had been said. She was appalled at herself.

He stared at her in dismayed astonishment. "I don't *know* you when you talk like this. How in hell can you say these things to me?"

She was silent, struggling between an aching indignation and that stubborn longing for him that no absence ever quite dulled, that nothing seemed to cure. Finally she asked, "Why is it that we never talk but always end up fighting? That's not a very good sign."

He seemed to sense a kind of relenting in her, because he said firmly, "There's never enough of the real conversation, that's why. Conversation like this."

And he reached for her, pulling her to him, lowering his mouth to hers.

For one wild instant the long and hungry kiss seemed to provide all the answers, make a mockery of any confusion. Melissa's mouth softened under the pressure of his hard, seeking mouth and she felt herself flowing, melting again, leaning backward in his grasp as he made an excited sound deep in his throat, his hands roaming free again, stroking her hair, tracing the shape of her shoulders, finding her breasts that had begun to throb and to bud under his masterful, unremitting caress. Her hands felt shaky as they crept up around his neck, stroking its lean strength, drawing his head closer and closer as she returned the long and savage kiss.

He was holding her so tightly now that it was hard to breathe, and she no longer cared. Now there was only his mouth, now there was just the strength of his pressing close to her surrendering body and she made no move to resist when his hands descended from her pulsing breasts to her quaking thighs. In that brief, stunning, timeless moment she felt as if she were being swept down a stormy river, floating helplessly toward its falls; soon she would be tumbled over the precipice and plummeting, drown.

"Oh, Melissa, my darling, my love," he was whispering against her hair, "this is the only answer to anything, this is the thing that answers all the questions."

She could almost see the triumph in his eyes, although they were hidden now from her; the momentary surrender, the helpless softness of her body were arousing him to new elation.

"Come, darling," he said in a low, coaxing voice, "we have a choice of rooms—we'll pick the one you like the best."

She stiffened, recalling the cruel but apt remark she'd fired at him about a "scullery maid." Suddenly that's what it all had become—another victory of seduction for him, an all too easy one, at that.

Sensitively he felt her withdrawal. His arms tightened and he asked, "Did I say something wrong? Tell me, Melissa . . . *tell* me, for God's sake."

She made no reply, simply asking for her release with a reluctant motion of her body.

Bart dropped his arms from around her. She reached with shaky hands into the cigarette box on the table and lit a cigarette with the knight's helmet—an object that she hated now. Suddenly the whole episode seemed sad and depressing and she cursed herself for letting it go this far.

"I'm sorry, Bart. I shouldn't have let this even begin. Will you take me home?"

Savagely he lit another cigarette. "I'm sorry, too, Melissa. It seems to me we've gone through this before, several times. You won't even let yourself do what you obviously want to do, so badly. We keep going around and around, like squirrels in a cage. I've tried to show you how much I love you, how much you mean to me. I've asked you to marry me, and you've turned me down . . . or at least, said 'Wait.' Which means the same thing to me as turning me down. And I've told you that I'm right on the point of solving the building-project dispute."

"But you've never told me," she commented, stung by his reproaches, feeling colder and colder, "why the president of his own company can't do whatever he likes about anything."

"You know it's because of that provision in my father's will. . . ." he said curtly.

"There's a great deal more, and you know it."

"All right, then, there *is.*" Now he sounded really angry. "And I can't tell you—not yet."

She thought, It's always not yet. What he means is never.

"You simply have to trust me," he said doggedly.

"When you can't trust *me* . . . to understand whatever it is?"

He looked at her sorrowfully. "You wouldn't understand it, Melissa."

They sat in uneasy silence for a long moment, then she repeated, "Will you take me home now?"

"Sure. Sure, Melissa." He put out his cigarette and after a quick glance around, gestured for her to precede him to the door. He left a light on, and by its beams they made their way to his car.

He opened the door for her and she got in. Slowly he walked around the car and got into the driver's seat beside her.

She was tempted to touch him, to say that she was sorry, to ask him to start the whole evening over, from scratch. Why did their encounters always end in this tangle of contention, of misunderstanding? The silent question ached in her. But she resisted the temptation.

He was still treating her like a stupid, irresponsible child without the ability to understand . . . understand whatever the hidden thing was. Wondering about that her imagination ran wild. Maybe it was something totally unethical, illegal, that he, as a businessman, would consider just a part of the business game. And that conclusion dismayed her; he'd always seemed so honest and open. But she didn't *know*.

Worse than that, there was the business with Edward Freeman. If Bart were really standing up to his family, he would have straightened that out by now, presented her to his family as the woman he was going to make his wife.

Melissa was so deep in thought that she hadn't realized how far they'd driven. They were turning onto the Verrazano Bridge, across its twinkling loop-the-loops, heading for Manhattan.

And Bart had still not broken the frozen silence.

Melissa remembered the way the beautiful old house had looked at sunset, thought of how different it all could have been.

And she realized bitterly that she herself had twisted the encounter into new confusion, new contention. She wanted to say all this to him but now she was tongue-tied with defeat.

In hardly any time at all he was pulling up in front of Time Was, getting out to open her door.

"You needn't see me in," she said from stiff lips.

"I'll watch until you're inside." Now his voice was only polite and cool. He sounded like a perfect stranger.

Unlocking the door, Melissa thought with a sinking heart, Now it's really, finally over.

On Wednesday morning Bartholomew Alexander Temple Freeman parked his brown Jaguar across from the tiny Greek church on Cedar Street and strode through the entrance of the Freeman Building.

He hardly heard the greeting of the guard and did not wave to his friend at the cigar stand; he merely grunted to the women in the outer office.

"Morning," he said brusquely to Roberta.

Her practiced and hypersensitive antennae must have picked up his mood at once, he reflected, because she only answered "Good morning" quietly, brought in a mug of steaming black coffee and went out again without her usual friendly remarks.

Bart closed the door softly, not wanting to offend his loyal secretary with a sharp slam, and threw himself into his chair. Letting his coffee cool, he swiveled the chair around for a view of the harbor.

It's already November, he thought, his least favorite month, one that always gave him the willies with its somber grayness. Even the harbor waters looked gray and forbidding, the Statue of Liberty's verdigris a sickly poison-green.

With an oath, he swiveled around again and took a swig of coffee. Even that didn't taste right.

Today was the Big Day, he thought with grim humor, and now it hardly meant anything at all. Up to now he'd looked forward to it like winning the biggest lottery in the world. Well, he'd better get on with it.

Carefully he went over all the folders—cost estimates, mounds of sheets full of the vital figures. And the evidence, including Brower's damning little tape.

Bart leaned over and buzzed Roberta. "Is my uncle back in town yet?"

"Oh, yes. I checked with Mrs. Cabot. He should be in at any moment."

Bart thanked her. The yellow-bellied old hypocrite had dropped his bomb on Melissa and then conveniently gone out of town. Well, it didn't matter now. He was back and he was going to walk into a cage of tigers this morning, Bart decided.

He buzzed Roberta again. "Board meeting all set for eleven?" She told him it was. He asked her to get hold of Edward Freeman, Brill and Paradine for a meeting at ten in his office. "Right away."

Bart glanced at his desk clock. It was now nine forty-five. And he was bright-eyed, bushy-tailed. And ready.

On the stroke of ten the three men were announced. Bart got up and went to the door, opened it and invited them in.

The attorney Brill was quite expressionless, but Paradine had a nervous manner and Edward Freeman looked grouchy.

They were hardly seated when Edward demanded, "What's this all about? We have a board meeting at eleven, remember."

"Oh, I remember." Bart kept his inflection slow and easy. "How was your vacation, Uncle Ned?"

"It wasn't a vacation," Edward corrected. "I just needed to get away for a few days."

"I'm sure you did." Bart paused and let that sink in. Then he asked sociably, "Coffee, gentlemen? I guess it's a little early for anything else." He shot a glance at Paradine, who was known to be a heavy drinker; the man's mottled face darkened.

A cheap shot, Bart thought, at that poor sick bastard. But he'd never felt quite so nasty or vengeful in his life.

The men declined, Edward and Brill with special impatience. Bart could see that the trio was getting more and more antsy. Well, let them squirm, he decided. He was not going to help at all.

Finally, after an awkward little silence that kept lengthening, Edward snapped at Bart, "You wanted us for something."

"Yes. For this." The tape was on his deck on a side table. He switched it on. Paradine's mumbling, tipsy words were eerily amplified. Bart's glance jumped from one face to another.

At first Brill and Edward just seemed bewildered, and even Paradine couldn't quite connect. But soon Edward and Brill were looking at the banker as if they'd like to assault him, right then and there. And Paradine himself turned an unattractive muddy color that made his mottled skin grotesque.

"What . . . what the hell is this?" he mumbled.

"That's just what I'd like to know," Edward Freeman said coldly, trying not to look at Paradine. "What's the meaning of this?"

"Why, it's only a tape of Mr. Paradine," Bart said softly, "at one of his favorite watering holes."

"But this is absurd!" Edward said sharply. "What

does it *mean?* Why have you been spying on a member of the board?"

"I took my cue from you, Uncle Ned," said Bart. Edward's pale cheeks reddened.

"But this is meaningless," Edward spluttered. "All this gibberish. Is this some kind of idiotic prank?"

Brill spoke out for the first time. "It has to be. If Bart, in his muddled way, is trying to prove something, he can't do it with that tape." His calm angered Bart.

"No, you're right, Brill. Not with that tape alone. But with *this,* the tape is damned significant." He passed to each of the three men a single sheet of figures. "There's quite a lot more, which I have right here." He indicated the piles of folders on his desk.

Their faces were a study. They'd gotten it right away.

Edward and Paradine were speechless, but Brill asked with a quietness that amazed Bart, "What are you going to do?"

"It's what *you're* going to do that concerns us," Bart retorted.

"Will you press charges?" Edward's face was stiff with fear.

"You know damned well, Uncle Ned, that's the last thing I want to do. You've banked on that. The trouble is you banked on the old Bart's inattention. No, of course I'm not going to press charges— disgrace my father's memory, devastate my mother, and make a monkey out of us on the market, and everywhere else."

"Then what are you going to do?" Brill queried coldly.

"Give you these papers to sign. That's all." Bart handed them three more sheets.

Brill studied his and said, "I'll be damned if I will. It's a resignation from the board."

"Come now, Harvey," Bart said softly. "You're a lawyer. You know I've got you all in a corner."

"That's true enough," Edward snapped. He hesitated for a long moment, his rage giving way to utter resignation. He got out his pen and signed. "You'd better sign, Harvey. You, too, Ferris." The other two signed and Edward handed the sheets back to Bart.

"And there's one other little thing," he murmured. They looked at him with hostility and growing dismay.

"And that is?" Edward queried curtly.

"I think you'll find your resignations from the board, if you recall, don't take effect until tomorrow. They'll be presented to the board at its next meeting. Meanwhile, today, you're still voting members."

"So?" Paradine asked belligerently.

"So . . . I think you'll agree that it would be politic for all three of you to vote with other members of the board in favor of my alternate building plan. Don't you?"

They were all silent. Brill was speechless; all he could manage was a reluctant nod.

"Very well." Edward could hardly contain his fury; he bit the words off. Then slowly Paradine nodded his head.

"Well, I guess that wraps it up, gentlemen," Bart said ironically. "You'll have to notify your cohorts yourselves."

"Too bad you couldn't have gotten that little shop-girl to marry you, Bart," Edward remarked maliciously as the three men got up from their chairs.

"That brings up another matter I'd like to discuss with you, Uncle Ned, in private," Bart replied coldly.

Edward flushed. When the others had gone he sank down into a chair.

"Did you really think you could get away with that?" Bart demanded. "I'm telling you right now, if you ever go within a mile of her again I'll take this evidence to the D. A., bring charges and see you rot in jail, no matter how much trouble it causes all of us. Have you got that?"

"I really think you would." Edward shook his head. "That's what all this was really about, wasn't it? All this was for that *déclassée* little—"

"Watch your mouth." Bart could feel his temper slipping. He took a deep breath. "No, that was not what this was all about, and you know it.

"This was about rottenness and corruption, the kind of thing my father wouldn't have touched with a ten-foot pole. This was about milking the company for a four-block extravaganza that is far better spread over only three. It's about disrupting a hundred lives and livelihoods—about concrete-foundation specs calling for a three-two-one mix that meets building code specifications and then, when the building starts, delivers a four-one-half mixture. It's about the possible risk of people's lives. And I-beams that meet specifications on paper but are delivered thinner, more fragile.

"No," Bart went on relentlessly, "above all else, it's about dealing out death so you could get your bundle."

Edward Freeman was on his feet now, glaring down at Bart. "You're just like my sentimental fool of a brother—too simon-pure to make a decent profit. I'm glad this has happened. That surprises you, doesn't it? But I'm glad. To be quit of it all. It was getting so I couldn't stand the humiliation another hour—the rotten humiliation of taking orders from a green boy when I should have been given the company, if there were any justice in the world at all. Well, I wish you joy of it."

He wheeled and stalked out of the office, slamming the door after him.

Bart rubbed his eyes, feeling drained. It had been a nasty encounter; he had done sneaky things, just like his uncle, to win. For one disturbing second he wondered if he were more like his uncle than his father.

But that was stupid; that was twisted thinking proceeding from extreme tiredness. He'd won, at last. Soon he would go into the board meeting and see the passage of his plan.

His uncle had said, "I wish you joy of it."

There was little joy in Bart Freeman right now, despite his victory. It was lonely, not having someone really to share it with.

But the bottom line was, he'd won.

So had Melissa, even if she didn't know it yet. He'd have to take care of that as soon as the meeting was over.

"I know it's outrageous," the woman said apologetically to Melissa. "But that watch is such a treasure I can't bear to part with it for long."

"I understand perfectly." Melissa did: The Geneva enameled gold watch was the most valuable piece she'd ever been asked to repair. "When would you like it back?"

The woman looked relieved and asked, "Do you think you can get to it today?"

Melissa smiled. "I'll have it for you this evening, by five."

The delighted woman went out, smiling widely.

Melissa held the lovely timepiece in her hands for a

moment, savoring its special beauty. It was set with half pearls; engraving in little scoops under the transparent enamel gave an effect called *guilloche*, a particular liveliness in color and texture.

The background enamel on the case was a warm golden color; in the center was a vivid bouquet of red roses, daisies and forget-me-nots and, delightfully unexpected, a coiled nautilus shell. The last, a sea symbol, inevitably recalled Bart, and Melissa felt a little drag of pain in her throat. The roses, too—she remembered the great bunch of red ones he had brought her the night they dined on the barge. And even the forget-me-nots made her think of their relationship, because she hadn't been too good at forgetting him.

But she'd better get her mind on business, she decided. She'd checked the watch while the client was there, and it was more of a cleaning job than any intricate repair. The watch dated back to 1850; it felt warm, almost silken, in Melissa's slender hands.

She hurried to her workshop and left the door open. Turning on the powerful overhead light she sat down and opened the back of the enameled watch, resting it on soft flannel to avoid the slightest scratch, and delicately began to loosen the minuscule parts. She handled the fragile hairsprings with accustomed ease and caution.

Delighted that there were no interruptions, she applied herself with such concentration that she finished the whole thing without taking a break. Handling something so exquisite was more like play than work.

But her neck was aching and her eyes danced. Glancing at a clock in the corner she saw that it was four. Amazing.

She decided to surprise the anxious client by calling

her right now, telling her the watch was ready. Its dainty beat was regular and strong; it glimmered from its fresh polishing.

The woman was delighted when she called, and she was pleased with herself and with the woman's pleasure. It wasn't often that she got an assignment so consuming that it brought her such forgetfulness.

She sighed. She should have a job like that every day for a while.

When the bell chimed and she saw Ria, Melissa rushed to admit her.

"I hope I didn't come at a busy time."

"Oh, no. Your timing's perfect. I just got through with a job a little while ago. You must see this beautiful thing before my client comes. She'll be here any minute."

Enthusiastically Melissa took her mother's hand and led her into the workshop. The trinket of pearl-studded gold lay twinkling on its flannel bed.

"Ooooh . . ." Ria leaned over and examined it closely without touching it. Then, as they returned to the front of the shop, she studied Melissa.

"You look very up today," she commented. "So much so you might not even need what I've brought." She sounded encouraged; Melissa had been hard put to hide her recent unhappiness.

"Don't say that." Melissa grinned. "Whoever had too much good news? Is it about the landmarks hearing?"

"I'm afraid not. I just checked that out. It's still not going on the Estimate Board's calendar until late December. And as far as I know, the—" She stopped abruptly.

. . . the building project moves on, Melissa completed for her, silently. She knew Ria had felt awkward bringing up anything to do with the Freemans.

"So tell me, then. What is it?" Melissa tactfully passed over the other matter.

"These." Ria reached into her handbag and brought out three airline tickets. "I was going to save this until Christmas, but it seems to me you've been needing something like this. A surprise we'd been planning for January."

Melissa looked at the tickets. They were stamped New York to London. She glanced up at Ria, who was smiling from ear to ear.

"From there, we thought France, maybe . . . Switzerland, so you can do some skiing, and take a busman's holiday." She was referring to the Swiss watches and timepieces that Melissa would want to see.

Melissa knew her pleasure must be absolutely beaming from her.

"And whatever else we can manage," Ria added.

"Oh, Mother! The Strasbourg clocks . . . the clock in Rouen!"

"Don't forget Salisbury Cathedral. And we can see the original of the one your grandfather made."

"This is heavenly," Melissa bubbled, throwing her arms around her mother. "I wish we could go *tomorrow*."

"So do I. But that's the best Mark could do. His sabbatical comes up then, so he may be flying off to other places to take care of his business. But meanwhile you and I can do our own thing—I'll nose around manuscripts and you can stare at clocks until you're slaphappy."

"You're wonderful, both of you. I'm very glad you didn't wait until Christmas to tell me. Now I'll have that much longer to anticipate it."

"That's what I told Mark. Look here, we've been

. . . worried about you. This . . . unfortunate affair with the Freeman boy—it's not going to turn into a Gavin tailspin, is it?" Ria looked worried.

"Never," Melissa said firmly, trying her best to reassure her mother. "Never."

She was glad that when Ria left she did look reassured, much happier. Soon after that the woman came for her renewed Geneva watch.

Melissa was overcome with warm gratitude to Mark and Ria. The trip would be the very thing to cure the deepest "Januaries." And by the time they got back she might not even remember him so much anymore.

But she knew that that thought of forgetting him had been an idle dream when a messenger came at five with a large package bearing a familiar return address.

When Melissa opened the package she found a beautiful old music box. Raising the lid she heard the tinkling strains of Vivaldi's "Four Seasons," the music that had been playing when Bart had first walked into Time Was on the bright September morning that now seemed an age ago.

She saw a scribbled note in his distinctive handwriting. "Time Was and is and shall be. All's well now. No more need to worry." It was unsigned.

He had won, then. What he'd promised her had come true after all. Her first impulse was to race to the phone and call him. But now it was after business hours; she wasn't going to risk calling him at home. What if he weren't alone? Besides, her shame was too great, her chagrin too deep. She hadn't believed him; she'd said awful things.

She'd write him a thank-you note and let it lie.

With that decision she burst into tears. Now she would trade all the European jaunts on earth for just one sight of him. Right now she wouldn't even care if she never saw another clock—if only things could be the way they had been before.

"Well, this is a treat, boy, to have you here with Claudia." Ralph Shepherd raised his highball glass in salute, his black, twinkling look shifting to Claudia and to his own blond daughter, Sue.

The four were seated in one of the several intimate dining areas of the Pendragon, a restaurant in a medieval-style stone castle in a suburb of Minneapolis. The mythical abode of Arthur and Guinevere had been transplanted intact to the midwestern spot, complete with tower, moat and drawbridge.

"It's good to see you, too, Ralph. And Sue," Bart said, including her rather belatedly. Her frank blue eyes, athletic looks and ultrachic air seemed enameled and hard in this romantic atmosphere. The widower Ralph made no secret of his admiration for Claudia, and had once inferred how cozy it would be if his daughter Sue and Claudia's son Bart could "hit it off."

That had been sternly discouraged by Claudia, and Bart, in his careless way, had totally forgotten about it until they were on the plane. Now he half regretted his impulsive decision to go along when Claudia told him she was flying out for a few days to see old friends.

Claudia had taken his decision to come the same way she took most of his other impulsive moves— quite calmly. When he had driven her to the airport and taken out his own bag, with the announcement that he'd decided to tag along, she had hardly lifted a brow.

Claudia had been genuinely glad, saying, "It'll do you good to get away for a little while." She had been too considerate to remark on his down-in-the-mouth attitude lately. However, she had warned him lightly that she wasn't going to have him "camping at the Shepherds'" without notice, and he had suddenly remembered the awkward little matter of Sue. He had agreed fervently that he wouldn't think of it surprising them.

Now, as the Shepherds debated solemnly about whether to have prime rib, duckling or steak Diane, Bart took a sip of his cocktail and looked around. The medieval artifacts inevitably reminded him of the Gothic house in Staten Island, and Melissa's somber remark about knights in shining armor.

But then, what didn't remind him? He took another swallow of his martini.

"I still think it's hogwash for you to stay in a motel, Bart," Ralph Shepherd said with his amiable persistence. "We've got enough room for the Twins," he joked, referring to the local baseball team.

"Oh, I couldn't do that, Ralph, thanks. This was all on the spur of the moment."

Ralph chuckled and gave their orders. Then with a glance at his daughter, he rumbled, "Same old Bart. I don't think you're ever going to settle down and be as dull as the rest of us."

"Someday," Bart muttered, his collar feeling tight. He gave Claudia a pleading look, which she picked up on immediately.

"Sue, I've been dying to ask you. *Where* did you get that wonderful dress? It's a million years too young for me . . . but I was thinking the store might have something suitable for me."

Bart blessed her quickness and tact. Sue launched into an enthusiastic recital of local boutiques, and attention drifted from him. What's more, Claudia's remark about the dress's being too young for her brought forth a flood of gallant disclaimers from Shepherd.

It was incredible, Bart reflected, how that friendship had gone on and on—Shepherd and Claudia had known each other from childhood, when they had lived in the east, and Claudia had become close friends with Shepherd's late wife. But the two were so different. He supposed it was the clock collection.

The clock collection—something else that had slipped his mind. Of course. But the very thought of clocks made him ache for Melissa. He'd really goofed, making this trip, in more ways than one.

After dinner, Ralph of course invited them back to the Shepherd house for a "little visit and nightcap," and Bart could not politely refuse.

Almost immediately after they had arrived, Ralph Shepherd said, "You've got to see my new treasures, Claudia. They'll probably bore your son to death— the children can entertain each other," he concluded with the subtlety of a bulldozer. In fact, Shepherd somewhat resembled a bulldozer, which item, sold by the gross, made it possible for him to pursue his expensive hobby of collecting clocks.

Bart repressed a grin, and said, "They wouldn't bore me at all, Ralph. Let's all take the tour."

He thought he caught an annoyed look on Sue's frank face, but he wasn't going to get stuck with that chic hockey player. She was about as soft and seductive as a puck.

Surprised, Ralph led the way into his study where his collection was housed.

Claudia forgot everything else in her enthusiasm. "Good heavens, Ralph . . . a Willard. Two Willards! Why, this lighthouse clock has to date back to 1800 . . . and that banjo clock is perfectly marvelous."

"Isn't it? Made in 1841, when they could still get that painted glass."

Claudia nodded with the excitement of the fanatic. *"Yes—the eglomisé."*

"Right," said Shepherd.

Shepherd, Bart thought, wasn't the kind of man you'd expect to be so freaked out over clocks. Maybe because their very delicacy, so opposite to his massiveness, attracted him. For the same reason Claudia did.

"I swear, Claudia, you must be the only woman in America who would know that."

Not quite, Bart retorted silently. Damn it, he couldn't take much more of this. It was like being in Time Was without Melissa. The athletic Sue looked insufferably bored by it all.

Bart got away as soon as he decently could, muttering something about looking up a business acquaintance, which fooled no one. Freeman had no business whatsoever in Minneapolis.

In his lonely motel room he switched on the TV, staring at it with unseeing eyes. Then impatiently he switched it off again and tried to read some magazines he'd bought at the airport. That was no better.

He decided to call Melissa. It was two hours earlier in New York, just about the perfect time. He put through the call and got no answer. He'd try again later.

Meanwhile he was going to write that letter that he should have written long before.

He looked in the drawer of the desk, found paper and envelopes and sat down to write.

"My dear one, I don't know if it's too late now. But I want you to know the whole story of what happened."

He wrote for a long, long time, signed the letter,

sealed and addressed it. Then he called the desk and asked if they had any stamps.

"Just leave it at the desk, sir. We'll be glad to mail anything for you."

Bart hesitated; he'd feel better mailing it himself. But then he shrugged and thanked the man, saying he'd leave the letter there when he checked out in the morning. That's when he'd be leaving. He was too impatient now to wait for Claudia to end her visit.

He called her to let her know and tried Melissa twice again. Each time there was no answer.

Bart Freeman had the devil's own time getting to sleep. He was haunted by her formal little thank-you note for the music box. Maybe he was the world's biggest cluck, to go on wanting her like this, when it seemed he didn't mean that much to her, after all.

And to have thought that merely "getting away" would get him away from himself.

When he checked out hurriedly the next morning, Bart said to the man at the desk, "It looks lousy out there." The sky was massed with darkening clouds, and a strong wind bent the trees.

"It is. A blizzard's on the way this afternoon, they say. If you're flying this morning, you're getting out just in time."

"Great." Bart would hate to get stuck here in the storm. "About this . . ." He handed the letter to the deskman.

"I'll take care of it, Mr. Freeman."

"Thanks." With a polite nod at the man's wishes for a good trip, Bart pushed at the wind-driven door and hesitated. He had a very strong feeling he should mail that letter himself. But sighting a cab, he went on out and signaled for it. The letter was forgotten, for the moment.

When the next traveler came in, he was accompanied by a galelike wind gust which swept all the papers off the counter. There was a new man on duty; with an annoyed exclamation he retrieved all the papers and correspondence. Jamming them impatiently into a basket, he didn't notice in his eagerness to greet the incoming guest that the letter addressed to Melissa Grey had fallen into an opening between the desk and counter.

It was almost the middle of November when Melissa decided to take an inventory of her wardrobe for the January trip. She had plenty of everything, but there were still a couple of items that should be replaced—her zip-in raincoat, which would be essential in almost all the cities on their itinerary, was looking a little shabby. The mean temperatures in France and the Netherlands, which Ria still called "Holland," would be in the upper thirties, and of course London promised to be wet.

Melissa's ski things also need replacing. She took off an afternoon to go shopping. When she was trying on raincoats she found to her surprise that her usual size was quite loose. Replacing the coat, she moved to the rack with the next smallest size. It fit perfectly.

She was struck with the realization that she had been so indifferent to herself she hadn't even noticed her loss of weight. Checking the coat out in the full-length mirror, she took a good look at her face. She was hollow-eyed and her face was much thinner. In the fluorescent lights she looked quite pale.

Melissa had ignored these changes in herself so completely that this was really the first time she'd seen them. She'd gone into the "Gavin tailspin" that Ria had feared.

She still could not think of Bart Freeman without an ache in her. And yet now it all seemed a thing of the past, far too final to do anything about. Since the delivery of the music box, she hadn't heard from him at all—no phone calls, notes, or anything. It was all too obvious, then, that the indomitable Bart Freeman had finally given up on her.

Melissa unbuttoned the coat and folded it over her arm, about to seek a saleswoman when she heard a familiar voice.

"Oh, this is marvelous! Do you have a four in yellow?"

Melissa poked her head around the screen of the three-paneled mirror and saw the minuscule Peg Linden. She was wearing an orange coat and a pixielike cap on her short dark hair.

"Peg."

"Melissa!" Peg came to her and gave her a strong hug. "Where have you been? I called you a couple of times last week but you were always out."

"I've been planning some redecoration in Time Was, and I've been all over the place." Melissa's heart skipped a beat; she wondered if Bart had been missing her, too. But no, if he'd really wanted to get in touch with her, he would have.

"You've gotten very . . . svelte," Peg said tactfully, observing her. "Are you dieting or something?"

"No. Just working hard, I guess."

Peg was still checking her out. Then she said hastily, "Well, it won't hurt you to have a snack with me. How about it? Are you through, or do you have to get something else?"

"This is it." As much as Melissa loved Peg Linden, she wasn't too eager for the get-together. She hoped it wouldn't turn into a gentle quiz about Bart. But her petite friend seemed so pleased to see her that she didn't want to make any excuses. "I'd love it."

Peg beamed. "Wonderful. Just let me slip on that gorgeous yellow coat and I'll be right with you." Melissa watched while Peg tried on the sunny garment; she looked like a breath of spring.

After they'd bought their coats and were seated in a café near the boutique, Peg ordered a meal and dived into it ravenously. Melissa made passes at a salad.

"How's Carl?" she asked, hoping to get Peg off on that subject.

"Perfect, as always." Peg smiled. "But what's *new* with you?"

Melissa told her about the projected trip, and listened to Peg's enthusiastic response. Then she remembered she'd come to the café that Peg had chosen several times with Bart, and her mind drifted. She came to attention, hearing Peg say something about "winter people."

Peg snapped her fingers kiddingly in front of Melissa, saying, "Come in, Melissa. Come in."

"I'm sorry. I was thinking about something else."

"That's all right. I was saying it's nice that you and Mark and Ria are all winter people, so January's a good time for you to travel." Peg studied her. "I must say you're taking it all very calmly. I'd be putting X's on the calendar if we were going to take off on a trip like that."

We, Melissa repeated silently. And she recalled that other occasion, the lunch with Peg, when her friend had mentioned the "party for two." Melissa could feel tears threatening and sternly tried to control them.

"Melissa." Peg put out her hand and touched Melissa's fingers lightly. "What's the matter? What did I say?"

"Nothing. Oh, nothing, Peg. You didn't say anything wrong. I'm the one who's wrong right now. You're absolutely right. I should be X-ing off the calendar, and not moping like this."

Peg took a sip of her coffee, her soft dark eyes full of sympathy and affection.

"May I say something?" she asked softly.

"Of course. When could anybody stop you?" Melissa teased her gently, with a shaky smile.

"It's Bart, isn't it?"

Melissa nodded.

"Oh, I was so hoping, that Sunday, that everything was going to work out."

"Well, it didn't, Peg. I don't think it was meant to." She told her something of their last encounter.

"I still don't believe that, Melissa. I think it *was*. When did you last hear from him?"

Melissa told her.

"Well, I'm going to stick my neck out," Peg asserted. "What's to stop you from calling him?"

"I've started to, a few times. Then I didn't," Melissa confessed.

"Oh, blast it. Call him again. If I ever saw a man who looked like he was really in love, it's that one. Call him, Melissa. Please."

To calm her down, Melissa said placatingly, "I'll think about it, Peg."

But deep down she knew she wasn't going to. It was far too late. The thing was ineradicably over, she decided, with a hollow feeling in her heart.

Chapter Ten

*H*is business concluded, Bart Freeman had time on his hands when he emerged from the office building opposite Rockefeller Center. It was cold, even for early December, and he turned up the collar of his overcoat and aimlessly crossed the short street, joining the crowds gathering around the big square, looking down at the ice skaters.

Bart had always liked to watch them, in their brief, bright-colored skating costumes, swooping over the man-made ice; it was as pleasant and soothing as the motions of fish in an aquarium.

It isn't today, he thought sourly. But what had been, lately? Watching them, he was just cold. And unrelentingly lonely. He turned away from an affectionate couple and looked at the shining statue of Prometheus, pure gold in the chilly sun. It had never failed to lift his morale, that handsome symbol of dogged aspiration. Even it, in his dark mood, worked only to depress him. Aspiration toward what? he demanded in irritable silence.

He abruptly rejected the skaters and Prometheus and walked off toward Fifth Avenue, his irritation increased by the sight of the delicate wrought-iron angels holding their Christmas trumpets aloft, erected on the famous rectangle between two buildings. The angels reminded him of Melissa.

Christmas, he decided savagely, began too damned early and went on too long. Thanksgiving was hardly over, and here it was already; the holiday would mock him for weeks and weeks before the trees and decorations, always a horror to the lonely, were taken down. What's more, his head was starting to ache. Claudia always said she didn't want to hear about it—she'd been telling him for twenty years to wear a hat, which he stubbornly resisted. The hell with that.

On Fifth people were already beginning to crowd the stores. Bart turned left, willy-nilly, and wandered in an uptown direction. He stopped, remembering the window of a travel agent in the Center; maybe he ought to go in and poke around. Maybe getting away was the thing to do. He'd always felt better when he was running. But somehow, right now, he didn't have the heart. Any day now she might come around.

Apologizing to a woman pedestrian with whom he'd collided, Bart walked on. *If* she ever came around. He might be making the biggest fool mistake of his career, handling it the way he was. But nothing had worked—the news, the music box, the letter he'd banked on. He'd finally realized there was nothing else he could do, concluded that if she loved him she'd find it out and come to him. Now that wasn't working, either.

Across the street, in a store window, he glimpsed

slender mannikins, dressed up in loose things of some kind, whatever they called them; lolling around in chairs and on a floor in front of a phony fire. That fire, he judged wryly, was probably just as about as warm as he was right now, inside and out. And the mannikins with their loose hair and look of seductive ease reminded him of things that were like a body punch— they hurt. Melissa, with her gorgeous hair down, spilling over her little shoulders, wearing one of those things like the papier-mâché women in the window.

He willed the poignant image away and stopped by a window on his side of the street. Might as well look for something for Claudia while he was in this neighborhood. There were a couple of things there that were nice, just what she might go for. Even the window display, with its theme of a long-gone era, confirmed that.

Something struck him, suddenly and wildly. That particular time—he looked at the tapestry at the back of the display. It was crazy—crazy as hell. Maybe he hadn't tried quite everything. Maybe he was a fool to wait for her to come to him. There he'd been, moping around, when the thing, for him, had always been action, taking the offensive. And what he was contemplating would be the ploy to end all ploys, or his name wasn't Bart Freeman.

It would be hard as the devil to bring off, maybe impossible. But he was surely going to try. He knew just the place to start, and that was nearly forty blocks away, uptown. All the cabs were headed downtown and he didn't have the patience at that point to wait for one. He'd walk it, all the way. Now he had a mission.

Bart walked so fast that he was climbing the museum steps in about twenty-five minutes. His headache was long gone, or forgotten. He headed for the particular display near the center of the massive building and walked around staring, fascinated. It had been years since he'd been to the display, he couldn't even remember how many, maybe since he'd been in school.

Sizing the displays up—literally, he thought, grinning—he decided it was going to be a tough row to hoe. Those things would just about fit Melissa, much less him. But he'd have to talk about it with an expert; get it from the palfrey's mouth, as it were.

He consulted a guard, who directed him to the offices on another floor. Bart chafed at the elevator's slowness in arriving, then ascending, but finally he was there, waiting to see the person in charge, Ms. Sophia Godfrey. Bart pictured a grim and forbidding type without the least sense of humor.

It was a pleasant surprise to see the small, compact and smiling woman come out to greet him. She examined him with twinkly gray eyes and ran a minute hand over her short salt-and-pepper hair with the distracted, gently reproachful manner of someone who'd been quite busy. But it was his fleeting supposition that anyone with her specialty might find the twentieth century, or anyone from it, slightly baffling.

He smiled at the thought, and her own smile widened.

"What can I do for you, Mr. Beekman?"

"Freeman," he corrected gently. "I need some expert advice."

"Well, come into my office, why don't you?" She led the way into a pleasant room furnished with a number of artifacts expressive of her specialty.

"Sit down, Mr. Beek—Mr. Freeman," she invited. "Now," she said briskly, "just what is it you want to

know? Are you a"—she studied him curiously—
"student, by the way?" She obviously didn't think so,
but he'd passed inspection.

"Oh, no." For a second he wondered if he should
make up a story; then he thought, I'll just tell her the
truth. Why not?

And he did, succinctly.

He watched Ms. Godfrey's expression, enjoying the
changes: first utter disbelief; then skeptical uncertainty, as if he were playing a prank; finally sheer enjoyment and a kind of sentimental empathy.

"Well!" Her small gray eyes were glittering like
Christmas ornaments. "Most original. Marvelous."
She laughed. "If any young man had planned such
a . . . caper, as they call it, to woo me, I daresay I
would not be a spinster today."

He grinned back. "But what about the practicalities
of it?"

"Ah . . . sadly, that is another matter. Even a
general knowledge, which is what I assume you
have"—he nodded—"will tell you that the sizes won't
do. Even a good hard look at the exhibit, for that
matter." She twinkled at him again.

"Where would bigger sizes be available?" he asked
eagerly.

"Nowhere, that I know of," she asserted firmly.
"Even if they were, there are other problems—even if
you could get on and off your transportation"—she
grinned—"without assistance, you'd still need a
Clydesdale to support you."

"Oh, like the beer ad," he said, enlightened.

"Exactly. What I would advise, Mr. Freeman, is for
you to go to a theatrical place. It makes more practical
sense."

Bart frowned. "I'd like to have the real thing."

Ms. Godfrey replied shrewdly, "You would. But I think that's the way to do it. I'm afraid I haven't been that much help . . . unless you'd like a lecture on the older, lighter versions of these things."

"No, thanks. You've been a lot of help. Thanks, Ms. Godfrey . . . very much." He stood up and smiled down at her.

"Well, good luck, Mr. Freeman. I wish you well on your quest," she said in her quaint fashion. "If it's successful—and I fail to see how it couldn't be—bring the lady to see me sometime. I'd like to meet her."

"That's a promise." Bart gave her a final salute and went out.

Before he left the museum he went back to the exhibit.

He remembered saying to Melissa that she reminded him of times gone by. Looking at the dull shine of the ancient artifacts, he thought sentimentally, Those were the days. But I guess they had their problems, too, having to drag a crane along when they went courting. He'd hate like the devil to have to cope with that on Eighteenth Street.

His idea was probably the nuttiest he'd ever had. But I'm going to go through with it, he thought, come what may. He hurried to the phones and consulted the Yellow Pages for two widely varying items. He'd have time to cab down there before they closed.

Then, incurable optimist that he was, he'd go to Saks or Tiffany's and choose a Christmas present for Melissa Grey.

Melissa had never felt less like celebrating Christmas; every fresh bombardment of holiday reminders left her lonelier and more oppressed. It had always been her favorite celebration, since she was a small child—until the one at hand, which was something to be gotten through, because she'd never felt more single and superfluous in her whole life.

If her family sensed it they did not let her know, but it seemed to Melissa that Ria and Mark, and many of her friends as well, were trying to involve her in every way they could.

Melissa had been unwilling to let Ria, above all others, know just how depressed she was feeling. So when Peg and Carl had invited her for a country weekend over Thanksgiving, where there was some- one "terrific" for her to meet, she'd gone along with it, even if it was the last thing she'd wanted to do. Peg's family had a huge and lovely house in Connecti- cut where their three grown children's former rooms had been converted into guest rooms.

Melissa met not only Peg's handsome single brother but a bright and charming colleague of Carl's. She tried her best to join in things, but it was so hard, when she thought of Bart, that it almost turned into an ordeal. She made up her mind not to commit herself to anything like that for Christmas; it would be ridiculous, it wouldn't work at all. Both the brother and the colleague vied for her attention, and both wanted to see her again in the City. Politely she turned them down.

She decided abruptly to have the shop redecorated and worked herself almost to exhaustion on the project. But at least, once it was done, the place looked wonderful, freshly painted with new arrange- ments of shelves and a far better distribution of the clocks. For a few days Melissa had gotten so involved in that she was able to forget everything else.

Then it was time to decorate for Christmas. And the memory of what the holiday might have been like suddenly assailed her. The pleasure that had gone into the redecoration had disappeared; it became just a chore she dreaded. Nevertheless, it had to be done. A shop without Christmas decorations would be unheard of. And if she didn't have any in the house, either, she knew it would disturb and sadden Ria as evidence of her continuing glumness.

So Melissa bit the bullet and put up her usual decorations in the house—gold and green for the downstairs, blue and silver in the bedroom and upper hall. She chose pure gold for Time Was, which had been repainted the happy color of crocuses, with white shelves. The gold would enhance the gilt and dark wood, the delicate multicolored enameling of the lovely old timepieces.

On one particular December afternoon, she was using an idle interval to wrap Christmas presents. The morning had been full and profitable; she had sold four clocks and three watches before noon.

She finished her gift wrapping and returned to the front of the shop, sitting down at her desk and looking around. It was one of those bright wintry days with a faint hint of snow that usually elated her, but the shaft of sun piercing the window, gleaming on the clocks and golden Yule globes, only mocked her mood of somberness.

She picked up the book of Ria's poetry from her desk—she'd taken to rereading it often lately—and opened it to one of her favorites, *The Shell of Gold,* reading the fragments that moved her unendurably now:

> Citied
> I was at moon's pouch,
> lulled within marigold; with winter's herb . . .

I stand at windowpanes.
Accented grave,
three insect segments drum the hour.

I sleep. Near maximum, I function and
endure.
Serve purpose, structure; hard autonomy . . .

I do my work.
Embrace the worlds I know . . .

I lie on winter's moon.
Dry at its molt;
with marigold, with larval change and promises:
three hours shed their skin.

Caro, I see your eyes,
brown in this dawn of reptiles, weep:
build sun on green green edge.
Quiet, I wait for you.

The singing, pictured words echoed to Melissa in
the silence broken only by the rhythmic ticking of the
many clocks.

Bart was so alive in that particular poem that she
could almost see him before her, with his brown, foxy
eyes, his ruddy skin, his fiery hair. And the vivid
picture tore her heart. She'd never known what it was
to miss someone so sorely, to feel so desolate in his
absence.

All these weeks, she suddenly realized, she'd been
waiting, hoping he would come back in spite of
everything. He always had before, no matter what
else happened.

The music box was on her desk; she opened the
cover, hearing the strains of Vivaldi in that wistful,
tinkling chime. Tears gathered under her lids. She
closed the box and the melody was cut off.

At first it had angered her, that implication of his that he would wait for her to come to her senses and get in touch with him. Then as the empty days had gone on, things had begun to look very different to her. She was ashamed to remember the bitter and cynical things she'd said. She was finding out how right Bart had been about so much—she had forgotten how to trust, had become unable to welcome the new and hopeful. She blushed to recall that nasty comment about "knights in armor."

A few weeks ago she'd given in and called him. But he had been out of town on business, his secretary had told Melissa. For some reason after that she hadn't had the nerve to call again; he had probably forgotten, she had concluded.

But a strong, growing desire to give it one more try was building within her. Abruptly, before she could argue herself out of it, Melissa picked up the phone and began to dial his office number.

While she was dialing, a customer appeared at the door, and she had to hang up.

The woman made a purchase, and Melissa wrapped it beautifully in Time Was golden Christmas paper. When the woman had left, extremely pleased with the gift watch she'd chosen, Melissa had to build up her courage again to pick up the phone.

Finally she did and dialed again. Bart's secretary answered, telling her that he was gone for the afternoon. The woman seemed strangely eager that Melissa leave a message.

But Melissa just thanked her, saying she'd call again, and hung up.

It had been a foolish idea, anyway, she thought darkly.

The latening sun had changed color. It would soon

be gone. Melissa thought of her trip, and was not cheered. Even the trip didn't seem wonderful any more.

To the accompaniment of good-natured laughter and cries of "Good luck," Bart Freeman gingerly headed east on Forty-eighth Street toward Eleventh Avenue, the route he would follow downtown. No point in getting into traffic before he had to.

What he was doing he'd handled with his eyes closed for years, but that had been in the country or the park or along western trails. This was a whole other ball game, he was finding out. And his vision was somewhat impeded by the highly unusual item covering his head.

Progressing in a downtown direction, he took it very easy at first; then as his confidence increased, he hurried it up. It would blow the whole thing if he didn't make it before dark; the sun was doing splendid things to his gear.

He would not cross town until he got to Eighteenth Street, thereby avoiding the Christmas crowds, the general mishmash of Forty-second and Thirty-fourth streets. His appearance, he thought as his mouth stretched into a wide and invisible grin, might cause quite a ruckus at Twenty-third, as well.

It was convenient that most traffic on Eleventh was composed of trucks or an occasional cab. Both truckdrivers and cabbies around New York had already seen almost everything and were not unduly impressed if they saw more.

His downtown trip was fairly peaceful, and he began really to enjoy himself. He was pleasantly surprised at just how warm his outfit was on this frigid day in December.

From time to time he heard a catcall or a yell of admiration from a passing trucker; there was a collective cheer from the Thirtieth Street terminal.

Ms. Godfrey knew her onions, as well as her history, Bart reflected; there was almost no one in New York who could fail to notice his particular combination—the outfit and the means of travel combined. It was the feet that felt the strangest, he decided; he had never worn such things on his feet. The rest was a comparative piece of cake.

At Twenty-third and Eleventh, a group of boys called out, "Hey, it's Hallowe'en!" Bart waved at them and let out a muffled laugh.

Things got a little sticky when he was heading east on Eighteenth Street. Thus far the few cops he'd encountered had reacted with amusement, waving and making remarks.

But when Bart got a little too close to a police car at Eighteenth and Broadway, an irritated officer rolled down his car window and stuck his head out.

When he saw Bart the policeman let out an astonished oath. The traffic light was about to change. Bart freed his mouth and explained his mission.

"All *right,*" the policeman said, grinning. "Way to go!" He raised his hand in a companionable salute and the car moved on.

Bart felt more and more elated: all the world *did* love a lover.

He was almost at the meeting point; he saw the four others waiting with smiles on their faces. One of them handed their discarded overcoats to someone in a car.

Bart had thought of everything, he was pretty sure. He mentally checked off items: A friend had called to make sure she'd be there, his car was parked in a nearby garage in case she kicked him out, one of the four hired helpers would dispose of his other transportation. And the ring was in the breast pocket of Bart's hidden flannel shirt.

Everything was ready. There was nothing left for him to do—except think about Melissa. And hope.

It was almost sunset. A roseate glow washed the Time Was window, transforming the golden globes and gilding inside to a wonderful fiery color that suggested a giant rose in flame.

Even Melissa's gloomy mood could not withstand that loveliness; she took a deep breath of sheer pleasure, exclaiming softly. The street was very quiet.

And then with great abruptness she heard the blazing note of brasses; they sounded like trumpets. From them was blown a majestic, triumphant air. Someone must be making a movie, she thought, and she wandered to the window to see.

Two splendid-looking young men, dressed like medieval pages, were marching down Eighteenth Street, as heralds to a single rider on a big white horse—a tall, strongly built figure covered from helmeted head to mailed foot in silver armor.

The helmet boasted a nodding golden plume; the rider's face was hidden by its visor. The setting sun glanced redly off the silver armor's scales, so the rider glowed with the fire of the rich, warm light.

Behind him marched two more pages, also blowing trumpets of shining gold. Silky banners of blue and crimson were attached to the trumpets and the two rear pages were dressed, like those ahead, in bright doublets and hose. All of the pages had long auburn hair.

At first Melissa was so bemused by the simple beauty of it, the startling pageantry, that she was almost too amazed to breathe. Then she felt her breath return in small, quick gasps.

It couldn't be—it was too incredible.

Transfixed, she stood at the window, staring. The pages gave one last great blast, then lowered their trumpets, standing at respectful attention. Then one of the rear pages handed his instrument to his companion and walked toward the knight. The man in the light armor slowly raised his right leg, preparing to dismount; the page stepped forward to support the knight in the middle of his back to enable him to get down.

The man in armor was on the sidewalk; he raised one of his mailed gloves in salute to Melissa.

She felt an incredulous, shaky smile breaking out on her lips. She raised her own hand in return.

Unable to take her eyes off the spectacle, she was only dimly aware of a few passersby and their stupefaction and delight. She watched the assisting page bow to the knight and then reach under his tunic and pull out a tiny pouch on a leather string. The page fumbled in the pouch for a coin, which he proceeded to drop in a parking meter, after which he carefully tethered the white horse to the meter's pole.

Melissa couldn't tell whether she was going to laugh or cry, most likely both at once. Her mirth was bubbling up to the accompaniment of something like a sob until she was almost hiccuping with confusion.

Then she caught sight of a familiar figure—the stocky, blue-clad patrolman Alan Stein, a favorite in the neighborhood. Melissa rushed to the door and opened it a crack to listen.

"What's coming off here, fellas?" Patrolman Stein was asking. He immediately seemed to question his own use of "fellas" as an inappropriate address to a knight and his pages. "You got a permit to park that horse here?"

The armored man pushed back his visor to free his

mouth, and Melissa's heart hammered against her ribs when she heard that well-known, deep and laughing voice. "Well, now, my page did put the money in the meter, officer."

Stein began to grin. "Who *are* you guys, anyway?"

The knight answered for them. "A lonely knight-at-arms, sir, and the best actor-musicians the union had to offer."

Patrolman Stein laughed out loud. "And," the knight continued calmly, "I checked out the state laws and municipal codes. A horse still has the right of way, officer, even in Manhattan."

Melissa was trembling now, both from cold and from an almost hysterical excitement. But there was no way in the world she was going to close the door now and miss the dialogue; she would brave the cold.

"I'll take your word for it," Stein said. "Sir Whatever. Where are you headed?"

"Right here." The knight indicated Time Was.

Patrolman Stein turned his head and saw Melissa. "Oh, Ms. Grey!" He touched his cap. "Do you want this visitor?"

She grinned at him, blinking to stop the gathering moisture under her lids. "I'll accept him. I've had some customers who were even stranger." Her laughter broke free.

An answering chuckle reverberated from inside the helmet.

"Okay, then." Stein gave them his blessing. "But what about the horse? It's cold outside today."

"Even now my trusty page is getting ready to take him back to the castle," the knight said. The page was untying the horse, preparing to mount.

"Well, then, I guess that wraps it up," Stein assented. "Merry Christmas, all of you . . . and Happy Hallowe'en." He touched his cap again to Melissa and strolled off down Eighteenth Street, swinging his nightstick for a moment before he shoved it back in his belt.

The page mounted the white horse and cantered away; the others walked off in his wake.

Melissa stood there in the path of the freezing air for an instant, staring at the tall knight in armor. She realized she was wearing one of her prettiest dresses; she was glad of that. It would have been a shame to welcome such a splendid occasion in something as banal as jeans.

"You'd better ask me in, my lady. The afternoon is chill." She smiled at the stately, dramatic inflection, made eerie and comic as it echoed in the helmet.

She held the door of Time Was wide and he strode through, his metallic shoes making a racket on the polished floor.

"This is quite a place," he said; those were the very same words he had pronounced the first time he had entered her shop. He looked around. "Even prettier than before."

When she closed the door he pulled off the helmet with one swift, strong motion, revealing his tousled, fiery hair and smiling face. The brown, foxy eyes sparkled down into hers. She was momentarily at a loss for words, drinking in the sight of him, the reflection of the golden Christmas globes in the shine of his thin, glittering armor.

From head to foot, he was shining, shining with the light of the season that promised, suddenly, to be so glorious.

"You said there were no knights, Melissa. I had to prove there are."

"I was so wrong," she murmured. "You've already slain my dragons. I was so wrong about so many things." Melissa paused, warm in the warmth of his gaze, the eyes that seemed to kiss her face. "You thought of everything."

"Not quite. I thought I had—I even have a ring under all this somewhere. But in this gear I can't even take you in my arms, which is what I'm dying to do, right now. Nobody reminded me that armor can bruise a lady." His expression was rueful.

"Then come upstairs, and let me disarm you, Sir Bart."

"For you that'll be easy, Melissa. You always were the most disarming woman I ever met." His brown look was still caressing her.

"I've been waiting for this, Melissa . . . a long, long lonely time. Come on, I can't wait for you to disarm me." He grinned.

"Not for just a moment yet." No, not for a moment, she thought. In this one brief half hour the shadows of the sunset had all been driven away; and there was, instead of a regretted past, life, becoming a splendid vista. But she wanted, in the last brief moment of the sun's setting, to see the glimmer of the golden light dance on his suit of silver.

"Not just yet," she repeated. "There are so many things to talk about. I've got to tell you how sorry I am, sorry for not trusting and believing."

"That was as much my fault as yours. I played my cards too close to my chest, from day one. I should have brought everything out in the open, laid all on those cards on the table, from the start. I told you I 'didn't have the heart' to identify myself that first day, because I thought it would turn you off. When we went to lunch, *I* was the one who was afraid—afraid to go into things too deeply for fear you'd mistrust me more than ever."

She started to speak but he held up his hand, smiling. "No, let me go on with my *mea culpa* before you say anything else. I should have told you about my uncle and about the provision in the will. Anybody with all his marbles should have known that Edward Freeman would try to pull something, try to spoil it all. So I left myself wide open for what happened. After what you suffered in the past, I couldn't have expected you to trust me after that—thinking my family 'disapproved' of you, which is ridiculous . . . learning about that crazy provision from my uncle, and not from me. No wonder you were doubtful."

"But I doubted too long," she protested. "You did everything to show me you loved me. I was so foolish to imagine that you wanted to *hurt* me. I didn't believe what my best friends told me . . ."—she smiled—"that history doesn't necessarily repeat itself, that one bad apple doesn't spoil the barrel. I was foolish and stubborn." She looked at him earnestly.

"But then," she continued, "when I didn't hear from you for so long . . ."

"What about my letter from Minneapolis? I thought, when you didn't even acknowledge that, things were really hopeless."

"Your letter?" She stared at him. "I never got it."

"Never *got* it?" He shook his head. "Well, I'll be damned. I left it to be mailed. It went into everything, explained everything down to the last detail. You see, I trusted the fellow to mail it. I was rushing off to the airport to get a plane back, trying to beat a blizzard. It serves me right. I should have done it myself, I see that now. Oh, darling, what a mess I made of that, with just that one small piece of carelessness."

"It doesn't matter now, Bart." She raised her face to his and they kissed sweetly and slowly.

When he got his breath back, he shook his head. "It *does* matter, Melissa. Everything does. It's things like that that kept us apart all this time. And from now on, it's going to be different. I'm going to be completely open with you about every little thing. I don't want to take any more chances. I want to be damned sure right now that none of this will come up again to haunt us. I couldn't take any more misunderstandings and hurt and questions. I don't have any more rotten relatives in my closet, I want to get that straight."

She laughed, feeling happier and happier by the second.

"As for Time Was, young lady . . . it's likely that my office window is going to overlook it, from a block away. I'll be able to keep an eye on you."

"I assure you that won't be necessary." She kissed his cheek, and he made a deep sound of contentment.

"I'm relieved to hear it. As for my family—my mother already loves you, after seeing you only once."

"At the auction . . . of course." Her happiness was growing and growing until she thought she would almost burst with it.

"Oh, yes, indeed," said Bart. "And she's probably waiting right now to hear how I've made out."

"Well, now that everything's settled," she said, "we shouldn't keep her waiting."

"But it isn't, quite. You haven't told me when we can get married. I think three days is the absolute minimum. Don't you think we'd better get to it, tomorrow? What do you say?"

She gazed at him, drinking in his charming, reckless face. "I say Yes. Oh, yes." His foxy eyes blazed with happiness; now all the wistfulness was gone. When he smiled it was a wide smile of utter delight, no longer the rather sad Piscean smile that had almost looked like a grimace.

The clocks began to strike the hour four times.

"Listen to the hour they're marking," he said softly. "The 'hour of the Maiden,' they tell me."

"And look what's marking it." She held out her wrist; her sleeve fell back. The hands of the moon watch were pointing to the tiny symbol of Virgo's Maiden, the sign of the season of her birth.

From the first, he had reawakened magic for her that she had feared no longer existed; then he had brought it back to them both from its imprisoned sleep. She saw the whole pattern at last; everything was clear.

"You told me once," she added, smiling, "that you'd be back some shining hour. I thought it sounded arrogant then. But I see now that you were right."

His look was like a long caress.

"Not entirely," he admitted. "You're the one who's made it shine, Melissa Grey, by saying Yes to me just now."

"We'll share the credit," Melissa decided. She looked around at the glowing decorations in the shop, then at their reflection in his silver armor. "Oh, Bart, it's really Christmas now. The best Christmas I've ever had in my whole life."

"The first of a lifetime of them, one day after the other," he declared. "I'm going to make every day a holiday for you, from this time forward." He slipped the ring on her finger.

There didn't seem to be anything left to say. Her heart was too full to let her speak.

And so they turned out the lights and made their way upstairs, to the next room full of gold and green, reflecting, like the last one, that glowing day of days, that shining hour.

Silhouette Special Edition

Coming Next Month

A Love Song And You by Linda Shaw

By all rights Laura Remington and country
and western star Dallas Jones should have
been enemies. But nothing seemed to matter
but the magnetic energy that charged the
atmosphere when they were together.

Gentle Possession by Melodie Adams

Caleb Stone and Randi Warner had a contract:
he needed a son and she needed to pay her
father's debt. Randi fulfilled her part of
the bargain, but how could she leave Caleb
when through their child they found the
promise of forever?

The Tangled Web by Tracy Sinclair

Trapped in a deception, Nicole never thought
she'd find herself drawn to the man she'd
schemed to deceive. But falling in love with
Flint Lockridge could put her at his mercy—
and completely destroy her plans.

Coming Next Month

A Ruling Passion by
Doreen Owens Malek

Try as she might, journalist Megan Fielding
couldn't keep her objectivity when she was
around Mike Henley. He touched her as no man
ever had, but could she do her job and keep
Michael as well?

Softly At Sunset by Anne Lacey

Tragedy had touched Cade Thornton's family,
and Jill had the task of healing his daughter's
pain. Soon her tenderness extended to the
father as well, and her job of healing was
complicated by new feelings of love.

Tell Me No Lies by Brooke Hastings

Maggie got a kick out of masquerading as
an eighteen-year-old student to get an audition
with director Carson McDermitt. But the joke
was on her, for how could her growing passion
for him be indulged when he was fighting
his feelings for the woman he thought of
as a young girl?

Silhouette Special Edition

£1.10 each

127 □ A WOMAN
OF DARING
Abra Taylor

128 □ STARLIGHT
Debbie Macomber

129 □ SEA OF GOLD
Melanie Rowe

130 □ PLAY IT
AGAIN
Eleni Carr

131 □ A FIRE IN
THE SOUL
Doris Lee

132 □ THE BEST
WAY TO LOSE
Janet Dailey

133 □ THE
CARPENTER'S
LADY
Billie Douglass

134 □ A MATTER
OF PRIDE
Margaret Ripy

135 □ A GIFT
BEYOND PRICE
Maura Seger

136 □ EXCLUSIVELY
YOURS
Joanna Scott

137 □ THE PERFECT
CHOICE
Laura Parker

138 □ SMILE AND
SAY YES
Carolyn Thornton

139 □ A HARD
BARGAIN
Carole Halston

140 □ WINTER OF
LOVE
Tracy Sinclair

141 □ ABOVE THE
MOON
Antonia Saxon

142 □ DREAM FEAST
Fran Bergen

143 □ WHEN
MORNING
COMES
Laurey Bright

144 □ THE COURTING
GAME
Kate Meriwether

145 □ SHINING HOUR
Pat Wallace

146 □ BY THE BOOK
Carolyn Thornton

147 □ APRIL
ENCOUNTER
Gena Dalton

148 □ LEGACY OF
FIRE
Lucy Gordon

149 □ APPALACHIAN
SUMMER
Eva Claire

150 □ LEFTOVER
LOVE
Janet Dailey

All these books are available at your local bookshop or newsagent, or can be ordered direct from the publisher. Just tick the titles you want and fill in the form below.

Prices and availability subject to change without notice.

SILHOUETTE BOOKS, P.O. Box 11, Falmouth, Cornwall.

Please send cheque or postal order, and allow the following for postage and packing:

U.K. – 50p for one book, plus 20p for the second book, and 14p for each additional book ordered up to a £1.63 maximum.

B.F.P.O. and EIRE – 50p for the first book, plus 20p for the second book, and 14p per copy for the next 7 books, 8p per book thereafter

OTHER OVERSEAS CUSTOMERS – 75p for the first book, plus 21p per copy for each additional book.

Name ....

Address ....

....